WIFE: *we are separate people*
each what he fears most each his own
trap his own bait his own victim
I am not responsible for your life
and you are not responsible for mine
                    —Richard Shelton

Doug Finn

Heart of a Family

State University of New York Press
ALBANY

1/1985
gen'l

The shell of this story is an actual incident. Everything inside it, including and especially the characters—their personalities, actions, and relationships—is fiction.

Published by
State University of New York Press, Albany

© 1984 Doug Finn

All rights reserved

Printed in the United States of America

No part of this book may be used or reproduced
in any manner whatsoever without written permission
except in the case of brief quotations embodied in
critical articles and reviews.

For information, address State University of New York
Press, State University Plaza, Albany, N.Y., 12246

Library of Congress Cataloging in Publication Data
Finn, Doug, 1946-
  Heart of a family.
  I. Title.
PS3556.I496H4   1984   813'.54   84-8474
ISBN 0-87395-861-6

10 9 8 7 6 5 4 3 2

For Kris, who made it possible

I

Jesse Landow stood under the shower in a kind of stupor, tired after work, feeling the steaming water spray on his hard, muscular shoulders. It had been a week since David's accident and the shock of its implications had finally reached him. It was like being awakened from a pleasant dream by a loud noise. "Jesus Christ," he said to himself. "My family's falling apart."

He had been thinking about his sons. They were all a little strange. Something less—or more, he wasn't sure which—than your typical all-American boys. He had pictured them, as he usually did for some reason, lined up according to their ages— eight, sixteen, and twenty—standing at a military at-ease, their faces wearing puzzled frowns, as if they couldn't figure out why he was looking at them. Whenever he saw them like that he became puzzled himself.

Well, hell, he thought. They were his kids. Why shouldn't he look at them? And as he thought this their expressions changed. They grinned, fidgeted nervously, looked at each other as if to say, "Hey, the old man sees us. He really sees us."

But, of course, he didn't see them at all. They were enigmas to him. He didn't know them. He worked too damn much, that was the problem. He wasn't around them enough to know them. Mary, he figured, might know them, but he wasn't even sure of that. Somebody ought to know them. And the thought that maybe nobody did, at least nobody that mattered, made a melancholy sadness well up in his chest.

It shouldn't be that way. He ought to change it. He would change it, he decided. Or at least try to change it. He would talk to Mary about it tonight.

A week later, the whole family sat around the dining room table. They were just finishing dessert.

"Goldwater knew what to do," Marty was saying. "If he was in now, the war would be over."

"You sound like a damn reactionary," Jesse said.

"Well, I don't like the idea that I might have to fight in a war that's only going on because Johnson is too chicken to end it," Marty said.

"It's more complicated than that," Jesse said. "We can't let the Russians get a foothold over there. If we let them have Vietnam they'll just go and try for more. They want to rule the world."

Marty's face was getting red. The rest of the family moved their eyes from one speaker to the other like spectators at a tennis match.

"That's what I've been trying to tell you," Marty said. "We have to stop them, not let it drag on forever."

Jesse shook his head. "No. It's not us. It's the Vietnamese who have to stop them. We're only there to help them out. It's not our war, it's theirs."

"Bull!" Marty said, exasperated. "It's our war. And anybody that thinks it's not is just naive—or stupid."

"Isn't there something on television tonight?" Mary asked.

2

Gary, sitting next to her, suddenly came to life. "Mission Impossible." He scooted his chair back and stood up. Mary stood, too, and started clearing the table.

"Just a minute," Jesse said. "Everybody sit down a minute. I have something to say to everybody."

Gary and Mary sat down, Gary on the edge of his chair. An awkward silence filled the room. The refrigerator hummed in the kitchen. Jesse studied the milky bottom of his ice cream dish, then looked up and cleared his throat. There was another instant of silence, then Marty said, "Mah fellow 'Mericans. Unaccustomed as Ah am to public speakin' . . ." Mary looked at him reprovingly. David chuckled. Gary didn't understand, but smiled. And Jesse grinned.

"Okay, smart-mouth," Jesse said. "This is serious though. I have something I want to say to everybody." There was another long pause. Jesse looked at Mary as if seeking some help, but Mary only smiled at him and nodded. He took a deep breath. "I've been doing a lot of thinking lately. No wise cracks," he said to Marty. He paused again. "There's, uh, something wrong—with us—as a family. I've been trying to figure out what it is. It's not really anybody's fault but mine, but the problem is that we're not together. We're not close like a family should be. Do you realize this is the first dinner we've had all together in over a month?"

"Two weeks," Marty mumbled.

"Okay, two weeks. But you see what I mean. Everybody just goes off in his own direction and nobody else knows what he's doing." He looked at David and David looked at his plate. "It shouldn't be like that. I think we should do something to change it." He stopped and looked around the table at them all.

" I don't know," Marty said. "I always thought we had a pretty good family. At least nobody burns flags or smokes dope or robs liquor stores."

3

"I know we're not bad," Jesse said. "That's not what I mean. But when was the last time we spent a whole day together as a family? Can anyone remember?"

Silence. Jesse waited.

Gary fidgeted in his chair, staring over the hutch opposite him at the clock, a huge pocket watch and chain with an electric cord hanging from it. "Mission Impossible is on," he said softly.

"What do you think we should do, Honey?" Mary said.

"Okay. Here's what we're going to do," Jesse said. "Tomorrow we're going to spend the whole day together. We're going to go out and look at campers. We're going to buy a camper for the truck. Then, in two weeks, when I get my vacation, we're all going together. We'll be together as a family for two weeks. We'll camp and fish and sit around the fire at night and talk to each other. There'll be no place to go. And no television. Just us. Maybe we'll get to know each other."

"I'm helping Connie's brother work on his car tomorrow," Marty said.

"You'll have to call him and tell him you can't come," Jesse said.

"But he can't do it without me. We're going to pull the block."

Jesse hesitated, but only a moment. "No," he said. "I'm laying down the law this time. You'll have to find some other time to do it, that's all."

"I told Aunt Roe I'd do her yard tomorrow," David said quietly.

"What about the two weeks?" Marty said. "I have to work, you know."

Jesse looked directly into Marty's eyes. "This isn't some game I'm playing, Marty. I'm dead serious. I want you to take the time off. Without pay if you have to. If they won't give you the time then give them your notice. There are plenty of jobs around as good as that one."

Marty looked a little astonished. Then he looked down and shook his head. "Jesus," he muttered.

Gary looked around the table from one person to another, trying to understand what was going on. "Are we going to go fishing?" he asked.

Jesse smiled at him, relieved to feel that somebody was on his side. "Yep," he said. "We'll catch some big ones, too."

"Can I get my own fishing pole and stuff?" Gary asked.

"Sure," Jesse said. "We'll get all that stuff tomorrow, too."

"I have to get ready," Marty said. "I have a date." He scooted his chair back and stood up.

"Two weeks from Monday," Jesse said. "Get the time off. One way or another."

"I'll see what they say," Marty mumbled, and walked back to his bedroom.

Marty stood at the bathroom sink studying his face in the mirror, looking for stray whiskers the electric shaver had missed. His face was full of little craters from a bad acne problem he had had when he was in high school. His dark brown hair was long, but not too long, and his brown eyes, set close together, drooped slightly and made him look sleepy. He'd been thinking about his father's idea and wasn't enthused. He didn't like camping. Living with the dirt and the bugs where you always felt like you needed a shower but could never take one. He would much rather the rest of them go and leave him at home alone. He would have the whole house to himself then, and Connie could come over at night.

He could always just refuse to go. Or he could say he couldn't get off work. But he would have to lie about that. There really wasn't any problem with his taking off for two weeks. He had a week's vacation coming and they had a high school kid filling in for people over the summer. Sure. Any high school kid could do his job.

He splashed after-shave on his face, ran a comb through his hair one more time, then turned to leave. He guessed there really wasn't any excuse and he couldn't just refuse. He had already disappointed his father enough by dropping out of college. His father was funny tonight. Different somehow. More serious? Not exactly. More alert maybe. Something. But the idea itself was typical. If there was a problem, there had to be a solution, and the solution had to be one big splash in the pan. Do this thing, solve the problem, and then get back to normal. But, Marty thought, one solution won't solve this problem, if it really was a problem. Well, it wasn't *a* problem; it was a lot of little problems. His father would count on the vacation to solve everything and then be disappointed when it didn't. And he, Marty, would have to be a part of the failure—again. He would rather just stay home.

David helped his mother clear the dishes from the table and take them into the kitchen. It wasn't something he usually did, but he didn't want to be around his father, who had gone into the den with Gary to watch television. He wished he had a date, like Marty, or something to do that would get him out of the house for a while. He felt uncomfortable, as if something itched where he couldn't scratch it. What his father had said was meant for him more than any of the others. It was his father's way of pointing out his failure. It was because of the accident. If it wasn't for the accident things would have gone on normally. Now they all had to go through this vacation thing when no one really wanted to.

Somehow he had made it through the last two weeks by keeping up his work for old man Whipple, who stood over him like a slave driver complaining about how he wished he could help—how he really had intended to dig out the pool himself but had sprained his wrist and now it was in a splint. And David had gone to see Aunt Roe twice, his only relief from the aching guilt he felt, the disappointment with himself, the humiliation of the accident. He didn't know if she knew about it. She hadn't mentioned it. They had talked, as they usually did, about books, about writing, about her past. The stories she could tell . . .

He laid the last dish on the counter and Mary smiled at him. "Thank you," she said.

"You're welcome," David mumbled. He stood there a moment, watching his mother rinse off the plates.

"I think Mission Impossible is on," Mary said.

"Yeah, I know," David said. "I think I'll go read for a while."

Camping was okay, he thought, walking from the kitchen, through the dining room, down the hall, and into the bedroom he shared with Gary. But he would rather do it alone, especially now. He would love to lose himself in some thick pine forest, to lie down on a bed of pine needles and stare up at the sky—the night sky, with the stars so bright they seemed to stare back. He would feel like he belonged there. There would be no people around to make things complicated. Just him and the forest and the sky.

He lay down on his bed and put his hands behind his head. This trip wouldn't be like that. He would have to go along with whatever everybody else wanted to do. He could picture them all lined up along some lake with their fishing poles propped up in forked sticks and their five bobbers floating one behind the other like a small fleet of red and white battleships. And he would sit there, bored stiff.

Well, he would take some books. That would help some. But he would rather just be by himself.

Gary watched "Mission Impossible" with his father. His mother came in when she finished the dishes and then they let him stay up and watch an old John Wayne movie on channel eleven. It was a good movie. John Wayne and two other guys were outlaws. They found a woman who had a baby in a covered wagon in the middle of the desert. The woman died and the three of them carried the baby a long way across the desert. They ran out of water and the other two guys died before they reached the town. John Wayne carried the baby on foot and the ghosts of the other two guys kept telling him to keep going, keep going. He finally made it to the town and walked into the saloon with the baby. He walked up to the bar and said, "Gimme a beer," in his hoarse, rattly voice and then the baby cried.

When Gary went into his room to get ready for bed, David was already in bed, with the light on, reading. David read all the time. Sometimes his mother called him a bookworm, which was funny because worms couldn't read books. He put his pajamas on, then went out to the kitchen for a drink of water. He always made sure to get a drink of water before he went to the bathroom because if he got it after, he would have to get up in the middle of the night, in the dark, and go to the bathroom again to get rid of it. Then, when he came back to bed, if he couldn't go back to sleep right away he would have to lie there in the dark listening to the quiet house and watching the door of his closet because something was in there. Sometimes he saw the door knob turn, very slowly, and once he had left the door open and he could see shadows moving in there.

He went back into the den, where his mother and father were watching the news. Usually on the news they showed movies of Army men fighting in Vietnam, but tonight there was just a man talking so he didn't try to get them to let him stay and watch it. He kissed his mother, then his father.

"Can I really get a fishing pole tomorrow?" he asked Jesse.

"Sure," Jesse said. "We'll go over to that fishing store on Lankershim. First thing in the morning we'll get all the fishing stuff out and see what we need. Go on to bed now." He smiled.

"Good night, Honey," Mary said. "Tell David to turn out the light now."

He left the den and went through the dining room to the bathroom. He sprayed a little on the floor because at first it didn't come out straight. Then he remembered that he forgot to brush his teeth. But no one had noticed, so he didn't. He went into the bedroom and got into bed. David was still reading.

"Mom said to turn the light out," he said.

"In a minute," David mumbled.

Gary waited, staring up at the light blue ceiling. He was wondering about the fishing pole, what it would look like. It wouldn't be a big long one like Manny had. Manny Martinez was his best friend at school, but he hadn't seen him since summer vacation started. Manny had a big surf fishing pole hanging on nails over the window in his bedroom. It was his father's, really, Manny said, but since his father didn't live with them any more he figured it was his now. His father had made it out of bamboo. He used to go over to Manny's house all the time after school. It was really fun because Manny's mother worked until five o'clock and nobody was home. Manny could do anything he wanted. They made peanut butter milk shakes in the blender. They heated up beans on the stove and made bean sandwiches. They wrestled on the living room floor and played cowboys in Manny's den where there was a real bar. Once Manny poured him a glass of real whiskey, but it tasted awful. When Gary told his mother how they had blown up some of Manny's model airplanes with firecrackers, she wouldn't let him go over there any more. Manny came to his house sometimes, but it wasn't as much fun.

Manny had gone to live with his aunt and uncle for the summer. He said they lived in Santa Monica and that he was going to go to the beach every day and fish off the pier with the big pole and catch a lot of fish. He said his aunt would give him money to take the bus to the beach all by himself and he could stay there as long as he wanted. Gary wished he could do that. That would be better than the vacation his father was talking about. They would be all together all the time and he could never do anything he wanted.

David switched off the light and Gary heard him settling down in his bed. Gary stared into the darkness for a while, thinking about Manny, then he turned on his side.

"David?" he said quietly.

"Huh?"

"You think we'll really go on a vacation?"

"Looks like it."

"You think it'll be fun?"

"I guess so," David said.

"You going to fish, too?"

"Yeah, I guess."

"Me, too," Gary said.

"Good night," David said.

" 'Night," Gary said.

He lay there for a while before he went to sleep, still thinking about Manny. He wished he could have a summer vacation like Manny was having, without his mother and father around to tell him what to do all the time.

Mary waited until Gary had left the room before she wiped the wetness of his kiss from her cheek. She smiled at the feel of his small, bony body, left behind like an impression in a soft cushion. She looked at Jesse and started to say that Gary seemed excited about the trip, but Jesse was staring at the television with a distant look in his eyes, as if he was watching his own thoughts instead of the news. He looked tired, too. She worried about him, probably more than he knew, and she could sense that he felt a kind of defeat already about the vacation plans. About that and all the other things that had been happening lately. David's accident and whatever was behind it. Gary's trouble at school. And Marty's apparent determination to do nothing worthwhile with his life.

She knew she felt it, too, but she thought the sense of failure must be stronger in a man, a man who felt the responsibility of his family as much as Jesse did. It was his life, she thought. He had dedicated himself to it after the other thing happened—the thing that made her realize she alone would never be enough for him.

She watched him sitting slumped on the couch with his feet straight out in front of him. His biceps bulged, making the short sleeves of his work shirt tight around his arms. His hair was black and curly, graying now at the temples. His mouth was firm, determined-looking, and his dark eyes, set beneath dark bushy brows, could make him look fierce when he chose to. The way he looked when he looked at Marty at the dinner table.

She looked back at the screen. The news was almost over. There was a story on about an old farmer somewhere in Nebraska who said that the family farm would soon be a thing of the past because a small farm just couldn't make enough money. Then the announcer came back on long enough to say, "And that's the news for July seventeenth, nineteen-sixty-seven. Good night."

An advertisement came on and Mary looked back at Jesse. "How about a drink?" she asked.

Jesse took a long, deep breath and sat up straighter on the couch. "No," he said. "I think I'll go take a shower and get to bed."

"Okay," Mary said. "I'll lock up."

They stood up together. She turned to face him and put her arms around him. She was shorter than he was and could rest her head just below his chin. She snuggled into him, felt his arms around her and his hands gently massaging her back. The scent of honest sweat surrounded her, a good smell. He was a good husband, everything any woman could ever want—strong, conscientious, gentle. When he held her like this she felt safe, like sitting in front of a fire in a strong log cabin while a blizzard raged outside.

He pushed her away a little and kissed her lightly. "I need a shower," he said.

She let go of him and he walked out of the room. Walter Cronkite was on the television now, hosting a special report about the war. She switched it off and walked through the house locking the doors and opening some windows. She went into their bedroom and opened one of the windows near the foot of the bed. A small, soft breeze floated through the room, bringing with it the sweet scent of night-blooming jasmine. She took off her clothes and put on her nightgown, the short yellow one with little ruffles at the bottom he had given her on her last birthday. Then she pulled the bedspread down and lay down between the sheets.

When Jesse came in he took off his robe, laid it over a chair, and climbed into bed beside her. Mary switched off the light and they lay there quietly in the darkness. Mary listened to Jesse's breathing, shallower and quicker than she was used to, and wondered what it meant. She spoke softly.

"I think we'll have a good time on the vacation."

Jesse grunted.

"You're not sorry you started it, are you?"

"They don't want to go," Jesse said.

"Gary was really excited."

"About the fishing pole, not the trip."

"It's still a new idea. Wait 'til tomorrow. They'll go."

"Sure," Jesse said.

"They'll want to go," Mary said.

"Sure," Jesse said. "They'll want to go whether they want to or not."

They were quiet then. Mary wondered if Jesse was right. They all had their own plans for the summer. Maybe it wasn't fair to interrupt them on the spur of the moment. Especially Marty. What if he did have to quit? She wondered what he would do then, when they got back. Where would he work? Maybe he wouldn't work at all.

"You know what I wish?" she whispered, and even as she whispered it she knew Jesse had fallen asleep. His breathing was slow and even—so quiet. She pulled the sheet up under her chin and settled down into the pillow. She had been about to say that she wished it could be just them, just her and Jesse, the two of them, by themselves who would take the vacation. But even if Jesse had not been asleep she wouldn't have said it. She did want it. She wanted Jesse all to herself. And yet, the boys were necessary. They were something between her and Jesse that kept them separated just enough to love each other. She had always known that, and had always wanted it that way. Yet she had always wanted it to be different, too. It was because of her that the separateness was there. It wasn't Jesse. She didn't really want him all to herself. She guessed she wanted to want him all to herself but she was afraid even of that. It was confusing.

She turned on her side, facing Jesse, and put her arm across his broad chest. "I love you," she whispered, and knew that that, at least in some sense, was true.

The next morning Jesse unloaded his tools from the back of the truck and they all climbed in (Jesse, Mary, and Marty in the front; David and Gary in the back) and started visiting the camper dealers in the San Fernando Valley. They ooed and ahed at the deluxe models with tiny bathrooms that had chemical toilets and showers, high overheads with chairs as comfortable as airline seats that made into beds, and front windows as big as small picture windows. They learned the different floor plans and decided which one was best for them. They looked at some with butane refrigerators that converted to electricity if it was available, and some with only small iceboxes. Jesse talked to the salesmen about construction—what size wood was used for beams, what supported the overhead, how much insulation was used, and even what size screws held the aluminum sheeting on the outside.

Jesse and Mary held periodical conferences about what they

could afford. Marty wanted to have a shower and bathroom, and the chemical toilet appealed to Mary as well. A butane refrigerator would eliminate the bother of buying ice every few days. But these things added so much more expense that in the end they decided on a simple, inelegant model with no bathroom, an icebox, an overhead just tall enough to sleep two comfortably, and a table with two cushioned benches that converted into a bed which would also sleep two, three if they squeezed a little. There was some counter space around the small sink, quite a bit of cupboard space, a three-burner butane stove and an oven, which was probably the only item that could be considered a luxury.

It took them all day to find what they wanted. Then it took all the next day for Jesse to haggle with the salesman and to have the camper installed on the truck. The salesman finally placated Jesse somewhat by throwing in a set of camper jacks for free.

When they got home that night they had to take the camper off the truck since Jesse needed the truck for work the next day. They unscrewed the tie-downs, which held the camper securely to the truck, and, with a jack at each corner, raised the camper off the bed. Marty crept the truck out from under the camper and the camper was left standing there in the driveway on four spindly legs. They all stood back and stared at it, half afraid to get too close. Gary said it looked like a Martian space ship and Jesse was afraid that if anybody breathed too hard it would fall. He knew that to be really safe the camper should sit on the ground, but the jacks wouldn't go down that far. Then Marty suggested the old redwood picnic table. Jesse got his tape measure and did some measuring and found that the table would just fit between the jacks. He and Marty slid the table carefully under the camper, then David and Gary helped them lower the jacks until the camper rested lightly on the table. Jesse still wondered about it, but at least it looked more stable. He cautioned them all to be careful when they went inside it, and said there was to be no roughhousing in or around it.

It was only after dinner that Gary mentioned his fishing pole. They had all forgotten about it. David said he would know what to get, that he would start getting all the fishing equipment together the next day when he was through working for Mr. Whipple.

The youth band Marty had belonged to before he started working was giving a concert that night, so Marty left after dinner to attend it. He was taking Connie, who had also belonged to the band. The rest of them watched television together for a while, then went out to the camper to look it over. They smelled its newness, examined little details here and there, and imagined the vacation and all the short week-end trips they would take later.

"We'll keep it stocked all the time," Jesse said. "That way when we want to go, all we have to do is put it on the truck and take off." He was feeling a kind of ethereal freedom, a gypsy-like desire for mobility. It was a new feeling for him. Most of his married life had been based on an opposite desire. They had bought the house from Mary's parents a year after they were married and had never moved. He had made enough moves growing up with his father's restaurant businesses that never lasted more than a year. He had attended five elementary schools. But this was different. There was still the house to come back to. It was only temporary escape.

The next evening Jesse came home late from work in an irritable mood and with some bad news. Somebody had botched up a job in Modesto and he had to go up there and make modifications on every hollow metal door Security Metals had installed. There were four hundred ten of them. He could have taken a crew up there, say ten men, and done the job in a couple days. But Modesto was a union town. The union wouldn't let him bring in a crew of his own and the union hall was full of a bunch of damn carpenters who didn't know anything about sheet metal. It was the damnedest thing he had ever heard of. He had finally talked them into letting him take one man with him. One man. Jesus Christ.

He sat at the kitchen table while he told Mary about it, and ran his hand through his hair. Mary was heating up the spaghetti the rest of them had had for dinner. It was one of Jesse's favorite meals and she had planned it as a kind of celebration after buying the camper, but Jesse had been late.

"Marty got the two weeks off," she said quietly.

"I suppose he's out somewhere now," Jesse said.

"The band was having a party. He took his trumpet."

"I'm glad he thinks he can still play it."

"He said they were going to jam." She set a plate heaped with spaghetti on the table and poured Jesse a glass of dark red wine. Then she sat down opposite him. He started eating as if his dinner hour was only two minutes long.

"Hey, slow down," Mary said. "We have all night."

Jesse put his fork down, picked up the glass of wine, and leaned back in his chair. He took a long sip, then held the glass in front of him, looking into it as if it was the future. "We'll go," he said softly, determinedly. "Just like I said. We'll leave in two weeks. Saturday morning. I'll have to do this job, but we'll go." He set his glass down, smiled, and started eating more slowly.

II

In his younger days, back when he was working at Universal Studios, Jesse would have thought nothing of working eighteen-hour days. Then, in fact, he had sometimes put in twenty-four-hour days, working the golden hours of overtime on top of overtime that gave him a pay check which quadrupled his normal one. But he was getting too old for work like that now.

He was driving his pickup south, through the darkness, on Interstate Five, going home after the job in Modesto. He felt tired, more tired than he could remember feeling before. And every so often he felt a stabbing in the middle of his chest. Indigestion. Another sign of age, he thought.

He was looking forward to the vacation. They would drive the first day over to Prescott and see Lyle and his family. Lyle was one of Jesse's buddies from Lockheed who had gotten tired of the city and moved to a small town. Jesse got letters from him every so often, telling him how great it was, telling him he should move, too. If it was as great as Lyle said, he just might move. From Lyle's they would go on to the Grand Canyon, then up to Yellowstone. They would take it easy. Stop whenever they felt like it. No schedule. And he would rest. Let the rest of them drive. Mary and Marty, even David a little, although it would be hard for him with the camper. Marty mostly. Marty was a good driver. *He* would just relax. Maybe sit in the back. Lie in the overhead and sleep all the way across the desert. That would feel good, to sleep.

Mac, the man he had taken with him for the job, sat beside him on the other side of the cab. He was talking now, in his characteristic laconic voice.

"Johnson already signed the bill. He's going to make them work. Like slaves."

"Back in the forties it wouldn't have happened," Jesse said. "There wouldn't have been any strike."

"Yeah, things were different then," Mac said. "There was a real war going on. Hitler was a killer and they bombed Pearl Harbor."

Jesse remembered. He had been pouring coffee for one of the two customers in his father's little restaurant in Oxnard. The customer was sitting at the counter looking bored and uneasy when Lopez, the fiesty little Mexican plumber from across the street, burst in with his eyes flaring. "Queek! Queek! Turn on the radio. The Japs are bombing us." His words shocked life back into a dreary, overcast Sunday. Jesse turned on the radio in the middle of a broadcast, just as his father came out from the kitchen. He watched his father's eyes. They grew instantly sad, as if he would cry, then he smiled. "There are forces at work we know nothing about," he said solemnly. Jesse could have predicted his father's reaction. Head in the clouds. He had studied too much metaphysics and listened to too much Aimee Semple McPherson. He could find what he considered Truth in the most insignificant happenings, but he couldn't make a restaurant successful, no matter how good the location.

Jesse glanced over at Mac. "There is a war on." He remembered Roosevelt calling it "righteous might." And the rest, "We will gain the inevitable triumph, so help us God." Brave words.

"Shit," Mac said. "There isn't any war. It's a goddamn stupid game."

"I suppose you would have voted for Goldwater, too."

"I don't know," Mac said. "Everybody's so hot on winning the war. They don't know what it's like over there."

"What's it like over there?" Jesse asked.

Mac shook his head. "I don't think anybody knows. All you ever see is a part of it. From what I could see, the Vietnamese don't give a shit."

Jesse wondered what part Marty would see when he went. He was sure Marty would go. It was only a matter of time, since he dropped out of college. He could have his draft notice waiting for him when they got home from vacation, if he hadn't already gotten it. No. Mary would have told him. Well, he might have gotten it today. He would go over there like Mac had, not knowing what he was doing there, not wanting to be there, bitter against the government for sending him there.

He stared out the windshield at the maze of red dots in front of him and watched the beams of his headlights eat up the asphalt. No matter how hard he tried he just couldn't understand that attitude. He had tried to enlist out of a genuine sense of patriotism and had been crushed when they turned him down because he had flat feet. He had had to be satisfied with working for Lockheed as a welder. And he had had to suppress his jealousy of his younger brother, Aaron, who went over as a forward gunner on a B-29 and then had hundreds of stories to tell when he came back. Jesse had wanted to enlist so bad he could taste it. Everybody wanted to enlist. Just like now, nobody did.

In that way, and in a lot of other ways, Mac was pretty typical, he guessed. Mac's mustache grew down over his upper lip and his stringy brown hair hung past his shirt collar. He was a good kid, though. He had worked hard, a lot harder than Jesse had a right to expect. Four hundred ten doors they had removed, modified, and rehung in ten days. They had had to take them off the hinges, haul them to the work site, cut three-eighths of an

19

inch off the bottoms, weld the channels back in place, haul them back to the frames, and rehang them. Forty-one times a day. They had started every morning at daylight and worked straight through, not even taking time for lunch, until it was too dark to see. Thirty-one tons of metal they had hauled around. All because somebody screwed up the specs. They could have started earlier, as soon as they got there on Tuesday. But Jesse had had to spend the whole afternoon arguing with the state inspector. Sure, they would fix the goddamn doors, but somebody else ought to sure as hell pay for it. They had made the doors according to their own specs. It wasn't their fault the air conditioning specs were different. It was only the air conditioning specs that called for three-eighths of an inch clearance at the bottom of every door. But the inspector said they were supposed to read all the specs. Jesus. Nobody did that. Why didn't the air conditioning company catch it then? They expect everybody to read the whole goddamn thousand-page book? They did. The bastard. You couldn't argue with him. Thinking about it made Jesse's heart race. Goddamn inspector thought he owned the world, with his loose jowls and beer gut hanging over his belt. Didn't know what it was to work for a living.

"You ought to tell your son to move to Canada," Mac said.

The words shot through Jesse's consciousness like an electric shock and his indigestion flared up again. "You really think that's the answer?" he said. "Run away from it? Jesus. Like a goddamn dog with its tail between its legs."

"It's *an* answer," Mac said. "It might be the only one. I don't know. A lot of 'em are doing it."

"They're all cowards," Jesse said. "Goddamn cowards." Was Marty a coward? It was the first time he had considered that Marty might run. What would he do if Marty just disappeared some day and then he got a letter from him from Canada?

"Maybe," Mac said. "When I went in it wasn't so popular. If I'd known then what I know now . . . I don't know. I might've ducked out."

"And where would you be today?" Jesse said. "Stuck in a foreign country. You couldn't even come home for a visit. You could maybe never come home."

"I know," Mac said. "But I was lucky. I might not have come home anyway."

"That's a chance you have to take," Jesse said.

"Yeah," Mac said. "But it would be nice to have some reason for taking it."

It was too much. Jesse tried to think of some way to change the subject but his mind swirled in circles. Bombs over Belfast, he remembered. When he had gone to Ireland with Lockheed Overseas. Hearing the explosions in the distance—always in the distance, and damn glad of it. Bill had been on Guam, shooting snipers out of palm trees. Bill and Marilyn were going to Texas. Mary had told him the first night he had called her from Modesto. Bill had had a sudden opportunity for promotion and he just couldn't turn it down. He worked for Union Oil doing something in an office that he could never explain very well. "Oh, I shuffle papers around," he always said. Well, hell. Jesse knew he wouldn't have turned down a chance for promotion either. It was life. But they would sure miss them. He had meant to talk to Bill about David. Bill seemed more like David. He thought maybe he could understand him, could give him some advice or something. Jesse remembered David when he picked him up at the highway patrol station the night of the accident. He looked so small and scared and humble. Embarrassed, he guessed. He didn't talk to him much then, but later he asked him, "What the hell were you doing driving back from Lancaster at one o'clock in the morning anyway?" He had just felt like driving around, he said. "Driving around. To Lancaster?" Well, he had some things he wanted to think about. "What things?" David had looked at the floor then. They were in the living room alone. Everyone else had gone to the store or something. David didn't say anything and Jesse could feel the wall between them, a wall that stretched clear to China and was as high as the moon and probably as old as David. "It's about Ellen, isn't it," Jesse said. He knew David hadn't seen her since the accident. And it was just as well, he had thought. She was two years older than David, with her own apartment and a job. David wasn't ready for that yet. But David just sat there staring at the floor. Jesse softened his face, reached his hand out and put it firmly on top of David's, an action that felt so strange to him it scared him. "I might understand if you tell me about it," Jesse had said. "I might be some help. I'd like to be some help." David looked up into his eyes and Jesse could see the tears there, and the confusion, and the helplessness that made Jesse feel helpless himself, and the pleading to leave it be, please, just leave it be. "It's personal," David had said. And that was it. Jesse knew he would never know what happened. But at least he had seen the wall. That was something. And the damn insurance company wouldn't even total the car. They were going to fix it and it would never be the same again. Gave them a loaner, an old clunker of a fifty-three Buick that used three times as much gas. And then Gary. Fooling around with Manny, that damn kid from a broken home and his goddamn firecrackers at school and his practical jokes that were just plain dangerous. Who knows what they were doing over at his house after school before Mary found out his mother wasn't home. It's a wonder they didn't burn the house down. And Mary . . .

Jesse glanced suddenly at Mac. "You hungry?" he asked.

"Starved," Mac said.

"We'll stop in Gorman and get something to eat. A steak or something. We deserve it." He paused for a moment, as if to catch his breath. "You're a good kid," he went on. "You can really work. I really appreciate your helping me out like that."

Mac grinned sarcastically. "Ah, gee. Thanks, old man."

Standing at the kitchen sink, a wet soapy glass in one hand and a soggy dishrag in the other, Mary stared into the darkened windowpane over the sink. In the daylight, she would have seen a distorted view of the yard, the large swing set, the grass, and the chain link fence, covered there with honeysuckle; distorted because she would have had to look through the thin branches of a large hibiscus plant which bloomed bright red flowers all year long. But what she saw now was like an underexposed photograph of her worried face. The image showed her light brown hair, which she always called blond because it used to be blond—all through high school it was blond—her small blue eyes and pug nose set in a round pudgy face above a wide mouth that smiled naturally much of the time and had caused her mother to nickname her Cheshire when she was a child. But the mouth wasn't smiling now. It was straight and the eyes squinted slightly. Two wrinkles moved up vertically from the bridge of her nose to meet the horizontal lines on her forehead.

A vague uneasiness had crept over her. But she couldn't think of anything she could have forgotten. She'd been trying to think of things all week, she and David. They had been loading the camper with camping equipment, cooking utensils, food, games, clothes, everything they thought they would need on the trip. She had gotten that boy Brian down the street to water the lawn and had asked Eleanor Trimble across the street to collect the mail. She had stopped delivery of the newspaper . . . . But what she felt didn't seem to have anything to do with all that. Someone had walked over her grave, as her mother used to say. She had been thinking of Jesse. The way he had sounded on the phone last night. So tired. But the feeling didn't really have anything to do with Jesse either, at least not directly. It was more general, as if encompassing her whole world, so much of which concerned this kitchen, this task, this unseen view through this darkened window. She remembered dreams where she would be running from something she couldn't see but which she could feel gaining on her from behind. She shivered again, more voluntarily this time, and tried to push the feeling away from her.

She looked at the image in the window and smiled at herself prettily. She was still pretty, although she could stand to lose some weight. The curl in her hair was still a little kinky, but it had been only two days since the permanent. Marilyn, in the midst of all her packing and the excitement of moving, had taken the time to come over and give her a permanent. God, she would miss Marilyn. Who would she talk to? It was really a good thing they were going on vacation at the same time Marilyn and Bill were moving away. She wouldn't have time to mope, to stand at the kitchen sink, like she was doing now, and think of all the good times they had had.

She washed the glass, finally, and laid it carefully in the rinse water. The house was quiet and peaceful tonight. Marty was gone, seeing Connie one last time before they left. David had gone to see Aunt Roe. Gary was in the den watching television. She could hear the faint murmur from the set. She wondered what was on. When she finished the dishes she would watch with him a little while, then it would be time for him to go to bed. They planned to leave early in the morning to get across as much of the desert as they could before it got too hot, but it didn't look like Jesse would get home in time to put the camper on the truck tonight.

She went on washing with quick precision, hoping her uneasiness wouldn't return. She thought about Gary. He was the only one who seemed excited about the trip and she was glad he would finally have something to do besides sit around missing Manny. Before Jesse talked to her about the vacation she had decided to call the parks and recreation department and see what kind of programs she could get Gary into. And she had decided she would take him to the beach sometimes, although she didn't know how that would work out since there were no other children she could take with him. All Gary's friends were from school and Manny was the only one he ever brought home. Manny seemed to her to be a bad influence on Gary. His mother was by herself and worked all day. Manny had two younger sisters but his mother kept them in a day care center. When she found out about the firecrackers she had gone over to talk with Manny's mother. She couldn't have Gary playing over there with no supervision and she didn't think Manny's wild kind of freedom was a good influence on Gary. It probably had something to do with the problems Gary was having at school. It wasn't that he was bad, his teacher had said at the conference. It was just that he didn't listen. He drifted off. He seemed to live in his own world and couldn't keep track of what was going on around him. And he didn't do the work. Or at least most of the time he didn't. When he did do it, he did it well, so it wasn't that he was stupid or anything. She just didn't know where he was most of the time. Jesse had talked to him about it for a long time one day. The two of them went out to get ice cream cones at the Tastee Freez and were gone about an hour. Just before school let out, the teacher said he was doing better, but it was hard to tell. He passed anyway. Next year would be the time to really watch him. The teacher said she would explain things to his new teacher.

She would like to know exactly what Jesse said to him. Jesse told her they had had a man-to-man talk and that he had told Gary he would have to straighten up if he didn't want to end up a working stiff all his life like his old man. It sounded like the same lecture he had given Marty and David—more than once. He had expectations for his sons, but they weren't very specific. To make a living doing what you want, Jesse always said, was the best life anybody could ask for. He had wanted to be a doctor, he said, but there was no money for college when he was that age. He ended up working at anything he could find just to make a buck, and he had been doing it ever since.

She wondered what he would have been like as a doctor. Not very good, she thought. He didn't have the hands for it. He had the personality, though. He was good with people. He had a kind of authority they respected instinctively. And he seldom disappointed them.

She felt her face growing warm. She swallowed. It was still there, she thought. After twenty-two years it was still there. Sometimes she hated herself for the way it made her feel. He had disappointed her once. Only once. But disappointed wasn't the right word. Disgusted, frightened, shamed, hurt. She had been hurt by the only man she had ever loved, and that hurt was enough to last her a lifetime. She just couldn't put it away permanently. It crept into her thoughts when she least expected it and made her face hot and tears edge dangerously close to the surface of her eyes.

It had happened before she knew Marilyn. If Marilyn had been there, things might have been different. She did talk to Marilyn about it later, but by then the hurt was ingrained in her so that nothing could get it out. At the time, there had been no one. Absolutely no one. She had never been so alone, and the loneliness frightened her. Just the bare facts—that Jesse was having an affair with a pert, sarcastic little extra at the studios—seemed mundane and stupid. They had only been married a year. There were no children yet. She could have divorced him easily. She had talked to a lawyer.

She wondered what would have happened if she had gone ahead. What would her life be like today? She wouldn't have the boys, at least not these boys. If she had children at all they would belong to some other father. Or maybe she would have never married again. She would have been one of those career women, a secretary probably. The lawyer had told her that good legal secretaries were hard to come by and all it took was a few years of schooling. Without children she could have done that easily. She wasn't dumb.

But she hadn't been able to bring herself to take the divorce proceedings any further than just talk. Mainly because she blamed herself for what had happened. After the miscarriage, sex became such a frightening thing to her. With Jesse on top of her, all she could think of was the little person who had been inside her and then had disappeared, as if to let her know she wasn't fit to be its mother. She couldn't help it, and she found herself sleeping as close to the edge of the bed as she could get. Just his touch unnerved her, made her shiver. Once he forced her, as good as raped her. But as she lay passively beneath him, her face turned aside, tears rolling down her face and wetting the pillow, Jesse suddenly got up and went into the bathroom. When he came back to bed his face was wooden and she knew that something—some invisible link that held them together—had been severed.

Time, she guessed now, had healed that broken link, but it had been a frightening convalescence. By the time Jesse told her about the affair, just before he left for Belfast, she had already guessed from a hundred tiny hints. And it was just after he had left that Marilyn came, the lifesaver, almost literally.

They had been like two peas in a pod, she and Marilyn. They did everything together. They talked endlessly. And slowly she came to understand that something was still left of her love for Jesse, that the affair, the miscarriage, didn't really matter. All that mattered was building back their love. They wrote hundreds of letters. When he came back they began again, and Marty was born as a kind of confirmation that life could at least be some semblance of what she wanted it to be.

But the memory of the hurt remained even when the hurt itself was gone. It was still there. Even now, as she drained the water from the sink and noticed that there must be an advertisement on the television because she could hear some kind of music, some cute jingle being sung about toothpaste or peanut butter or something. She wiped her hands on the towel, looked again at the darkened window, and left the kitchen.

"What did we go there for?" Connie asked.

"I don't know," Marty said. "It was supposed to be good. That's what I heard."

"It stunk."

"I know."

They walked down the sidewalk away from the movie theater holding hands. Connie's long black hair sparkled with the reflection of neon lights dancing in it. They reached Marty's car, a white sixty-three Impala, and Marty opened the door for her. Then he went around and got in himself. She scooted across the seat close to him and he looked at her a moment before he turned the key. He wanted to smile. He knew he should smile. He smiled.

"I just thought we should do something," he said. He was awkward with her and he couldn't understand why. He had known Connie for five years, ever since he joined the band. And they'd been going together for two. They were really very good friends. "I should have known it would be a drag," he said.

"It's okay," she mumbled.

"That score," Marty went on. "Typical Hollywood mush."

"Not a Mancini," Connie said.

"Hardly." Marty started the engine and pulled away from the curb. "It's still early," he said. "You want to go down to the beach?"

"Okay," Connie said.

She laid her hand on his thigh and he became aware of her presence, as if he had been talking to a figment of his own imagination which had now suddenly become solid. Watching the road, he pictured her in his mind, her slim, almost frail body; her dark soft eyes; her small, round mouth beneath a nose just slightly too large; the thin line of dusky hair above her lip, barely perceptible against her dark skin. He wondered if he loved her, if he would marry her. He knew it was assumed by them both—and by everyone else. But the way things were now, he couldn't be sure of anything.

He turned on Coldwater and drove past the high school. The band and choir rooms sat off by themselves, near the student parking lot, ostracized. Marty looked at the rooms and a wave of nostalgia washed over him. Then a smile broke across his face. He looked over at Connie. "Hey, remember . . ." But Connie was ignoring the school, her head turned to look the other way. The smile left Marty's face. He turned right on Roscoe Boulevard, drove a few blocks, then turned right again on Sheldon and got up on the San Diego Freeway.

He relaxed then; there wasn't much traffic. He put his hand on Connie's thigh. She wore a thin nylon dress. Her legs were bare. He could picture them dark, shapely, and soft beneath the dress. She snuggled closer to him. Cool night air rushed in through the partially opened window and after a time, as they approached the ocean, Marty could smell the damp saltiness that flooded him with sensual memories.

He pulled into a dark parking lot that overlooked the beach. Another car was parked at the other end of the lot. He turned off the lights and the engine, then sat a moment, drinking in the air, the slightly musty odor from the car, and Connie's Persian Wood perfume. Then he put his arm around her and his mouth searched for hers. They kissed passionately, but not violently. Marty slid his hand down her shoulder and gently rubbed her braless breast. Her hand was at his crotch. Electricity surged through his body. They kissed again. He slipped his hand under her dress, slid it up her legs to her panties, and she moved away from him to lie down on the seat. He gave himself over to his body then, and stopped thinking, embracing this release of his mind in the form of Connie who received him with the same kind of abandon.

Later, they walked barefoot along the beach, in the soft sand near the water. It was, as Marty knew, the time when Connie talked incessantly, saying nothing in particular, letting the sound of her voice drown out something within her, something Marty couldn't fathom. He let her talk, lost in himself again, making responses when appropriate, not listening. He felt himself suspended, like a blob of seaweed, drifting, at the mercy of the tides and the constant motion of the ocean. And he could see the possibility of being washed ashore to lie helpless in the sand, the sun beating down, drying, killing. He shivered, then became aware of Connie's words, that she was talking about him.

"Do you practice any more? You don't, do you. You're giving it up. Because it's easier to go to work and collect your pay check so you can pay off your car and take me out to dinner. Why should you give up the only thing you love? I know. I don't know what you really love. I think you're just lazy. Doing what's easy for you now. Taking the easy way out. It would make a good song. You ought to write it. You could do that. You have too much talent to give up now. You shouldn't have quit the band. John Mellon is playing with Ray Conniff now, and Rocky started his own group. Phil is playing solo in a little restaurant on Sunset Boulevard. Colby filled in for somebody or other who was sick as Shelly's Manne-Hole. He played with Joe Pass. And you're better than any of them."

"I'm going to get drafted," Marty muttered. "Any time now."

"And you're going on vacation for two weeks. And when that's over, there'll be some other excuse. There's always some excuse."

"I'm not that good. Why do you think I was always second chair?"

"Because you never challenged. You let Grobin sit there like a god or something. You could have done Blue Skies a lot better than him."

"I don't see you out there tearing up the world with your great talent."

He looked at her and saw her smile. "I know," she said. "I'm lazy, too."

They walked on in silence. So Colby played with Joe Pass at Shelly's, Marty thought. His mind drifted into a familiar daydream. He saw himself standing on a small stage, a microphone in front of him, a small group behind him—drums, bass, piano, a tenor sax, a trombone. He played his trumpet into the mike, leading the group through complicated riffs and slurs, feeling the rhythm, ad-libbing mellow, cool sounds that drifted over the small audience like an ethereal canopy that slowly settled upon them. And when he finished there was the applause, but it wasn't important. Only the music was important.

She was probably right, he thought. He probably was just lazy. It was true, he didn't practice much any more and he had given up his lessons when he started working. He had never really considered trumpet playing a possible profession. It was always just a hobby, a pleasant pastime. Sure, he thought, that way it didn't matter if he was any good or not. It would be terrible to have to be good at something. But there was so much competition. Grobin really was better then he was, and when he listened to people like Gillespie or Miles Davis, the thought that he could play professionally seemed absurd. When he started college right after high school, he decided to prepare to be a forest ranger. It would be easy, he had thought, and pleasant. He had pictured himself tramping through pine forests all day, giving little lectures around a campfire at some national park. He smiled at that picture now. He didn't even like camping. Who was he trying to kid? Besides, there were chemistry and physics courses that he just couldn't seem to grasp. He didn't know what to do. He had to change his major, but he didn't know what to change it to. He took the job stacking crates at McMichael's Egg Company to give himself time to decide what to do. He could have gotten a better job, probably, but when he didn't go back to college they changed his draft classification to one-A. Nobody would hire a one-A. So, even though he knew there were these decisions he ought to make, in the back of his mind was the thought that the draft board would make them for him and that would make things much easier. He had stopped thinking about his life and resigned himself to waiting for his draft notice.

What he did think about was the lectures he got from his father. Jesse had been disappointed when Marty took the job at McMichael's. "You don't want to spend your life doing something you hate just to make money," he had said. "You'll get stuck in it. You think you can get out whenever you want, but then, before you realize what's happening, it's too late. It's a hell of a way to live, believe me."

Sure, Marty thought. Do what you want, he always said. It was easy for him to say. *He* never had to decide what *he* wanted to do. Besides, things were different now than they were when his father was his age. For one thing, going to college wasn't the big deal his father made it out to be. You could make just as much money without a degree.

He and Jesse had argued it back and forth, over and over again, and he just couldn't make his father see that what he was doing was all right, that he wouldn't turn out a failure just because he didn't go to college. He needed time, that was all. He needed to see a little more of life before he made any permanent decisions. Just because his father had these feelings of inadequacy and blamed them on his lack of a college education, he tried to make Marty feel like a failure, too. Well, he wasn't a failure. Not yet anyway. He wished his father would ease up and get the hell off his back.

They had almost reached the Santa Monica Pier and Marty glanced at his watch. "We'd better start back," he said softly.

They turned around and followed their footprints slowly the other way. Connie clung to him as if afraid, and Marty felt muddled stirrings of fear himself. The war, he thought. He wondered what it was like over there, and his wondering stopped at a blank. He became aware of the shuffling of their feet through the sand, and the gentle crash of the breakers, the hiss of the foam reaching toward the dry sand, and the indiscernible noise that went on incessantly beneath all the others, the noise of an active, living sea.

None of his friends would ever believe that he came here voluntarily, David thought. That this house, with its musty smell and old-fashioned furniture, was one of his favorite places in the world. That this old lady, his mother's aunt, sitting properly straight on the couch opposite him, her thin, ancient face smiling at him through a thousand tiny wrinkles, was his favorite person, maybe the one person he loved unequivocally. His friend, Jeff—the crack reporter on the school paper for which David wrote features, who had dug up that story about Mr. Reddleson selling marajuana to students right in his own room during lunch—would find sitting here with Aunt Roe unbelievably boring. And if David told him how Aunt Roe had helped the police break up a whole ring of dope dealers who were using the vacant house next door as a drop, he wouldn't have believed it.

The living room, where they sat drinking coffee from delicate china cups, was overfull of furniture—three easy chairs, a long, high-backed couch, a large table under the windows, and a piano backed up to the fireplace. There was a coffee table and several end tables, all loaded down with books, some just lying there, others propped up with elegant book ends. The walls were hung with dark, classical-looking paintings.

The books in the living room were only a sample of what David knew was in Aunt Roe's reading room, a small room on the east side of the house with windows to catch the morning sun and floor-to-ceiling bookcases. It was David's favorite room. He watched the house for her when she made her frequent trips to Trona to see old friends or to Ridgecrest to see her son, and he sometimes sat in the room for hours, losing himself in some old book that sucked him into itself like a vacuum cleaner while the sprinklers outside went untended until water ran down the street. It was there that he had become enthralled with Goethe's

The Sorrows of Young Werther, and when he asked her about it, she had given it to him.

The book had a strange effect on him. Werther's extreme romanticism seemed sloppy to him at first, but the more he read, the more he became a part of it and began to understand how Werther felt. After he had read it the second time, he started writing poetry. That was about six months ago. Now he had a stack of about forty poems in his desk drawer that no one except Aunt Roe had ever seen. He considered them his most important work. Much more important than the silly features he wrote for the school paper.

"The crack in the floor under your chair is a potential feature," Mr. Novotny, the journalism advisor, told him one day. So David wrote a feature about the crack in the floor under his chair. It was a wild fantasy about microscopic, two-dimensional creatures whose whole world was that single crack. They were extremely intelligent, with art and poetry that strove toward three dimensionality, a complex system of government modeled after Plato, and scientists who tried to tell everyone that two dimensionality was all there was. Then one day the maintenance people filled in the crack and the world was destroyed. David had written it as a joke, but Mr. Novotny printed it anyway. David was never sure if Mr. Novotny really liked it or if he had done it to teach him some journalistic lesson. But his poetry was different; he was serious about that.

He had told Aunt Roe about the vacation and where they planned to go. Now, she was telling him about the time she and her husband had visited Yellowstone and about their guide. Her stories usually centered on some unusual character.

"He was magnificent," she said. "Simply magnificent. He wore leather breeches and moccasins and, for photographs, a war crest of eagle feathers. He wore no shirt at all, and when he stood erect with the sun streaming down on his gleaming brown skin I could feel all the simple majesty of his race. He was full-blooded Shoshone and spoke very little English. We rode all over the park on horseback, camping at various places which were particularly beautiful or which had good fishing. At one place, there was another party there ahead of us. We camped several yards from them and joined them around their campfire that night. Sun Tree—that was his name. Actually a more correct translation, I believe, would have been Tree of the Sun or Tree full of Sunlight, something like that, which really has an entirely different connotation, don't you think? Sun Tree sounds too much like an orange juice brand. Well, but Sun Tree seemed very taken by a sweet blond girl of about eighteen who was with the party—she was a daughter, I believe. The next day, as we were leaving, I caught him looking after her with a wistful expression on his broad, noble face. 'Why Sun Tree,' I said. 'All this time I thought you were my beau.' He looked at me rather fiercely—which frightened me a good deal, I don't mind admitting—then shook his head and growled, 'No. No shoot. No shoot.'"

She laughed, with her low, throaty laugh that was infectious. David laughed with her, although he knew his heart wasn't in it tonight. This was the third time he had seen Aunt Roe since the accident, and every time he wondered why he had come. She had seen it, he knew. No one could size up a person better than Aunt Roe. And he knew from some of the things she said that she was trying to help without prying. It was one of the reasons he loved her, he guessed.

"You will enjoy Yellowstone," she said. "It is really very beautiful."

There was a lull in the conversation then, something Aunt Roe only allowed when she chose to for some purpose. David looked toward the heavy, flowered drapes that covered the front windows and sensed her watching him inquisitively.

"So tell me," Aunt Roe said. "How is your writing coming?"

David took a folded piece of paper out of his shirt pocket, unfolded it, and handed it to her. "I wrote this last night."

Aunt Roe read the poem carefully. It took her a long time. Finally she looked up at him, smiling only slightly. The floor lamp behind her chair shone directly on her white hair and made it glow softly.

"This is very different," she said. "It's lovely, but very different. I sense a violence here that I have never sensed before in any of your poems." She folded the paper and handed it back to him. "You should never stop writing," she said, as she always said. "It is in your blood, in your soul. Your expressions are so sensitive and you have insights into things that seem beyond your age."

David raised his eyebrows at that. That was something she had never said before. She went on.

"I think perhaps it is time for you to leave off poetry, for a while at least, and try writing a story. Think about it while you are on vacation. Perhaps something will happen that will light a spark in you that will grow into a story. I believe you are ready for that now."

"Because of the violence?" David said.

Aunt Roe smiled. "No. Because of the form your poems have been taking lately. They are really little stories. The violence . . . ah, well. I don't know about that." She looked into his eyes, reading his mind, he couldn't help believing. She probably knew all about him, more than he knew himself even.

"A little violence may be a good thing," she said, "if it is directed properly. It is a form of energy, like all emotion, but it is difficult to control. Violence is, by its nature, destructive. We must be careful to use it to destroy the proper things."

What was he destroying? David wondered. Himself, maybe. Or Ellen. Or both of them. No. It probably wasn't that general. Only a part of each of them. Some part that would never grow back. Well, it was already gone. Whatever had been there with them was gone now. He hadn't seen her since it happened. He had only talked to her on the phone. She told him she thought it was best for them not to see each other any more. Yes, he had said, she was probably right, and he had resisted the almost irresistible urge to tell her he had almost died because of it.

And what violence was behind that? Something more than he could put into a silly poem. That violence had been real, so real he could still feel it, still dreamed about it, could still see the sparks flying around his head as he rode upside down in the spinning car that scraped along the highway on its top, then rolled upright into a ditch on the wrong side of the road. And he could still see himself getting out of the car, looking at the top, flattened as if a wrecking ball had fallen on it. He had slammed his hand down on the top so hard his palm throbbed and burned because of the stupid, asinine thing he had done. And Ellen . . .

"Would you like some more coffee?" Aunt Roe asked.

David shook his head. "No. No, thank you." He wanted to go now, but something kept him there, staring at Aunt Roe dumbly. Then suddenly it hit him. He couldn't believe he hadn't realized it before. He wanted to tell her. He wanted to tell her all about it, even what happened with Ellen. And he wanted to tell her how he felt, about the muddy churning water that flowed through his brain instead of blood, and about the questions that went on and on, making his head spin like a globe on its axis.

But he knew he wouldn't tell her. He would never tell anyone. Maybe he would write about it someday, after he had it all sorted out and organized. When he could put the hurts, the questions, the stupidities into some kind of order he would probably understand them better. It wouldn't ease the pain any, but at least he would be able to see what was causing it.

"Well," Aunt Roe said. "I'm going to tell you one more story, if you can stand to listen to me babble on, then I'll let you go. I know you must have important things to do. You may be able to use this story in your writing sometime. It happened when I was a girl in boarding school. I had been there quite some time and I was becoming upset with some of the other girls. You see, they were very hypocritical, or so I thought, so full of gossip about one another, evil gossip that hurt me to listen to. There were many petty little jealousies. Well, you can't imagine what it was like. One day, one of the mistresses found me off by myself crying, moping probably. The mistresses, I think, considered me a sensitive young creature, when actually I was just very self-centered. They thought I was sensitive because I was so skinny then." She laughed quietly. "At any rate, they sent me to the headmaster to talk over my problem with him. I found him seated behind his huge mahogany desk in his high-backed wicker chair. He was just a young man, and extremely handsome. Every girl in the school had an intolerable crush on him. 'Well, Miss Griffith,' he said. 'What seems to be the trouble?' Standing there, stiff and rigid, I poured out everything, all my feelings, all the problems I felt I had. They all must have seemed very petty to him, but looking into his bright blue eyes I could see genuine concern that prompted me to go on and on." She chuckled again. "Oh, dear. I must have bored him to death, the poor man. Well, when I had finished my lament he said, 'Miss Griffith, come around here, will you please?' Trembling—I had never been that close to him before—I went around the desk and stood beside him. He took a sheet of paper from a drawer and laid it on his desk. Then he quickly drew a very good picture of a tree, a maple tree, as I recall. He was really a very accomplished artist. 'There is a little lesson in this tree,' he said. 'Let us say the tree itself, as a whole, represents God. You, Miss Griffith, are one of the branches. Let us say this one here.' He pointed to a particularly thin one. 'You see, the branch remains attached to the tree throughout the life of the tree. Attached to the branch are leaves. The leaves grow out of the branch in the spring, then wither and fall away in the fall. The leaves represent the friends you will acquire as you pass through life. Those friends who are not meant for you will simply fall away. But you, the branch, will always remain a part of the tree.' He looked at me and smiled. 'Do you understand this, Miss Griffith?' I said I did, although I wasn't at all sure at the time. He handed me the paper and told me to keep it. 'Think of this little illustration the next time you see faults in others,' he said. 'The others are like leaves. They serve a purpose while they are there, but they will fall away.' Well, I kept that little picture for a long time, many years, in fact. And I still think it is a beautiful little lesson."

She paused and looked off into space. The memories she must have, David thought. And he couldn't help wondering what memories he would look back on when he was eighty.

Finally, she stood up slowly and took David's coffee cup. "Well, you must have some last minute things to do before you go."

David nodded and stood up, anxious to go but sorry to leave. He felt strange about this parting—a projected nostalgia, as if he was remembering this moment even while it happened. He kissed her wrinkled, powdered cheek lightly and hurried out the door.

Driving home in the old loaned clunker, he mulled over the story she had told. He didn't think it really worked the way she had intended it to because if he was a branch, it didn't seem logical for his friends to be leaves. He thought of all the people he worked with on the school paper. They were branches, too. A tree has more than one branch. If the other branches weren't people, what were they? No, wait. There are different kinds of people. That must be it. If the leaves are the people who will fall away, then the other branches are the people who will remain, who are strong enough to remain, who are also connected directly to the tree. Carl and Jeff were probably like that, although he couldn't be sure. Their friendship had never been tested. But they seemed more like branches than leaves to him. Wait. That was it. He felt his mind light up. It all depends on your point of view, he thought. When he looks at the picture, he is a branch. But if someone else looks at the picture, say Carl or Jeff—or Ellen. Say Ellen was looking at the picture. Then she would be the branch and he, David, would only be one of the leaves. So you can be a branch and a leaf at the same time. It all depends on whose tree it is. He laughed out loud. Well, he thought, we're all self-centered. Aunt Roe's headmaster was a smart man.

He had been driving very carefully. The old clunker was a Mac truck compared to the little Renault he was used to. It seemed wider than the lanes; it drifted to the left and every so often he had to jerk it back with the power steering; the power brakes nearly sent him through the windshield whenever he touched the pedal. He was glad there wasn't much traffic. Finally, he turned down his own street, drove to the house, and turned into the driveway. He touched the brake pedal to stop, but nothing happened. The pedal wouldn't go down. He braced his back against the seat and pushed down on the pedal as hard as he could, but the old car lumbered on ahead like a stubborn elephant. There was a dull clang as the car hit the chain link gates. The latch snapped and the two gates swung forward and around, banging against the fence. About halfway through the gates, the old car rolled to a gentle stop, and it was only then that David thought of the emergency brake. He swore at himself.

The porch light came on and his mother ran out. "Are you all right?" She almost shouted it, even though she was only ten feet away. David could hear the frantic worry in her voice.

"I'm okay," he said. He started to say, What'd they loan us a damn car with bad brakes for? But he remembered that it was his fault they had the old car in the first place. He inched the car through the gates and up the driveway a little way. Then he got out and looked at the gates. The end pipes on both gates were bowed in like two letter "C's." He tried to close one and it scraped on the cement driveway.

"What happened?" Mary asked.

"The brakes went out or something. I couldn't push on the pedal." He was still trying to close the gate, not thinking about what he was doing, straining against the scraping.

"Why don't you leave them open," Mary said. "Your father will be home pretty soon."

"Oh, yeah," David mumbled. He shoved the gate back off the driveway and onto the grass, stood back, and looked at them again. His heart was beating fast. His stomach churned. There was a lump in his throat. He couldn't tell if he was going to cry or be sick. He turned and walked away from the gates and his mother, around the house, through the back door, and into his room. He wanted desperately to be alone, but Gary was there, lying in bed, his eyes wide. Gary started to say something, but David left the room and went back outside. He barely avoided his mother as she walked around to the back door. When she had gone into the house, he went back and climbed into the camper.

He sat on one of the cushioned benches and laid his head on the table. The darkness of the camper closed around him and he felt himself sinking, sinking into himself, as if his mind was a living dough kneading itself—flattening itself, folding itself over, flattening, folding over, constantly changing its shape but never leaving itself, never attaching itself to anything outside. It was an endless, senseless motion. And he was tired. Suddenly he felt very tired. He wanted the motion to stop. He wanted to sleep. The darkness was like a drug.

The door opened. He could see the upper half of his mother, silhouetted, peering into the camper as if into a dark cave.

"David?" she called softly.

David didn't answer. He felt the camper shake as she climbed up the steps. She stood beside him for a moment, then stroked his thin, sandy brown hair, the way he remembered she used to do when he was a child.

"Don't be so hard on yourself," she murmured. "We all make mistakes sometimes."

David turned his head and looked up at her with what he

knew must be a vacant stare. The words he mumbled were dead. "It wasn't my fault. I told you the brakes went out." And as he said it he suddenly came back to life. Even though he knew what he said was true, he had the feeling he was lying and he hated himself for it.

"That's what I mean," Mary said. "It wasn't your fault."

There was a long silence. David felt as if he had been burned all over. The raw flesh was exposed and he flinched at the lightest touch. Mary's hand dropped to her side, but David was still acutely aware of her presence. It was all he could think about, her standing there, a foreign body that grew into the darkness and enveloped him like mud. He was finding it hard to breathe.

"You'd better come in and get some sleep," Mary said finally. "We'll be getting up early tomorrow." She went to the door and quietly climbed down the steps.

David breathed easier. He sat there in the darkness for a short time, then realized he should get to bed before his father came home. He wasn't up to facing him tonight.

He had been in bed less than fifteen minutes when he heard his father's truck pull into the driveway. Then, through the open door of his bedroom, he heard the voices.

"What happened to the gate?" Jesse asked.

"David hit it with the car," Mary said.

There was a short pause, then Jesse exploded. "Jesus Christ! What the hell did you let him drive for? Damn that kid! How are we going to close the gates before we leave tomorrow? Damn!"

"He didn't do it on purpose," Mary said. "The brakes went out."

There was a long silence. He might as well have done it on purpose, David thought. But then, maybe it was more on purpose than he realized. Destructive violence. He could hear their voices again, softer now so that he couldn't make out all the words. He caught them in little snatches. ". . . upset lately . . ." ". . . Jesus . . . get a hold . . ." ". . . the trip . . . help to me . . . he feels . . ." The voices became softer and he couldn't make out any words at all. After a while he heard his father walk across the den and go into the bathroom. The shower turned on.

He wondered how his father would act the next day. Distant, he figured. He would avoid a direct confrontation, but there would be small actions no one else would notice that would tell David how he felt. There would have to be some discussion. Everyone would see the gate. Marty would see it when he came home tonight. Marty would do it. He would check the brakes and find out what was wrong. Then he would argue with his father about how they ought to get the garage to pay for the gate for loaning them a car with bad brakes. And his father would say, "We're going on a vacation now. We'll worry about all this when we get home." David knew he would feel relieved and apprehensive at the same time, because he would have that hanging over his head for the whole two weeks. That along with everything else.

He settled down in his bed and pulled the sheet up to his chin. He could hear Gary breathing softly in the darkness. Gary, the baby of the family, the one everybody spoiled. Sometimes he wished he could be a kid again. Things were so much less complicated then. There weren't all these dark questions that had to be dealt with. Right and wrong were what Mother and Father said they were and you did what you thought you could get away with. Like Gary and his firecrackers. He smiled. Gary was so innocent, even for a kid his age. He didn't think his father or mother realized what kids were like these days. Hell, kids in the fifth and sixth grades were selling marijuana and popping bennies, getting drunk after school, having sex.

And that's what it all boils down to finally, in the end, isn't it, he thought bitterly. Every moral issue in the universe finally becomes, "Thou shalt not fornicate." Every day it taunts you. Every pair of tight jeans, every breast bouncing under a loose blouse, on television, in movies, on billboards, says, "Hey, come

on, let's fornicate." If it ever became as natural as it was probably meant to be, like in *Brave New World* or something, Madi-
son Avenue would go out of business.

But, of course, the Brave New World wasn't really utopia. It
was dehumanizing. That was Huxley's point. Sex just for the
sake of pleasure brings humans to a level lower than animals.
But he had thought that with Ellen it was more than that. He
had loved her. Still loved her, he thought. But what he had done
was wrong. He knew that. God, he knew that. Because it had violated her. It violated *him*.

He was thankful that his father had been so quiet when he
picked him up at the highway patrol station after the accident.
But later, when his father tried to talk to him about it—cornered
him, almost, in the living room—he felt intimidated by his father's bulging muscles showing through his tight T-shirt and by
his stern face. He knew his father would never understand.
Things were black and white for him. There would have only
been condemnation. No. He had to work it out himself, had to
sift through everything and try to make sense of it all. That was
enough to worry about without worrying about what his father
thought of him, too. But he knew he would worry about what
his father thought about him anyway. His father was just there.
He was always there. It would be easier, maybe, if he wasn't;
like Gary's friend, Manny, who only had to worry about a soft
mother who was easy to fool, easy to manipulate.

Well, it would never happen. He didn't want it to happen.
He only hoped, as he felt sleep drifting over him, that he
wouldn't dream about the accident again tonight. That he would
rest a little. A short reprieve from everything.

The next morning, as the sky was turning from black to
gray, Mary came in to wake up David and Gary with her soft,
pleasant voice. When they went into the kitchen, Jesse and
Marty were already there, drinking coffee and looking sleepy,

and Mary was scrambling eggs to give them all a good breakfast before they started.

There was little conversation around the kitchen table. Marty and Jesse discussed the best way to get the camper back onto the truck. There was really only one way, though. Raise the camper off the table with the jacks, move the table, back the truck under the camper, and lower the jacks again. Thinking about it made Jesse nervous. Those damn spindly little jacks.

The sun was just peeping over the foothills when they went out to do it, leaving Mary inside to do the dishes and straighten up the house a little—she would hate to come home after two weeks to a dirty house. Outside, each of them stationed themselves at one corner of the camper and raised the jacks until the bottom of the camper cleared the table. Then Jesse and David carefully pulled the table out from under the camper while Marty climbed into the pickup.

David glanced at his father, but Jesse was watching the edges of the table, absorbed in what they were doing. No one had mentioned the gates yet. Marty must have talked to them about it when he came home last night, David thought. The table cleared the last jack and Jesse went to the other end. He and David carried the table back to the patio.

When they got back to the camper Marty was already backing slowly toward it. Jesse stood at the right front corner and motioned with his hands for Marty to keep coming.

"Easy," Jesse said. "Take it real easy."

The truck crept backward. Marty stared intently out the back window. Jesse motioned with his hand. "A little to the left," he said. Then, "A little more. A little more . . ." Jesse held up his hand. "Hold it," he said. But the truck kept creeping. "Hold it. Stop!" Jesse yelled. But Marty's stop was too late. The right rear corner of the bumper nudged the jack Jesse was standing next to. The camper swayed. Jesse grabbed the bottom edge of it, trying to steady it. David and Gary ran around beside him, not sure what to do. The camper quit swaying, but the bumper of the truck still rested against the jack.

"Goddamn," Jesse breathed, still gripping the edge. Then, "Okay, pull it forward. But take it easy."

Marty pulled on the emergency brake, shifted gears, then let up slowly on the clutch and the emergency brake at the same time. But even so, the truck rolled back about an inch, pushing the jack with it, before it began creeping forward. The bottom of the jack slid along the smooth cement driveway. The corner Jesse held dipped and he strained to keep the camper steady. David grabbed the edge next to his father just as the jack snapped in two and clanged to the ground. David and Jesse were left holding up the corner. David could feel the edge digging into his palms.

"Steady," Jesse said softly. "Hold it steady."

Marty jumped out of the truck and ran around to them. He grabbed the edge next to David and the three of them stood, straining against the weight.

"Gary," Jesse said. "Get your mother to help you bring the table back."

Gary scurried around the camper like a scared lizard and headed for the back door. Mary recognized the excitement in Gary's voice and ran outside with him. They grabbed the table and carried it to the camper as quickly as they could.

"Right at this corner," Jesse said when he saw them coming.

Mary and Gary shoved the table under the corner of the camper and they lowered the corner carefully onto it. Then they all backed away, breathing hard, and watched apprehensively as the camper swayed gently back and forth. Finally it was still, resting precariously off balance.

Jesse rubbed the center of his chest. "Almost lost it," he muttered.

"What do we do now?" Marty asked.

Jesse stared at the camper. He never would have thought that table would hold. It was a sturdy table, but he had built it twenty years ago. He would have to find some better system of getting the camper onto the truck, better jacks, at least. But that was later. What was he going to do now?

"American Bricks," Gary said.

"What?" Marty asked.

"Yeah," Gary said. "If we had some great big American Bricks, that would hold it up."

"Sure," Marty said. "Or you could build us something with your Erector set."

"Or Lincoln Logs," David added.

"Okay," Mary said. She looked at Jesse. "What *are* we going to do?"

"That's not a bad idea," Jesse said. "Bricks, logs, something." He could build something, he thought. If he had the wood, and the time, he could make a permanent frame, good and sturdy, with removable braces so they could drive the truck right under it and then pull it away. Build it out of four-by-fours.

"Yeah, logs," Gary said. "Down the street on the way to Manny's they were chopping down some big trees. There was a whole bunch of great big logs there."

"Are they still there?" Jesse asked.

"Yeah, I think so," Gary said.

Jesse looked at Marty. "It's worth a try. If we could put a big enough log where that jack was we could probably all keep it steady long enough to get the truck under it."

They all piled into the truck. Gary showed Jesse where the trees were. They were huge eucalyptus trees growing on a vacant lot between two apartment complexes. It looked like the city had topped them to keep them out of the way of some power lines. Scattered around on the ground were several big logs, about a foot in diameter and about six feet long. Jesse picked out the straightest one and he and Marty loaded it into the truck. It was heavy and green.

Back at the house, Jesse did some measuring and sawed off

the log so it would fit where the jack had been. He made it about two inches longer than the distance from the ground to the bottom of the steel sheath that had held the jack in place so they would be able to pull the table out. Then he backed the truck up directly in front of the camper.

"All you have to do is come straight back now," he told Mary. He wanted Marty to help steady the camper. "And remember," he told the rest of them, "if it starts to fall, just get out of the way."

The men grabbed the bottom edge of the camper at the corner where the table was. "On three," Jesse said. "But don't jerk it. Lift easy. Okay. One . . . two . . . three."

They lifted and Mary slid the log into place. Then she and Gary moved the table out of the way. The camper swayed a little as the log wobbled almost imperceptibly. "Steady," Jesse said. "Keep it steady."

Mary climbed into the truck and backed, inches at a time, under the camper. When the front window of the camper was about an inch away from the back window of the truck, Mary stopped. Jesse steadied the camper while the three boys slowly lowered the other three jacks until the camper sat in the bed of the truck. Then Jesse let go and took a long, deep breath.

"We did it," he said.

With the blunt side of an ax, Jesse knocked the log away and the camper dropped into the truck like a foot settling into a well-worn shoe. Then they all stood back and admired it silently.

"Well, let's tie it down and get on the road," Jesse said.

III

They had only been on the road three hours, and already it was hot. Jesse's hands were sweating and the steering wheel was slippery. It would have been good to put air conditioning in the truck, he thought, but they didn't have the money for that. Besides the unit itself, he would have had to get a bigger radiator to handle the extra load. Even as it was, he wondered how the radiator would stand up under the weight of the camper. He glanced at the temperature gauge. It was only a little past the middle. Well, so far, so good.

Mary sat beside him with Marty next to the window. David and Gary were in the back. Every once in a while Jesse glanced into the rear view mirror and could see skinny bare legs under the table. They had said they were going to play cards, but he couldn't tell if they were or not.

They had just driven through Indio and were back on the freeway again. Mary's eyes kept closing and her head nodding forward. Then she would jerk her head back and open her eyes again. Jesse patted her leg. She was wearing yellow shorts and a loose white blouse. Her legs were white. She hadn't had a chance to get any sun yet this summer. Her legs always looked best with just a slight tan, but it was hard for her to get. Usually she burned.

"You can go in back and lie down for a while if you want to," Jesse said.

She looked at him, her expression sober. "I'm all right."

"If you get tired, I can drive," Marty said.

"Maybe later," Jesse said. "We'll stop for lunch before too long."

They drove on in silence. Outside, the desert rolled on and on monotonously. Jesse rubbed the center of his chest. The damn indigestion had been bothering him all morning. He didn't feel all that tired, though. Not as tired as he expected to feel. He had slept well last night. He woke up with a slight headache, almost as if he had a hangover, but it was gone now. Things were working fine, he thought. They really were doing it. All together. It was too bad someone had to ride in back, but he had made sure they had pencil and paper so in case they needed anything they could pound on the window and hold up a sign.

It would be good to see Lyle tonight—and his wife, Ruth. They had two kids now. They didn't have any when Lyle left Lockheed. A boy and a girl, he thought. He couldn't remember their names. They must be about two and four now. The first one would be four, anyway. Ruth got pregnant almost as soon as they moved to Prescott and that was about five years ago. Lyle was working construction over there then, and studying for his real estate license, too. Things were pretty tight, he wrote. But since he started selling houses, they were doing pretty well. Hell, Lyle would be a great salesman.

Jesse remembered him from Belfast, where they worked together with Lockheed Overseas. He could talk anybody into anything. Outgoing, you'd call him. Always raising hell with those two-bit whores. The only one who could drink that warm beer and like it. Yeah, he'd be a good salesman. Jesse could picture him wearing a polyester suit with white shoes and a white belt. "This house here is a beauty," he'd say, turning on that little half smile that drove women crazy. And for the men, he would make it man-to-man, would talk about the construction. "Nothing but quality lumber. And the electrical, all number twelve copper wire fed through conduits. None of this Romex shit." Yeah, he's probably doing all right.

Jesse turned on the radio. He moved the dial around until he found a good country-western station, then settled back to strains of some mournful Hank Williams song.

"Do we have to listen to that maudlin stuff?" Marty asked.

"Go ahead, find something you like," Jesse said.

Marty turned the dial up and down the band, but ended up back at the same station Jesse had. There were only three or four others, two of them Mexican. A twangy disk jockey rattled on for a while, then there was another song.

Marty shook his head. "Must be Hank Williams day."

"Nothing wrong with a little Hank Williams," Jesse said. "Reminds me of Spade Cooley."

Mary smiled.

"Yeah," Marty said. "Spade Cooley shot his wife."

"That was later," Jesse said. "He wasn't so popular then."

"He was crazy then," Marty said.

"Yeah, I think he was a little crazy then," Jesse agreed.

"All those lovesick songs went to his head," Marty said.

"Well, he could sure play that fiddle," Jesse said.

"Sure," Marty said. "So can Jack Benny."

There was a pounding on the window behind them. Jesse looked in the rear view mirror and saw David holding up a sign. It took him a while to read it backwards. WHEN ARE WE GOING TO STOP. HUNGRY. Mary was turned around holding up her hand to them to wait a minute. Jesse looked at his watch.

"It's only a quarter to eleven," he said.

"We ate pretty early," Mary said.

"Okay," Jesse said. "I'll stop at the next rest area."

Mary took a pad from the dash, wrote PRETTY SOON on it, then held it up to the window. David nodded to her and sat back up on the bench at the table.

"We ought to have an intercom system for this thing or something," Jesse said.

"Yeah," Marty said. "Just like Star Trek. 'Bridge to Captain Kirk. Bridge to Captain Kirk.' Click. 'Kirk here.' Click. 'Sir, there's a Klingon ship, a yellow and blue Cadillac with some cool dudes in it, approaching at warp ninety-seven point four seven five.' Click. 'Sound shuffling alert and turn on Ramsey Lewis. I'll be right there.' Click."

"Who's Ramsey Lewis?" Jesse asked.

"Oh, man," Marty said. "You ain't got *no* cool. They just the biggest thing goin' down, that's all." Marty shifted his voice back to normal. "What we really need in here is a good tape deck."

"You didn't bring your trumpet, did you?" Jesse asked.

"No," Marty said. "What for? Reveille in the morning? Taps at bedtime?"

"You could have played some songs for us around the campfire," Jesse said. "I brought my harmonica. We could have played duets."

Marty looked thoughtful. "Never thought of that. A trumpet and a harmonica. Maybe with a mute . . ."

"It would have been nice," Mary said.

"When I have my own group I'll have to have a harmonica player in it," Marty said.

"You two could start your own group," Mary said.

"I mean someone who can play jazz harmonica," Marty said.

"I guess that's something I don't understand," Jesse said. "What makes jazz any different from any other music?"

"Well, for one thing you ad-lib a lot," Marty said. "There's no music. You just have the chords and then you play notes that fit into the chords. Anything you want."

Jesse smiled. "You mean you fake it. I can do that. I played tenor sax in the high school band and could never read a note. Always faked it."

Marty leaned forward a little and looked at Jesse. "You never told me that."

"Where do you think you got your talent from?" Jesse said.

"And from his grandfather," Mary put in.

Marty settled back in the seat. Had he really never told him that? Jesse wondered. A lot of things he had never told any of them, he guessed. Well, one thing he would do when they all sat around the campfire is tell some stories. He could tell some whoppers, and they would all be true.

Like the time he had saved that little boy from drowning. The boy fell off the boat dock and the tide banged him against the pilings. He had dived into the cold water—it was the middle of winter—and almost been swept into the pilings himself. But he saw the boy's small body dangling there like a jellyfish and he scooped him up and struggled to the surface gasping for air. Some other people lifted the boy onto the boat dock and gave him artificial respiration until the ambulance came. Everyone congratulated him and told him what a brave thing he had done, but when it was all over he found it hard to believe he had done it. It had been an instinctive reaction, he guessed. No thought behind it. He remembered how good it felt to be doing something like that, something so natural and basic you didn't have to think about it. And it worked. The boy was all right, he found out later.

That would be a good story to tell them. And he could think of others. And they could tell stories, too. They could all tell stories. It would be a good way to get to know each other. The only rule would be that the story had to be true.

A blue and white sign approached as if pulled toward them

by an invisible rope. REST AREA 1 MILE. Then: REST AREA
NEXT RIGHT. Jesse pulled off the freeway, followed the short
frontage road, and parked in front of a big beige building with
restrooms. It was a small rest area, with only two ramadas, sitting in the middle of the hot desert like a dry oasis. Everyone
piled out of the truck and into the beige building.

They ate bologna sandwiches because they were easy to fix,
and drank some of the pop Mary and David had stocked into the
icebox. Jesse studied the map. They had about two more hours
before they reached Blythe, which was, as near as he could figure, about half-way. Then they would have about four more
hours before they got to Prescott. All desert. Damn, he'd like to
get out of this heat. But they had to cross it. It would be cool in
Prescott. Lyle said it was almost always cool there. They would
just have to brave it out, that's all.

Jesse was sweating when they got back into the truck and
started off again. His stomach felt a little queasy and his breath
was short. He had never had the heat affect him this way before.
Hell, he thought, driving the truck back onto the freeway, he'd
worked in hundred-and-ten-degree heat before, all day, drinking
gallons of water, for weeks at a time. Like that time he did that
job in Phoenix in the middle of August. And it was humid, too.
Sometimes, in the afternoons, they would have thundershowers
that would cool things off some, but usually it was just the heat
bearing down on you like a hot iron. It was a lot worse than this.

He settled in the seat and watched the road, rubbing the
center of his chest absently. Not much of a vacation yet, he
thought. But it would get better. If he could just get rid of this
damn indigestion. It was worse now. He wouldn't have thought
a bologna sandwich and a Coke would cause indigestion. Getting old, he thought. The thought splintered off into a thousand
different directions. What had he done all his life except work?
What had he accomplished? He had made enough money to hold
his family together and that was about it. There wasn't anything

bigger he could point to and say, "There, you see? I did that. That makes it all worth it." He could have been a doctor. Hell, he could have been anything. A musician. A salesman. A policeman. A politician. Anything. All he would have had to do was settle his mind on something. But he hadn't and now he was a sheet metal worker and he guessed he would have to be satisfied with that. It was all he'd ever be.

Marty turned on the radio again in the middle of another Hank Williams song. "I'm so lonesome I could cry," Hank wailed, and just then, a burning pain stabbed Jesse's chest. He gasped, then grimaced and tried to grab his chest as if he could pull the pain out with his fist. Mary looked at him, startled.

"Are you all right?" she asked.

The pain subsided, leaving Jesse weak and limp. His breathing was quick and shallow. "Yeah," he said. "I'm all right. Indigestion. Must be something I ate up in Modesto." He rolled his window down some more and felt the hot air blasting into his face. He took deep breaths of it, trying to get some strength back.

"Want me to drive a while?" Marty asked.

"Maybe in a little while," Jesse said.

He had to fight it. Couldn't just give up. It was the enemy, trying to sap his strength and stab into his weakness. And he did fight it. All the way to Blythe and beyond. On through the hot, miserable desert. Mary said he ought to stop. Marty said again and again that he would drive, but still Jesse drove on. He did recover some of his strength, but just as he was feeling good, the pain would strike again, like a relentless boxer jabbing away at him. Finally, he had an overwhelming craving for a big glass of cold milk. He pulled off at Quartzsite and they all went into a little restaurant. He drank a glass of milk and ordered another while the rest of them drank Cokes and iced tea and sat in the air conditioning like half-dead fish finally put back into the water.

When they started out again, Jesse let Marty drive. Gary sat in the front and Jesse sat in back with David.

David was apprehensive about his father sitting in back with him. If somebody else was there, even Gary, it would have been okay, but just the two of them . . .

He was relieved when Jesse said he was tired and just wanted to sleep a while. David watched him crawl up into the overhead and lie there breathing hard, as if the crawl had been a mile run. The truck started off across the desert again and David settled on the bench, his back against the wall of the small closet, his shoes off, his bony knees, showing beyond his cutoffs, pulled up under his chin. He watched the scenery, what there was of it, through the open window, and felt the hot air blow against his face.

He was bored. He had been bored since they started. He had tried to read but the bouncing of the truck made his stomach queasy. He had played cards with Gary, but the only games Gary knew were Fish and War. He had tried to teach him Five Hundred Rummy but it was too complicated for Gary's simple mind. Now he just wished they were there, Prescott, or anywhere but in this God-forsaken desert. He was tired of the heat.

Finally, his eyes closed and his head nodded. He fell into a light sleep, still feeling the bouncing truck and the hot wind in his dreams.

He woke up suddenly, startled by what he thought was a strange noise, but he couldn't be sure. The front of his T-shirt was wet with sweat and he could feel the sweat trickling down the back of his neck. His father was still lying in the overhead, his eyes wide open, rubbing his chest. David watched him move to the edge of the bed and climb down.

"Hot," Jesse said. "Too hot to sleep."

He stood up, steadying himself against the bouncing truck, took a glass from one of the cupboards, and pumped some water into it. Then he sat down opposite David at the table. Jesse's dark maroon T-shirt was wet and his curly black hair resembled coiled springs. He looked past David out the window.

"Shouldn't be much longer 'til we're out of this desert," he said.

David didn't say anything. He didn't know what to say.

"You guys been playing cards?"

"Yeah," David said. "Part of the time."

"When I was a kid we used to play by the hour. Poker, mostly, or blackjack." Jesse smiled in a strange way David wasn't expecting. "We played for marbles. That way when the teacher came we could hide the cards and start shooting them."

David didn't understand his father's attitude. It wasn't like him. But he felt himself warming up to him a little. "We do something like that sometimes, too," he said.

David watched his father gaze out the window. Then Jesse seemed to come to. "What do you do?" he asked.

"In the journalism room. During lunch sometimes. We play poker. But we play for nickels."

"What if you get caught?"

"Mr. Novotny knows about it. Besides, nobody would do anything anyway."

"Yeah," Jesse said. "I guess they wouldn't any more. When I was a kid, you'd never get away with it."

"I guess things must have been pretty straight-laced," David said.

Jesse smiled and David couldn't help seeing how tired he was. "In some ways," Jesse said. "But we raised a lot of hell. Got into some good fights." He smiled again. "One time, Walt Feldon and I got into it with some cowboys at the Double L Bar. That used to be in downtown Oxnard. I don't think it's there anymore. Walt tried to pick up some cowboy's girl and the next thing I knew he was lying on the floor rubbing his jaw. I tapped the guy on the shoulder and asked him to step outside. I went out first, then he followed me, then about ten more cowboys followed him. Jesus, that was some fight. Walt and I backed up to the wall and fought them off as long as we could, but there were just too many of them. Kicked the shit out of us. I was laid up for a week. And then, after it was all over, some cop came by swinging his night stick and told us we ought to have better sense than to mess with cowboys at the Double L. That was some fight, though. Jesus."

David could see it. He could see his father throwing his heavy arms around punching jaws and stomachs. It made him proud. And it made him remember his own fight, the only fight he'd ever had. In junior high, when he met that kid in an empty garage. He couldn't remember the kid's name or what the fight was about, but he remembered the sharp pain that shot through his jaw when the kid hit him, the close heat in the garage, the nausea as the fight went on, and his astonishment that the kid was serious—he was really fighting. The humiliating knowledge that he was going to lose the fight to a kid at least a foot shorter than him but who had strong arms, like he lifted weights or something. It was only after a teacher broke it up and he was walking home that he realized the kid wanted to hurt him— would have hurt him bad if the teacher hadn't come—and he couldn't understand why. Why would anybody want to hurt anybody?

"So," Jesse said. "Think you'll be a newspaper reporter?"

"I don't know," David said. "Maybe."

"You ought to start thinking about it," Jesse said. "You can be anything, you know. Anything you want. All you have to do is fix your mind on it and you can have it, be it, whatever." He looked off out the window again. His eyes were glazed over, as if he was looking at something inside himself. "Funny how that works," he said, so softly David could barely hear him. "The only thing is, you never know how it'll turn out."

"What do you mean?" David asked.

"Well, you can wish for things. Hard. You can want things. If you want something bad enough, you'll get it. But it's the way you get it . . . Well, hell. You can never know that. And then when you have it you wonder why you wanted it so bad."

David was confused. For an instant he forgot it was his father he was talking to. Some instinct made him prod. "Did you get something that way?"

"Yeah," Jesse said. "And it killed my best friend."

David's eyes widened. He hadn't expected that.

Jesse took a long drink of water. "Funny," he said. "I never told anybody this before, not even your mother." He looked perplexed for an instant, then his face went blank and he told the story in a strange, tired monotone.

"It was Walt," he said softly. David leaned forward so he wouldn't miss anything. "I was nineteen then. Walt was older. Twenty-one or twenty-two, I think. Anyway, Walt's family had money and one day his old man bought him a big Indian Four motorcycle. The Sewing Machine they used to call it, because that's what it sounded like—smooth. It had four cylinders in line lengthwise along the frame with a big black gearshift knob and a suicide clutch. Damn, that was a beautiful machine. Riding it was like driving a sports car with only two wheels.

"All I had was an old belt-drive Honda I'd bought used. It was all I could afford. But I used to look at Walt's Indian and think about what it would be like to own it. I could see myself purring down the highway at about eighty, the wind whipping into my face so hard it would sting. Damn, I wanted that motorcycle. I wanted it so bad I could taste it. I used to lay awake nights wishing for it.

"Well, one night Walt was riding down the main street in Oxnard doing about fifty, probably, trying to make a yellow light that turned red before he got to the intersection. That's what we always figured he was doing. Walt didn't like to stop unless he had to. Anyway, a big semi pulled out right in front of him.

59

There was nothing he could do but lay that big bike down and hope for the best. The driver of the semi saw him and stopped. That's what saved the bike. But it didn't do Walt much good. He caught his chin on the running board of that truck. His body went flying underneath the truck but his head stayed right there."

David swallowed, staring at his father's blank face.

"We were living in San Fernando when all that happened. I didn't go to the funeral. I didn't hear about it 'til later. I'd sold my Honda because I couldn't find a job in San Fernando right away and I needed the money. So I hitchhiked up to Oxnard and went to see Walt's mother. When I went to leave we were standing on the front porch and Walt's Indian was sitting down below us in the front yard. The only thing wrong with it was some scratches on the tank. 'Jesse,' she said, 'you'd be doing me a favor if you'd take that motorcycle and get it out of here. I can't stand to look at it every day.' And just like that that motorcycle was mine. I rode it for a couple years and then sold it."

There was silence between them. The truck rumbled on down the highway and the hot air hissed through the screen on the camper window. Had she really said that? David wondered. Just out of the blue? Or had he gone there to ask for the motorcycle. Had he said, "How much are you going to ask for Walt's motor?" and she said, "Why don't you just take it. I can't stand looking at it every day." Or maybe he'd tried to pay. "All I have is fifty now, but I can pay you ten dollars a week 'til it's paid off." "Oh, just take it. Get it out of here. I can't stand looking at it every day."

David was looking down at the table, half aware that his father was watching him. When he looked up he caught his father's eyes for an instant, then looked back down.

"Well," Jesse said. "That's a pretty morbid story for a vacation."

David nodded. He didn't know what to think of it, wasn't even sure if it was true, or only partly true, and what part was true and what part wasn't.

"Tell me," Jesse went on. "What do we have in the way of fishing gear?"

Gary wanted to sit by the window but his mother said no, that she was tired of being in the middle. So Gary had to sit in the middle, between his mother and Marty, who was driving the truck. Marty was a good driver. That's what his dad was always saying. But Gary couldn't see that driving was so hard, anyway. All you had to do was keep the truck in between the two white lines on the road.

It was fun being in the front, though. More fun than sitting in the back with David. David couldn't even play cards very good. Gary had won two games of War. But David had won the game of Fish. They should have played Slap Jack. Gary could have won that easy. But then David had gotten tired of cards. He read for a while and then just sat and stared out the window. Gary was thinking of getting out his Matchbox cars and his crayons. He was going to lay some of the papers on the table and make roads and stuff for the cars to drive on. But then they stopped and went into the restaurant.

Now he sat and tried to read all the signs they passed. His favorite one was a big billboard that showed a picture of a girl with a dog pulling her pants off. He was so busy looking at the girl's bare bottom he forgot to read the writing. Copper-something, it said. Copper butt, Gary thought. She has a copper butt and the dog is going to lick it. That sign was back on the freeway and they weren't on the freeway anymore. They were on a highway. Gary knew the difference. His dad had told him once. On a freeway you can only get off at certain places.

On the highway, they went through this desert town that

was only two or three houses—all beat up and run-down with old cars sitting beside them. His mother said Indians probably lived there, but there weren't even any horses. He wished they could have stopped to see them. There weren't very many big signs on the highway. All there were were signs that told you how far it was to someplace and signs that said what the speed limit was and signs that said there was going to be a curve in the road. One sign said Wick-something. Wicked city, Gary thought, like in a western. It would be the town where all the bandits lived and they would sit around the saloon all the time, with those girls on their laps, playing poker. He knew when they came to it, it wouldn't be like that though. It would be just another city like all the other cities, like the city he lived in where kids would have to go to school and all that other stuff.

Manny always said he wanted to be a truck driver when he grew up. That way you could see the country and have a different girl in every town. But Gary could never see what fun that would be. They were all the same anyway. Even the girls. At school Joyce said she loved him once and poured salt on his head and all it did was make him mad. Joyce was kind of fat, anyway.

Well, he didn't have to decide what he wanted to be for a while. He might be a secret agent like Barney Collier in "Mission Impossible." It would be more fun than being a truck driver. If you were a truck driver you'd have to sit like this all day. Boy, what a drag that would be.

Now someone was pounding on the back window. Gary turned around to see his father holding up a sign.

"He wants to stop at the next town at a drugstore," Mary said.

"We're almost to Wickenburg," Marty said. "Keep your eyes open."

Mary nodded to Jesse. Jesse grinned and waved to Gary, then disappeared from the window again.

Pretty soon they stopped in front of a drugstore and Jesse

went in and bought some medicine for his stomach. Then he wanted to drive again. They let Gary stay in the front and Marty went and sat with David in the back.

"I don't see why he has to drive all the time," Marty said. "An eight-hour trip and I only drove two."

David looked at him from across the table. "He doesn't trust anybody else to do it."

"Shit," Marty said. "He's always saying what a good driver I am."

"It's not you," David said. "He wouldn't trust anybody. Mom can drive, too. So can I."

"Well, I was getting tired of that damn country music anyway. You'd think they'd at least play some Woody Herman or something. Even Glenn Miller. I was getting desperate."

David grinned. "Nothin' wrong with a little country music, son."

"Don't start," Marty said.

"It's where the money is."

"Yeah, I know. That and hard rock."

"And green berets."

"Oh, Jesus."

That's what he ought to do, Marty thought. Join the Green Berets and have his own jazz group. They could all stand at attention and play *Over Hill Over Dale* in swing time. Switch off to blues once in a while, just for variety. Jesus.

They were finally getting out of the desert. They had driven out of Wickenburg down a narrow two-lane road and through a dusty little hovel of a town called Congress. Then they started climbing. The road was steep and the desert dropped away beneath them. The shrubbery changed from sagebrush and cactus to small oaks and, as they neared the top, to scrubby little pines. The air was at least ten degrees cooler.

Jesse pulled off the road before they reached the crest of the mountain so they could look down over the desert. Marty and David got out of the camper while the rest of them got out of the cab.

"What did we stop for?" Marty asked.

"Just to look," Jesse said.

The five of them stood there for a long moment, drinking in the view. They could see for miles, could follow the road they had just come up down into Congress and almost all the way to Wickenburg. The land was dotted with ranch houses and tiny pools of water and criss-crossed by dusty dirt roads. The whole thing resembled some fine old tapestry with a rich mixture of greens and browns.

"That's really something," Jesse muttered.

"It's beautiful," Mary said.

Jesse could feel them all drawn together by the beauty. Sharing the experience. Something they hadn't done for a long, long time. He felt like a king pointing out his kingdom.

"Hey, look at that," Gary said. He hunkered down and poked at a small red bug with a twig. They gathered around him. "I never saw an ant like that," Gary said. Its body was bright red velvet.

Jesse knelt beside Gary. "It's a spider," he said. "It has eight legs."

"Do we have a jar? Can I save it?" Gary asked.

"Better not," Jesse said. "It might be poisonous. It's hard to tell about things out here."

"Aw . . ."

"This is its home," Mary said. "It belongs out here in the open, not in a jar."

"How would you like to be put in a jar?" Marty said.

They all got back into the truck.

"It'll probably just get run over," Gary muttered.

The truck pulled back onto the highway and kept climbing. It was only then that Mary realized she had never seen Gary interested in anything like a bug before. She looked at him. He sat there, a glum expression on his face, his long brown hair hiding his eyes. She wished she had let him take the spider and she wondered what had come over them all to gang up on him like that. Something to do with the land, the view, this vast expanse of deep blue sky.

"Hey, Grumpy," she said. "You can have the next bug you find."

"As long as it's not poisonous," Jesse said.

"It will be," Gary muttered.

The truck rolled over the crest of the hill and started down into Yarnell, a small community built on the downward slope of the highway. It took two minutes to get through the town, then they wound through scrubby oaks and pines and huge granite boulders and when they came out of that there was a green valley spotted with cattle and ranch houses nestled beneath mushrooming cottonwood trees. The scene could have been a picture on some calendar.

"Jesus," Jesse said. "Lyle was right. We ought to move up here."

"I wonder what it's like to live here," Mary said.

"Peaceful," Jesse said. "Just peaceful."

They watched the valley approach them. A little way from the highway a man was digging with a post hole digger at a barbed wire fence. His horse was tied to the fence near him.

"I'll bet these ranchers work hard, though," Mary said.

"The hired hands work hard," Jesse said. "The ranchers sit back in the shade and drink beer."

Jesse's tone made Mary uneasy. She looked at him. His face was clouded over. Cynicism wasn't like him. "Well, anyway," she said, "it's a different kind of work. Out here on the land. Out in the open, in the fresh air. Not like working in the city."

"Work is work," Jesse said bluntly. "Sometimes it's good, and sometimes it's not."

Mary let it drop. She settled back in the seat and watched

the scenery. They were driving through the little valley now. Peeples Valley it was called. The highway threaded its way through high grass. The roads leading to the ranches were dusty and the gates needed paint. But the sky was big and blue and inviting, as if it wanted you to float up and melt into it.

Then they were out of the valley, climbing to a high plateau where the grass was shorter and the ground rockier. Small houses and mobile homes sat randomly, as if someone had picked them all up together and flung them down. Then they were in the pines—bigger pines than they had seen around Yarnell, a real forest of them. The air was filled with pine scent and the road twisted and turned, following the shape of the mountains. They were still climbing and the air became cooler still.

They reached the crest and started down. Jesse had to put the truck into second gear several times to get around sharp switchbacks. Then the road straightened and they began to see houses, a large mobile home park, stores and motels and a restaurant with a big plate glass window sitting in the pines. They were in Prescott. Jesse stopped at a Circle K store and called Lyle.

They followed Lyle's directions that Jesse had scribbled down on a piece of paper, driving slowly, admiring Prescott. There was the town square with a huge old block courthouse surrounded by grass and cement walkways and shaded by overgrown elm trees that billowed against the blue sky, and the old bars and stores on Whiskey Row with false fronts like something you'd see in a western movie. "It's like going back in time a hundred years," Jesse said.

They turned on Mt. Vernon Street, a quiet residential street lined with hundred-year-old houses perfectly preserved with immaculate yards and more elm trees. They followed the street until they left the houses behind and climbed up a winding road into a thick pine forest.

"I thought Lyle's house was in town someplace," Mary said.

"It was," Jesse said. "But he sold that one and built one up here."

"He never wrote about that."

"I know," Jesse said. "But his letters haven't been all that detailed lately, anyway."

"Are you sure he wants us to come?"

"We're coming, whether he wants us or not," Jesse said. "But I think he wants us. He's still the same guy he used to be. Maybe a little stuck-up from being a big fish in a little pond."

"Can we fish up here?" Gary asked.

"I don't think so," Jesse said. "There isn't any place close and we won't have much time. We want to see Lyle and Ruth and the kids, whatever their names are."

"Yeah, and talk," Gary said.

"Well, grownups like to talk," Jesse said.

"Yeah, I know," Gary said, rolling his eyes.

Mary laughed at him. Sometimes he seemed almost grown up himself.

The road climbed higher into the mountains. Pine trees towered over it, casting spindly shadows on the pavement. Finally they came to Spruce Mountain Road. Lyle stood at the intersection waving to them. Jesse had to look twice to be sure it was Lyle. He had put on weight since he saw him last, had, in fact, the beginnings of a good-sized beer belly. He wore jeans and a plaid western shirt, cowboy boots and a wide-brimmed, brown cowboy hat with a feather in it.

"A cowboy hat?" Jesse said. He drove onto the small dirt road. Lyle came to the truck and Jesse could see that his face was still the same. A little older maybe, but the same mischievous, boyish smile was there, the same big round eyes that always looked a little amazed.

"Howdy," Lyle said. "Welcome to the great outdoors."

"How you been?" Jesse asked.

"Great," Lyle said. "Just great. Look, just follow me. It's re-

67

ally not so far. I was just afraid you'd think you were going to some old gold mine or something instead of my house."

"Okay," Jesse said.

Lyle left the truck and climbed into a shiny new jeep, open at the top, with wheels as big as airplane wheels.

"He really plays the part, doesn't he?" Mary said.

"Maybe that's what he was looking for," Jesse said. "Some part to play."

They followed Lyle up the little dirt road, full of ruts where water had washed down it. The truck and camper lumbered after the jeep like an elephant after a bobcat. They drove for several miles with no sign of any houses.

"He was right," Jesse said. "I probably would have turned back by now."

Finally Lyle pulled onto a cement driveway in front of a large log cabin, got out, and motioned for Jesse to pull in between the jeep and a little Volkswagen bug that sat off the cement. Jesse parked the truck and they all piled out.

"Jesus, Lyle," Jesse said. "A log cabin?"

"Nice, isn't it," Lyle said. "Wait 'til you see the inside. Airlock Logs they call them. You buy them all cut and treated, then just fit them together, like Lincoln Logs or something. Easiest house I ever built."

They all looked at it a moment, then Lyle said, "Come on in. Ruth has been dying for you to get here."

Ruth met them at the front door. Looking at her, Jesse was astounded. When she and Lyle had left the Valley Ruth was a kind of dumpy woman, bordering on fat, who seemed bored most of the time, whose hair usually looked like she just got out of bed. Now she was beautiful. Her red hair was long and flowing and her figure, like a model's, molded into tight jeans and an embroidered western blouse. Even her freckles looked somehow more wholesome, and her bright blue eyes sparkled.

"Come in, come in," she said as she reached down to scoop

up the baby who had crawled up behind her. "It's so good to see you all."

Mary was worried about Jesse. She had been worried ever since they left—since before they left, really. When she saw the way he looked when he came home from Modesto, she was ready to forget the vacation, or at least postpone it for a day or two. But Jesse was stubborn, as she knew he would be. Once he got something into his head it took a twenty-mule team to get it out.

He had looked better that morning, though, after a good night's sleep. But after lunch she got worried again. He wouldn't stop. He kept driving, as if he was the only one who could and they were running from an invasion or something. She was relieved when he went into the back and slept for a while. He looked better when he started driving again, and as they were getting close to Lyle's he really perked up.

She wasn't looking forward to the time they would spend at Lyle's. She had never liked him very much, even though he was Jesse's best friend. When they came back from Belfast they made arrangements to work in the same Lockheed plant building in Burbank and Lyle had moved from someplace in Long Beach to a cute little house in Van Nuys. That was before Van Nuys was so built up. When he sold the house to move to Prescott, he sold it for three times what he paid for it. And he couldn't wait to come over and brag about it.

She knew he would like to take them on a tour and show them every house he had sold since he went into real estate. "Made five thousand bucks on that one," he would say, pointing to some shack, and Mary would cringe thinking about some young couple who were in debt up to their ears.

Jesse never had been very good at picking friends. They were all kind of like Lyle—self-centered, egotistical—and they all took advantage of Jesse's soft heart, borrowing money, keeping him up until all hours in some bar telling him their sob stories. None of them were like Marilyn and Bill, good, solid people with their feet on the ground, who would never do anything crazy, like packing up and moving to a town like Prescott with no job lined up. She guessed it rankled her a little that Lyle and Ruth had done so well here.

They did tour the house that Lyle built—it really was a pretty nice house—and now they were sitting on the deck that went out from the sliding glass doors in the living room. They sat in lounge chairs and looked out over the forest, a sea of dark green, full of shadows now as the sun was getting low in the sky. Lyle had started the barbecue and the blue flames from the lighter fluid danced in the air.

"How 'bout a beer, Jess," Lyle said. "Anyone?"

"As long as it's cold," Jesse said.

"Aw, shucks," Lyle said. "Warm is all I have."

The two of them laughed, as if it was a private joke, when really it wasn't. Lyle went into the kitchen and came back with the beer. Then he stood over the barbecue poking at the coals with a stick.

"Jesus, Lyle," Jesse said, looking out over the forest. "I can't believe you actually live here."

"Yeah, I know," Lyle said. "Sometimes I can't believe it myself. We feel kind of privileged, like we really don't deserve all this, but here it is." He gestured with his hand toward the forest. "It's like somebody knew we needed this, so he gave it to us."

Jesse looked at Lyle. "You haven't gone and got religion, have you?"

"Naw, nothing like that," Lyle said. "It's just that living here, you get the feeling there's something a lot bigger than you, know what I mean?"

"Yeah, I think so," Jesse said. He looked away and took a long drink.

Ruth stood up. "I'm going to start the salad," she announced.

"Can I help?" Mary asked.

"Sure," Ruth said.

Mary followed her into the kitchen. It was small and poorly arranged. Mary couldn't help thinking that Lyle hadn't consulted with Ruth before he built it. It would be like him to do that. There was only a few feet of counter space and the cupboards were so small she wondered where Ruth kept pots and pans.

Mary stood at the sink, which had a window over it that looked out over the forest, peeling carrots, while Ruth chopped an onion.

"I really like your house," Mary said.

"Yes," Ruth said. "It's nice. The house we had in town was bigger, though. More room for the kids to play. And the kitchen was bigger. We had to make some concessions when we decided to move out here. After we bought the land, we couldn't afford a mansion."

"It's not a bad kitchen," Mary said.

"Well, I don't spend much time in it anymore anyway. Too much to do."

"Oh," Mary said. "Do you work?"

"Well, yes, as a matter of fact," Ruth said. "I'm the mayor."

The carrot slipped out of Mary's hand and clunked into the sink. "I . . . I didn't know that."

"I didn't think you'd expect it, and I knew Lyle hadn't written about it."

"You . . . how . . . ?"

"Prescott's a pretty small town. Not much in the way of industry or anything. It's almost all retired. That, and tourists that come up from Phoenix. Being mayor is only a part-time job. And even at that it doesn't pay very much. And, well, to tell you the truth, I wouldn't care if it didn't pay anything at all. As soon as we moved here I fell in love with the town—so quiet and quaint. I want to try to keep it that way."

Mary caught herself staring at Ruth, trying to remember the

slouched, muumuued woman with the messy hair she had known in the Valley. That woman would never have said anything like that. That woman wouldn't have cared that much about anything. She picked up the carrot.

"What do you, you know, do?" Mary asked.

"Not a lot, really," Ruth said. "I try to keep up with all the reports and memos from the city staff, and I go to council meetings every Monday night. It's mainly making decisions—seeing the way you want the town to be in, say, ten years, and trying to move in that direction."

"How did you, I mean, did you have to campaign and everything?"

"Oh, sure. Lyle was my campaign manager. He knew how to advertise and all that, how to handle the press. Not that he ever told me what to say. Nobody tells me what to say."

"But how did you ever get elected? I thought small towns were supposed to be conservative."

Ruth slid the chopped onion off the cutting board into a bowl, stopped a moment, and looked at the cupboard in front of her. "Prescott's a funny town," she said finally. "You probably couldn't find a more conservative town in Arizona, and Arizona's a conservative state. I mean, we don't want a lot of growth; we like to try to preserve the old things; we want government to stay out of our business. There's even some thinking about the race and sex questions that dates back fifty years. But overriding all of that is a kind of western practicality. I was the best person for the job, so I was elected. It's really as simple as that."

Mary laid the peeled carrots on the counter by Ruth. "I think I'll have a beer," she said.

Ruth laughed and nodded to the refrigerator. "Help yourself," she said. "Oh, and while you're in there, get the lettuce."

Nothing more was said about Ruth's new career during dinner. The news left Mary with a strange, edgy feeling, as if she had just awakened in the morning and wanted badly to throw the covers off and stretch and yawn, but she knew if she did she would wake up Jesse who, after all, needed his rest. The conversation during dinner and afterwards was trivial, mostly Jesse and Lyle reminiscing about the old days. What ever happened to so-and-so, and remember that crazy so-and-so. Mary didn't listen. Her mind was pounding ahead at a gallop. She kept looking at Ruth and Lyle, wondering what it was like between them; how much they talked and what they talked about; what Lyle thought, really, about being married to the mayor of Prescott, about being the "first man;" what they did with the children and how much of that responsibility was Lyle's . . . Her questions went on and on.

Marty and David sat quietly listening, bored to death, she imagined. Gary was off playing with Dawn, the little four-year-old girl. When the conversation came around to the war, Marty joined in with his pet theory.

"Goldwater would have ended it once and for all," he said.

Ruth looked at him soberly, her pretty, freckled face intent. "Goldwater is a dangerous man. You've been snowed by all the campaign rhetoric. In Arizona, we know him better. I'd like to see him out of the Senate for good."

"Arizona was one of the few states he carried," Marty said.

Ruth sighed. "I know. Barry Goldwater is an institution in Arizona. He's been around so long most people just don't know any better. If his voting record in the Senate was every publicized adequately, he'd be voted out in the next election."

"I don't think so," Lyle said. "People wouldn't pay any attention to it. It'd take something really monstrous to overcome that image he's kept up over the years."

"Well, being president would have done it, then," Jesse said. "It would have been World War Three for sure."

Ruth smiled. "I don't know if I'd go that far."

"I just don't think the man can think straight," Lyle said.

"Have you ever read *Conscience of a Conservative?*" Marty asked.

Lyle shook his head.

"I have," Ruth said. "I didn't believe a word of it."

"Goldwater didn't write it anyway," David said.

Ruth smiled at him. "No, he probably didn't."

"Some speech writer or something," Lyle said. "I'm not sure Goldwater can write his name."

"Not a very good speech writer, either," David said.

"Well, I'd just like to see the thing over with," Marty said.

"So would I," Jesse said, looking straight at Marty, "if that's what you're waiting for."

Marty glared at his father and Mary cringed. Don't start in now, she thought, please.

"Well," Ruth said. "You people must be tired. And want to take showers. It must have been terrible driving across that desert today."

"It was hot, all right," Jesse said. "Nice and cool here, though."

"Perfect weather," Lyle said. "It's been dry this summer, though. Usually we start getting thundershowers this time of year."

Mary stood up. "I think I'll take a shower," she said.

Ruth stood up, too. "I'll get some towels."

Mary followed her down the short hallway to the bathroom. Ruth opened a cupboard in the hall and pulled out several towels.

"You don't talk about it much, do you?" Mary said.

"What?" Ruth asked.

"About being mayor."

"Oh, well, it's really not all that interesting. All the everyday problems are kind of boring. Zoning decisions, water rates, parking downtown, things like that."

"I think it sounds exciting," Mary said.

"Well, yes, sometimes it is. Water rates have been a problem because we really do have to raise them, but we know that when we do people will . . . But you don't want to hear all this."

"Yes, I do," Mary said.

"Well, I'll tell you all about it tomorrow morning."

It was decided that since Lyle and Ruth had a nice hide-a-bed in the living room, Mary and Jesse would sleep there and the boys would sleep in the camper. Mary made up the bed for them after her shower. Marty would sleep in the overhead and David and Gary down below in the bed that the table and benches converted into. Mary was anxious to go to bed. She wanted to find out if Lyle had told Jesse about Ruth being the mayor. It seemed like something he would want to brag about, like everything else, if he was really proud of it.

When everyone was settled for the night, Mary lay close to Jesse on the hide-a-bed. They had left the drapes open and moonlight drifted in lazily through the sliding glass door. Mary raised her head a little and saw the moon, a soft, white ball in the sky over the forest.

"Nice place here, isn't it?" Jesse said softly.

Mary couldn't wait. "Did Lyle tell you about Ruth?"

"What, is she pregnant again?"

"She's the mayor," Mary said.

"What?"

"She's the mayor of Prescott."

"You sure?"

"She told me. She campaigned and everything. Lyle was her manager."

"Jesus," Jesse said. "No wonder his business is so good."

Mary hadn't thought of that. "Is his business that good?"

"He says he sells a house about every week and a half, on an average. I guess that's pretty good. But I don't know anything about real estate."

That would be like Lyle, Mary thought. He would give in to his wife's crazy idea if he thought it would improve his business. But she couldn't believe that was Ruth's motive. She sounded so sincere—almost idealistic.

"What if I did something like that?" Mary said.

"What, be the mayor? of Los Angeles? Come on."

"I don't mean that," Mary said. "What if I got a job?"

"What for?" Jesse asked.

"I don't know," Mary said. "I just might want to some time."

"You already have a job," Jesse said. "A damn important one."

"I know," Mary said. "But what if I did want to get one? What would you do?"

"Jesus," Jesse said. "Ruth isn't a women's libber, is she?"

"No," Mary said. "Don't be silly."

"Well, it sounds like she is. The mayor. Jesus."

Mary felt something welling up inside her, some vague frustration that she had been fighting most of her life without even realizing it, as if she had been living in a cage so long she had almost come to believe the cage was the world. But it was an iron cage. She couldn't get out.

"I could do something like that," Mary said. "Something important. Something worthwhile."

"If you want to do something worthwhile, get some sleep," Jesse said. "I think we'll leave right after breakfast tomorrow. This place is a bad influence on all of us."

"You too?" Mary asked, a little surprised.

"Sure," Jesse said. "I keep thinking how good they have it here. I keep thinking what it would be like if we lived here, what a good place it would be to raise the kids. And then I think, why not? Why not just pick up and move like they did? But there's nothing to do here. All I could do is work construction, hammer nails. But I'd only work about two-thirds of the year and the pay is lousy. There's no union. We'd never make it. But it's tempting. It's really tempting."

"We don't know what it's like here," Mary said. "We haven't even spent a whole day here."

76

"All the more reason to get out now," Jesse said. "Before we find out."

There was something confusing about it all to Mary. What had she been thinking? Get a job. What a stupid idea. What would she do? How could she leave the boys, the house? At one time, maybe she could have done it. Had almost done it. On her own she would have gone to school and been a legal secretary, maybe worked with a criminal lawyer, been in on exciting court cases, investigated things for him. It probably would have been more exciting than being the mayor of Prescott. But it was too late now. She had made her decision and she had to stick with it. She was needed where she was. But that didn't stop her from thinking—from wishing.

"Got to get some sleep," Jesse said.

Mary sighed. "You must be tired."

"I am," Jesse said. And, as Mary listened, his breathing slowed to a regular rhythm.

She really did love him, she thought. He'd been so good over the years. It made her warm and cozy thinking about it. His broad chest and strong arms meant so much. They represented safety, security, strength to cope with the world, a shield protecting her from the world, a blindfold keeping her from seeing the world—a cage.

In her mind she paced back and forth like a lioness at the zoo. Then she drifted into muddled dreams where she could feel the truck rumbling beneath her as she drove along the little road in Peeples Valley. She drove past green cottonwood trees where a man slept propped up against one of the big trunks, a cowboy hat over his face. As she passed, the man took off the hat and waved to her. It was Jesse. She was still moving but the scenery didn't change. Jesse stood up, put on his cowboy hat, and stood beside a barbed wire fence digging with a post hole digger. She drove on down the road watching him in the mirror grow smaller and smaller and smaller . . .

She woke up reaching for Jesse, but he wasn't there. He was in front of the bed, pacing back and forth, holding his left shoulder. In the moonlight his face looked pale and moist—ghostly. She sat up suddenly.

"What's wrong?"

"Pain," Jesse said. "This goddamn pain. It's like somebody stuck his fist in my chest and squeezed—hard."

"Oh, no." She could feel herself getting ready to cry or scream. Help me, she thought, but there was nobody there. She got up and went to him. "What can I do?"

"I think I better get to a doctor," Jesse said.

She ran back to Lyle and Ruth's bedroom and shook Ruth's shoulder gently, trying to control herself.

"Ruth," she said. "Ruth. Jesse's sick. How do we get a doctor?"

Ruth opened her eyes. "What?"

"Jesse. He's got terrible pain. He needs a doctor."

Lyle sat up in bed. "Where is he?"

"In the living room," Mary said.

Lyle got out of bed and padded down the hall. Mary followed him.

"Where is it?" he asked Jesse.

"It was in my chest," Jesse said. "But now it's in my shoulder, going down my arm."

"My God," Lyle said.

He went to the telephone in the kitchen and fumbled through the phone book. He dialed, waited, looked disgusted, and hung up. "I forgot," he said. "The damn doctor's on vacation." He ran his finger down the page and dialed another number, waited, then spoke. "I have a friend from out of town who's having pain in his chest." Pause. "Yeah, into the shoulder and down his arm." Pause. "God. That's what I was afraid of." Pause. "No. I'll get him there. It'll be faster." He hung up. "Get some pants on, old man," he said to Jesse. "We're going to the hospital."

David couldn't sleep. He had been lying in the darkness of the camper, staring at the black ceiling, feeling the cool breeze float over his face, thinking, thinking. He couldn't stop and couldn't control his wandering mind, as if it was some machine gone on a rampage.

For a long time he had thought about Ellen, remembering her in detail, inch by inch, with a sodden ache in the pit of his stomach, loving her more now that he couldn't have her than he ever had when he thought he could. He missed her, longed for her low, soft voice, her laughter, her full, wide mouth that had touched his . . . He could hardly stand it.

And then, for the millionth time, he went over that last night. He remembered the way she looked when he left her, lying naked on her bed, her back to him, curled up in a fetal position, white, vulnerable. And he could see himself walking quietly out the door, glancing back one last time before he closed it, knowing even then, in the deepest part of him, that it was over, that he had destroyed something beautiful.

He saw the road in front of him as he drove down the highway, back from Lancaster, although he had never really reached Lancaster, had never intended to reach Lancaster, had never intended to reach any place—going too fast for the curve, feeling the front wheels bounce over the raised median, slamming on the brakes—the wrong thing to do—and the rest, until his fist was gripping the sheet and his whole body was tense.

And his father sitting in the living room interrogating him. What were you doing? Where were you going? What was wrong? Why are you such a stupid, asinine jerk? The rough, calloused hand on his, the stabbing guilt that he feared would turn to hate, knowing it was possible because he had read it in *Werther*, had memorized the lines: "Love and loyalty had turned into violence and murder." The silent plea to his father that he knew now his father had heard, at least partially, but not enough to let him forget, never enough for that, so that more than anything else he wished to get away, just to be gone from them all.

Then running into the gates with that old tank of a car, helplessly pushing on the brakes and watching the gates bow in like in a slow motion movie, and having that to add to everything else. Kneeling down watching through the camper window as his father and Marty closed the gates after backing out of the driveway, the bottom of the gates scraping on the cement, his father and Marty both sober, the whole family carefully observing a pact of silence so that David could stew in his own embarassment. His father observing it even when they were alone in the camper rumbling across the desert, his father only telling him that crazy story that he couldn't understand except on the surface, and couldn't understand why it was told.

After what seemed like years, he drifted into a fitful sleep. But he was awakened by the roar of Lyle's jeep next to the camper. He looked out the window just in time to see it back out of the driveway and speed down the road in a cloud of dust, his father sitting next to Lyle and his mother in the back. And at the same time Marty bounded down from the overhead and scrambled into his pants.

"What's going on?" David asked.

"I don't know," Marty said. "I'm going to find out."

Marty rushed out of the camper, leaving the door open, and David saw him go into the house. Gary sat up in the bed.

"What happened?" he asked.

"I don't know," David said.

They waited.

Marty came back out of the house, climbed into the camper, and stood looking at them silently, his lanky frame silhouetted in the doorway like an apparition.

"Dad had a heart attack," he said.

The three of them looked at one another.

IV

The ride down the mountain in Lyle's jeep left Jesse shivering from the cold. He had been wet with sweat before they started and the cool wind felt like a blizzard to him. His teeth chattered as they pulled up to the emergency doors and screeched to a stop. Two nurses met them with a wheelchair.

"I can walk," Jesse said. But when he stood up, his legs crumpled beneath him and the two nurses, one large and round, a mountain of a woman, and one old and frail-looking, caught him as he fell and helped him into the chair.

"What's his name?" he heard the older one ask on the way into the hospital.

"Jesse," Lyle said. "Jesse Landow."

The hospital air was just as cold as the air outside. Jesse kept shivering and he couldn't stop his teeth from chattering. It was embarrassing. The pain surged through his neck and shoulders and left arm. They wheeled him into a big room and drew white curtains around him. The old nurse looked him over carefully, like she would a roast in a butcher shop, Jesse thought. The mountain took his wrist and held it gently in her enormous, soft, freckled hand while she studied her watch.

"It's all right, Mr. Landow," the mountain cooed absently. "Just relax and take it easy. We're here to help you. Everything's going to be all right."

The old nurse shook down a thermometer and stuck it into Jesse's mouth. Then she wrapped a blood pressure cuff around his other arm and pumped it up. Jesse looked around frantically for Mary. She was standing beside him. He caught her eyes and she put a hand on his shoulder. She was trembling. The old nurse took off the cuff and left the room. Jesus, Jesse thought. This is it. I'm going to die. Just like that. I'm going to die. They all stand around me like a bunch of vultures. He looked back at Lyle.

"It's a heart attack, isn't it," he mumbled through the thermometer.

Lyle started to say something, but just then the old nurse came back wheeling a pole with a bottle hanging from it upside down. A young man wearing a white smock and gold wire-rimmed glasses was behind her.

"You feel weak, Mr. Landow?" the doctor asked.

Jesse nodded while the doctor unbuttoned his pajama top and probed his chest with a stethoscope. The old nurse had positioned the stand near Jesse's left shoulder. Now she slipped off his pajama top and picked up his left wrist.

"This will just be a little stick," she said.

Jesse felt the needle slide quickly into his vein. The doctor turned to the nurse. "Get him right up to CCU. You called Blackwell?"

The nurse nodded. The doctor left.

"We're going upstairs now," the old nurse said in a harsh, cracked voice, smiling at Mary. "If you'll go over to admissions they'll need some information. Then you can meet us in the coronary care unit. It'll only take a few minutes."

Mary nodded absently, then touched Jesse's shoulder again. "I'll be right there."

The mountain pushed Jesse out of the curtained room, down a hall, and into an elevator. They went up one floor, then down another long hall, past a row of pulled white curtains, and into a small, three sided room with a bed, a big green oxygen bottle, and a brown box with a screen sitting on a shelf against the wall. There was a window, but the curtains were pulled. They stopped beside the bed. The mountain walked around in front of him and eyed him curiously.

"Feeling better?" she asked. She towered over him. Her eyes, set deep in the valleys of her face, seemed to peer out of a cave.

"Yeah," Jesse said. "I think I am." The pain was easing up now. A vague sense of relief stole through him.

"We're going to take your clothes off," the mountain said. "Then you can lie down on this bed and rest."

"Must have been a false alarm," Jesse said. "I'm okay now." Take his clothes off hell. He looked down at himself. He was wearing Levis over his pajamas. He decided to get the hell out of there. But he couldn't move. Nothing would move. Not his arms or his legs or his butt. Goddamn, he thought. He was tired. So damn tired. If he could get back to Lyle's he could rest. He looked around for the way out.

"It's all right," the mountain said soothingly. "Just relax. You need some rest. You deserve that, don't you? We're here to help you. Just relax and everything will be okay."

"You had a heart attack," the old nurse said. Jesse's eyes travelled lazily over to her wrinkled face, splotched with age marks, her springy gray hair sprouting out from beneath her cap. "You need rest. Lots of rest."

Jesse looked into her old, gray eyes and suddenly started to cry. Tears flooded into his eyes and rolled down his cheeks. The mountain smoothed back his hair with a light, soft touch, then helped him stand. He leaned on her shoulder while the old nurse unbuttoned his Levis and slid them and his pajamas down to his knees. He sat on the bed, helplessly exposed, while the old nurse took them the rest of the way off and the mountain checked the needle in his wrist. Then they laid him down gently and covered him with a sheet.

Mary sat on a bench near Jesse's room, rigid and still, her hands folded in her lap, her full, round face composed, like an Egyptian death mask. At first, Lyle sat beside her. He had tried to talk to her, saying soothing words about how Jesse was strong as an ox, he'd pull through this, hell, he'd watched him work in Belfast welding until his fingers were raw and his eyes burned, twenty-four hours at a stretch sometimes, Jesse was one of the unsung heroes of the war, he was a good man, the best friend he'd ever had in his whole life, he was great, just great . . . When his voice started to crack, he stood up and paced back and forth in front of her, his cowboy boots squeaking softly with every other step and making little clicking sounds on the shiny beige tile.

Mary watched him, or stared at the wall, or watched the nurses scurry about, in and out of Jesse's room, and felt that she was with Jesse, loving him and soothing away some of the pain.

Once an old doctor rushed into Jesse's room behind the huge nurse with the squinty eyes. When he came out, the young doctor who had first checked Jesse met him at a nurses' desk. They stood with the old nurse studying a long strip of paper, mumbling to one another.

". . . that ST segment. Twenty milimeters off the baseline . . ."

". . . deep Q waves . . ."

". . . no severe arrhythmia, though . . ."

Then the young doctor nodded in her direction. "Get that damn lab up here," the old doctor said, and walked over to Mary, smiling. "Mrs. Landow?" He held out his hand. Mary stood up and shook it automatically. Lyle stopped pacing.

"I'm Dr. Blackwell." He was old and thin, with a bushy gray mustache, thinning hair, thick glasses with heavy black frames, and gray hairs protruding from his ears and nostrils. His breath reeked of stale coffee and tobacco smoke.

"As soon as the lab gets here, you can go in and see your husband if you like."

Mary nodded. "Yes. I'd like that." Jesse was in someone else's hands now, she thought. In the hands of this old doctor and of that big nurse. People she didn't know. Strangers.

"You probably realize your husband has had what is commonly called a heart attack."

Mary nodded.

"The way it appears to us now is that he has had what we call a myocardial infarction. That's just a fancy name for the fact that one of the arteries that supply blood to the heart has clogged up so that no blood is pumped to a certain area. Without blood there is no oxygen. Without oxygen, the cells in that part of the heart can't live. Their struggle for life is what caused the pain your husband had. The cells have probably died now, and the worst is over. But that area of the heart has to heal and while it's healing the heart's pumping action is slightly impaired. Your husband must have complete rest. That's the most important therapy. The heart will heal itself in time. There will be some scar tissue, but unless the infarcted area is extremely large, your husband will be back to normal, pretty much, within six to eight weeks."

Mary nodded again. She didn't understand a word of it. The doctor might as well have been speaking a foreign language.

"That's the way it looks now, at least," the doctor went on. "I wouldn't want to give you false hopes. The situation could change—drastically and suddenly. That's why we're constantly watching his heart out here on the monitor." He motioned toward the nurses' station. "This is our job. But you have a job, too. It's extremely important that your husband rest emotionally, as well as physically. Your job is to see that he stays calm. Reassure him that things are all right, that you are in control of the situation. As much as you can try to keep him from worrying. And if something is bothering him let us know. His emotional health is extremely important."

Again Mary nodded. She knew she should ask him some questions, but she couldn't think of any. What she really wanted to know was how she was going to raise three boys all by herself. How was she going to put them all through college and give them all the things Jesse wanted them to have so badly? How was she going to get a job when she couldn't even type? She would have no time now to wait while she went to school. How would she even pay the hospital bill? She stood there staring at the doctor dumbly.

"Do you have any questions?" the doctor asked.

Mary shook her head.

"I do," Lyle said. "Are you going to call in a specialist?"

"I am a cardiologist," the doctor said. "I understand you're from out of town. I assumed you had no family doctor here. If you have someone in particular in mind I'd be happy to consult with him, of course."

Lyle shook his head and looked at the floor. "My doctor's on vacation."

"Well, perhaps when he comes back he would like to look in on the case."

"Yeah, maybe," Lyle said.

"I assure you we're doing everything we can. Unfortunately, we are not gods or magicians. The main things we do in cases like this is monitor the patient closely and allow him complete rest. The heart is an amazingly strong muscle. It can take a pretty tough beating and come out of it like a champ, as long as we give it the chance. It just needs time. Time to heal."

A pretty young nurse with short black hair had approached the nurses' desk. The doctor noticed her.

"Here's the lab," he said. "Excuse me. If you have any questions, please feel free to ask."

He went to the nurse, spoke to her briefly, then followed her into Jesse's room. Mary sat back down on the bench.

Lyle sat down beside her, wringing his hands nervously. "He'll be all right," he said. "He'll get some rest and then be as good as new. You'll see."

Mary looked at him. His face was drawn, almost haggard, in spite of its boyishness. There was genuine concern there. She knew Lyle liked Jesse, but there was more in his face than just maybe losing an old working buddy. He seemed desperate. She caught his eyes and they looked at each other for a time in silent commiseration.

The pretty nurse, and then Dr. Blackwell, came out of Jesse's room.

"Rush it through," the doctor said. "I'll be waiting for it."

The nurse nodded and scurried down the hall toward the elevator carrying a sample of Jesse's blood.

"You can see him now," the doctor said to Mary. "But remember, he has to stay quiet—physically and emotionally. Keep him calm as much as you can."

"Can I see him?" Lyle asked.

"Are you some relation?" the doctor asked.

"No," Lyle said, a little sheepishly. "Just a friend."

"I think it best if you wait," the doctor said. "He really must stay calm. This is a crucial period in his recovery."

"I understand," Lyle said.

The doctor nodded to Mary, then walked over to the nurses' station.

"I'd better call Ruth and tell her what's happening," Lyle said. "I'll be right out here if you need me."

Mary stepped hesitantly into Jesse's room. She felt her stomach ball up into a knot and her heart beat violently against her chest. She swallowed. Jesse was laid out on a bed, covered with a white sheet up to his neck. Wires ran from under the sheet up to a machine with some kind of screen on it which sat on a shelf against the wall. There was a plastic thing in his nose connected by tubes to a big green oxygen tank. Another tube went from the IV bottle down to Jesse's left wrist. The big nurse held Jesse's other wrist, checking his pulse. She smiled at Mary, then laid Jesse's wrist down.

"He's doing fine," she whispered. "He's a strong hunk of man."

Suddenly Mary wanted to laugh. The laughter bubbled up from her stomach into her throat and she covered her mouth. Her eyes watered. The nurse looked at her strangely, then smiled again.

"Sit down there," the nurse whispered, pointing to a chair next to the stand that held the IV bottle. "Try not to wake him."

For the first time since she came into the room, Mary looked closely at Jesse's face. His eyes were closed and he seemed to be sleeping peacefully. But he was old. Her laughter stopped abruptly. He was so old. There were wrinkles in his forehead and loose folds of skin around his jaw. And he was white. His lips had a bluish tint to them.

She half stumbled over to the chair, sat down slowly, and stared up at the nurse. The nurse was smiling placidly.

"He really is all right," the nurse said softly. "The worst is over now. All he needs is rest. Lots of rest."

Mary nodded. Her eyes followed the nurse as she left the room. Then she looked down at her hands—small hands, with short, pink fingernails. The diamond ring on her left hand sparkled from the overhead lights. She remembered the day he had given it to her. The happiest day of her life. His proposal had been almost formal, and she felt again, now, as she had then, her self pouring out to him. Her reply had been without hesitation.

She took a long, deep breath, mentally gathering courage to look at him again. She followed the tube from the IV bottle down to the needle stuck in his wrist. Then followed his bare arm, still full of potential strength, to his broad shoulder, over to his neck, and finally to his face.

Yes. He was still Jesse. Still her Jesse. And yet he was different. He looked older, but that wasn't all. She sensed something. She had sensed something from the moment she entered the room, before she even looked at him. Something that reached deep into her, into that part of her that she was dimly aware of only at odd moments; when she was stuffing wet clothes into the dryer, stirring a pot of soup on the stove, watching television, or washing dishes.

His eyes slowly opened, as if it took all the strength of his arms to lift the lids. His pupils moved slowly toward her. "Mary?" he asked.

She touched his arm lightly. "I'm here," she said. "Don't try to talk. You have to rest. The doctor said."

"Look . . . Mary." He spoke very slowly, and suddenly her mind shot back to the stroke her father had had. To her father, lying in a coma for two weeks until he died with a strange, distorted smile on his pale lips. "Don't let . . . Lyle . . . take that . . . camper off."

She smiled at him and stroked his arm gently. "I won't," she said. "Don't worry about it. Try to sleep. You need to rest."

His eyes closed again. She let her hand rest lightly on his arm, conscious of the contact, feeling her own strength flowing into him.

V

Jesse's recovery followed normal expectations. "A classic case of the heart healing itself," Dr. Blackwell told him. They watched him closely. They kept the EKG wires connected to his chest and a bottle of oxygen handy beside his bed. But after the second day they disconnected the IV bottle and let him feed himself. It was mush, though. Baby food, Jesse called it. And they let him go to the bathroom on a bedside toilet that Jesse figured overworked the air conditioning system getting rid of the smell.

They kept him sedated. It was like being on a permanent drunk. Not too much mattered. He laughed at the big nurse, Martha's, stupid jokes when he knew they weren't funny. He even laughed at the old nurse, Ethel's, granite face when she came in to check his pulse and blood pressure. During the day there were other nurses he didn't get to know so well. For some reason he slept most of the day and stayed awake most of the night. And there were nurses' aides, mostly young and inexperienced, who changed his sheets and filled his water bottle. He joked with them, sometimes in veiled obscenities that made them smile and blush, and that made Mary angry twice when he forgot she was there and said them anyway. You don't make passes at pretty nurses' aides when your wife is in the room, he told himself over and over.

Mary wasn't there the first day the head nurse looked in on him. She was a tiny, ancient nun named Sister Elizabeth who looked like a penguin in her black habit. Seeing her was the first inkling Jesse had that he was in a Catholic hospital. He told her she scared him, that he thought he was in heaven already. She smiled amiably, like she was used to comments like that, then asked him a few questions. Where was he from? What kind of work did he do? Where was his family staying? How did he get here?

When he told her they had driven over from the Valley she looked at him sharply, her tiny eyes narrowing, sighting down her beaked nose at him.

"And I suppose you did all the driving."

"Oh, no," Jesse said. "My oldest son drove for a couple hours."

"And I suppose you had pain while you were driving."

Jesse lowered his eyes to protect himself from her gaze. "Yeah, sometimes."

She launched into a strident lecture. "Don't you realize, Mr. Landow, that you could have killed your whole family? What would have happened if you had lost control of your vehicle, if you had passed out at the wheel going around a curve? Your truck would have careened off the road, perhaps falling down a steep cliff, catching fire. The highway patrol would have found nothing but charred remains of the five of you. Don't you care about your family, Mr Landow? Is your pride more important than their safety? You deserve a good thrashing for that."

Thinking about it, he had to agree with her, but he couldn't think about it for very long. He couldn't think about anything for very long. Either somebody would come in and distract him or he would fall asleep.

She saw him every day after that, and he came to appreciate her thin, puckered smile radiating out from under her bonnet like light from a shaded lamp. She would lay her wrinkled claw on his arm and ask, "How are you feeling today, Jesse?" as if some important, life-changing decision depended on his answer. They would talk for a while, and she would ask him to pray with her. He would close his eyes politely and listen to her thin voice mumble a brief prayer for his health.

Mary came into the room once when this was going on. She had seen the sister before, had talked to her briefly about where she could stay if she didn't want to impose on Lyle and his family. There were Catholic relief workers who knew of people who volunteered their homes for just such cases as hers. But she had told the sister that Lyle had said they could stay there as long as necessary and she knew Lyle would be hurt if they stayed anywhere else.

She wasn't surprised to see the sister praying with Jesse. Was glad, in fact, for any kind of help anyone offered to make Jesse well again. She was still in a kind of daze. All of her attention centered on Jesse—how he felt that day, how quiet he had been, how much cooperation he was giving the nurses and doctors. She knew he could be obstinate and while he was under sedation he usually had to be treated like a child. He scared her when she talked to him. He was distant. He treated her like she was one of the nurses, joking with her about his dying and whether he would go to heaven or the other place. He said it in a stage whisper, smiling mockingly and watching her to gauge her reaction. And about how they might as well cut off his penis because he sure wouldn't be able to use that any more. There was a good amount of evidence that sex was the root cause of heart attacks and if everybody abstained they could eradicate the disease. He needed somebody to pray for him, Mary thought.

It wasn't until Wednesday that she finally came out of her daze enough to realize she ought to call some people to tell them what had happened. She wanted to call Marilyn. That would have helped *her* the most. But Marilyn and Bill were on their way to Texas and a whole new life. Marilyn would make other friends, and their lives would drift apart until there would be only the cards at Christmas to remind them they had once been close.

But she ought to call Aaron, Jesse's brother. She knew he would be upset if she didn't call him soon. He would probably wonder why she waited so long as it was. Wednesday, she decided to do it. She was sitting in the waiting room, down the hall from the coronary care unit, where she spent most of her time. She realized she knew every square inch of the room by heart, had thumbed through every magazine on the coffee table, had memorized the view from every window. Sometimes she could see the room while she was eating dinner or talking to Ruth. She dreamed about it. And she realized she hated taking deep breaths because the smell of the hospital was becoming nauseating to her. She wondered if she secretly feared she might catch some sickness herself if she breathed enough of the air. She needed to get out of the hospital for a while. She talked to Jesse about it the next time she saw him.

"Yeah," Jesse said dreamily. "You're not sick. Go out and do something."

"It's just that I feel so helpless."

"Yeah," Jesse said. "If I was feeling better you could climb in here with me. That would help a lot, I think."

"Help you have another heart attack."

Jesse's eyebrows furrowed, as if he was forcing himself to think straight. Mary watched him, her whole body tingling with the desire to leave. "I probably won't be much good for you after all this," Jesse said finally.

"Oh, baloney," Mary said. She stood up and smoothed back his hair. "The doctor said you'll be good as new."

"The good doctor doesn't want to upset me," Jesse said. "That old fart."

Mary thought she saw tears coming to his eyes. He was so easily hurt. She shouldn't have said what she did. "Don't think about it," she said. "All you have to think about is resting. You really will be good as new. You'll see."

"Old Martha says so," Jesse said slowly, his eyelids fluttering. "Good old Martha." He closed his eyes.

Mary leaned over and kissed his forehead softly, wondering absently how long it would be before he could have a haircut. He had needed a haircut before they left. By the time he was out of the hospital he would look like an old hippie. She looked out the window, at the parking lot below and the funny little mountain in the distance that Lyle said was called Thumb Butte. Then she sat down in the chair again.

But she couldn't stand it. She couldn't stand sitting there any longer. She wasn't doing Jesse any good watching him sleep. Maybe Ruth would be home. It would be somebody to talk to. She really ought to call Aaron. And she ought to see what the boys were up to. She could make sure they were cleaned up to come down to the hospital tonight. Dr. Blackwell said they could see Jesse tonight if they came in one at a time and only stayed a few minutes. They were anxious to see him. They weren't satisfied with the reports she gave them every evening. He really was getting better, she would say. All he needs is rest and he'll be okay again. Marty wanted her to explain what exactly had happened and she tried to tell him what Dr. Blackwell had told her about heart attacks and what she had read in the pamphlets. Then she gave him the pamphlets and he and David read them voraciously. Gary just looked at her with little squinty eyes, not comprehending, she knew, anything she had said; not believing, she felt, that she was telling the truth about Jesse getting better. She wondered if he would believe it tonight, when he saw Jesse hooked up to that machine, the wires running out from under the sheet, and all the equipment sitting around as if at any moment they would have to rush in and bring him back to life. Maybe a nurse could talk to him. Or that pretty blond social worker she had talked to once, or maybe even Sister Elizabeth. She would try to find someone tonight with a little authority, and hoped Gary would believe them.

She stood up slowly and picked up her purse. She looked at Jesse, sleeping peacefully, and resisted the impulse to stroke his forearm, lying limp outside the sheet. She didn't want to wake him. She walked quietly out of the room.

She went outside and climbed into the truck. She worried, as she had for two days, about backing the truck out of the parking space. She didn't like using the side mirrors. There was a blind spot immediately behind the truck that didn't show in the mirrors. She always imagined backing over something—like a small child—that she couldn't see. Sunday, Ruth had lent her the Volkswagen to drive to the hospital, but Monday Ruth had needed the car to go to some kind of meeting in town and, even though she offered to drop Mary off at the hospital and pick her up again, Mary decided to drive the truck. It wasn't so bad. She had to learn that there was almost no pickup to it with the heavy camper on it, that it would creep away from stop lights until it gradually built up enough momentum. And she drove carefully, doing everything she could to avoid sudden stops. She figured it would be all right as long as she never had to parallel park it.

When she got back to Lyle and Ruth's there was no one home. The house was locked up tight. She opened the door with the key Lyle had given her, went into the living room, and sat on the couch. The drapes were pulled over the sliding glass doors and the room was dark and cool. She stared at the drapes, following the dark green, leafy pattern around and around. She wondered where the boys were. She knew they were all right. Marty was old enough to take care of them. She trusted Marty. He had a good head on his shoulders for practical things. The first born. The one who had always had responsibility shoved onto him. She could hear Jesse saying it, clear back when Marty was only ten. "You're the oldest. It's your responsibility." In a way he was lucky for that. She had been an only child. She had moved out of her parents' house only to marry Jesse. She had never been without someone to lean on.

There was a dull ache in her stomach. God, she wished she could call Marilyn and listen to her strong, even voice telling her not to worry, that everything would be all right. She would say that, and a lot more that she couldn't imagine because Marilyn wouldn't just try to make her feel better; she would try to make her strong. She could use some strength now.

It was funny, she thought, that she hadn't cried yet. Right at first was when she should have cried. Now Jesse was getting better. Things would get back to normal again. There was no reason to cry now. It was true, what she knew Marilyn would say. Everything really will be all right.

She unsnapped her purse and pulled out her address book. She had intended to send post cards to people—a few neighbors; Jesse's boss, Angelo; Aunt Roe; Aaron and Sybil.

She went into the kitchen and dialed the operator. "I'd like to make a collect call . . ."

She was surprised when Aaron answered. He was probably working the night shift again. He was a guard at the state prison in Soledad. She could hear his gruff, bored voice talking to the operator, accepting the call. Aaron was okay, except he drank too much and liked to throw his weight around. And he had a lot of it to throw. He was pleasant when he talked to her, though.

"Hi ya, Sis. What's up?" He always called her Sis. It irritated her.

"Listen, Aaron." She hesitated. How was she going to do

this? "We're . . . we're up here in Prescott, Arizona on vacation."

"Prescott?" Aaron said. "Don't know where that is. Having a good time?"

"Listen," she said. "Jesse had a heart attack."

"What?"

"Jesse had a heart attack Saturday night. I thought you'd want to know." There was a long silence. Mary waited. Then she said, "Aaron?"

Aaron coughed. "Yeah, Sis. Look. You sure? Is he all right?"

"He's in the hospital," she said. "In a coronary care unit. He's resting. That's what they do. They make him rest."

"Goddamn," Aaron said. "A heart attack? How bad is it?"

Mary felt heat rising to her face and her eyes filling with tears. "I don't know," she said, trying to control herself but unable to keep her voice from shaking. "They're watching him pretty close."

"Jesus," Aaron said. "A heart attack." There was a long silence then. Tears rolled down Mary's face and tickled her nose. She wiped them away with her free hand and sat down on the chair under the wall phone. Then she heard a female voice, soft, like a sexy Hollywood model. It was Sybil, Aaron's wife.

"Hello, honey. Are you all right? Where are you staying?"

"With some friends here."

"Give me the address, okay? Wait a minute."

"You really don't—"

"Here. Okay. What is it?"

Mary gave her Lyle and Ruth's address and told her how to find the house.

"We'll be there tomorrow," Sybil said. "Probably late afternoon or early evening, okay?"

Mary took a deep breath. "Okay," she said.

"Keep a stiff upper lip," Sybil said. "We'll . . . wait a minute."

Mary heard mumbles in the background, then Sybil saying

to Aaron, "Of course you can. You're his brother, aren't you?"
Then she spoke into the phone again. "We'll see you tomorrow,
honey. Oh, and don't worry about us. We'll get a motel or
something."

"Okay," Mary said.

She was composed again when she went back into the living
room and sat on the couch. She would call Angelo later. It
wouldn't do to break down on the phone with him. She would
call tomorrow, before Aaron and Sybil came. It was no good having them come, even though they really did care. They meant
well, but they were so different. Aaron reminded her of a gorilla.
He had worked at that prison so long he almost acted like the
animals they kept caged there. And they didn't have any children—never intended to have any, Aaron had told Jesse. They
spent their vacations in Las Vegas drinking and gambling and
lived in a little shack of a house in Gonzales, a little town near
the prison filled mostly with wetback migrant workers.

But they would come and try to make her feel better, would
say all the right things, all the things they were expected to say,
and she would suffer through it until they left again, knowing
they didn't know, could never know, like Marilyn had, back
then, when it was so important for someone to know. She shivered a little. She would have to take them to see Jesse, like he
was some museum piece on display, and she would say, "There
he is. There's the man I married. See what I've made of him?
Isn't he a fine specimen? Isn't he a strong hunk of man?" And
Jesse would grin and babble and sleep.

She sat stiffly on the couch, her hands folded tightly in her
lap. She felt the closeness of the room, listened to the steady
tick of the battery-operated wall clock just over her head, looked
at the blank face of the television off to her right. Then she
stood up, went to the drapes that covered the sliding glass doors,
and drew them.

The deck just outside the doors was cast in shadow, but the

99

sun shone on the forest below. The trees stood out distinctly, shimmering, iridescent, the brown pine needles of the forest floor sloping sharply downward until they blended with the more distant trees. Her gaze centered on a lone gray pine towering over the other trees. Unconsciously, she wrapped her arms around herself and hugged herself tightly.

She started when she heard the door open, and turned to see Lyle walk through the door carrying his small, brown briefcase. He set the case down, took off his cowboy hat, and smiled automatically.

"Home early today," he said. "How is he?"

Home, she thought. This wasn't home. But it was becoming home. "Okay, I guess," she said. "He sleeps most of the time."

"Well, that's good for him, to sleep," Lyle said.

She turned her back to him and looked out over the forest again. Lyle walked over and stood beside her. They were silent for a long time. Then Lyle said, "Beautiful, isn't it."

"It's so big," Mary said, almost whispering. "It's scary. It's like it's alive."

"It is," Lyle said. "It's full of life."

"It might die," she whispered, gazing again at the lone gray tree.

Lyle shook his head. "No. It might be killed some day, by a forest fire or something. But it won't just die."

The tears welled up in her eyes again and she tried to blink them away. Lyle put his hand on her shoulder and squeezed it lightly. "It's all right," he said softly. "Don't worry. Everything will be all right."

"Where are the boys?" she asked.

Lyle took his hand away and opened the sliding glass door. Pine scent drifted in through the screen. "I dropped them off at Goldwater Lake to do some fishing. Probably won't catch much, but it's nice out there."

"Thank you," Mary said.

100

"Don't worry," Lyle said. "They're earning it. Dawn and Lyle Junior are with them. Marty's playing baby sitter. Saved us having to pay the day care center."

"Where's Ruth?" Mary asked.

"Some kind of a closed meeting. Personnel matters. She wouldn't even talk to me about it. I think it has something to do with the police chief."

"Did you sell any houses today?"

"Naw. Couple of good prospects, though, if I work it right." He grinned. "You got to do your best to give them what they want—whether they know what they want or not."

"How do *you* know what they want?"

"They tell me," Lyle said. "In subtle little ways that they don't even realize. Sometimes what they say they want and even what they think they want isn't what they really want. Nobody thinks of the consequences. Everybody thinks they want a mansion, even though they'll both have to work to make the payments and won't even have time to clean it."

Mary looked at his funny round face and smiled. "You have it all figured out."

"I been doing it a while," Lyle said.

She walked away from the doors toward the kitchen. "What can I do to start dinner?"

"Aw, don't worry about that yet. Ruth said she'd stop and get some hamburger. I'll barbecue it."

"The boys are going to the hospital with me tonight."

"That's right," Lyle said. "We better go get them. I'll show you the lake. It'll do you good to get outside for a while."

They hadn't caught any fish. But Gary had gone wading in the lake—with his shoes on—and he and Dawn had built a little city around a big rock on the bank. The rock was a house, Dawn had said, and she sat her Barbie doll on top of it. But Gary knew that the rock was all out of proportion to the roads they had

101

made and the stupid Barbie doll reminded him of a movie he saw on television once about a woman who grew into a giant. He wished he had brought his cars. Next time he would bring his cars. Marty had his hands full watching Lyle Jr. He had to change his diapers twice and it took him a while to figure out how the disposable diapers Lyle had sent with them worked. He and David had pondered over it, a little embarrassed that neither of them understood them. Marty remembered watching his mother change Gary when he was little, but Gary never wore things like that.

They all took turns taking showers while Lyle barbecued the hamburgers and Mary and Ruth puttered around the kitchen, making another salad. She would buy groceries tomorrow, Mary decided. She couldn't let Lyle and Ruth feed all four of them all the time, and she would make the dinner, a big batch of spaghetti.

After dinner the four of them climbed into the truck and Marty drove them to the hospital. They went through the visitors' entrance and rode up the elevator to Jesse's floor. The three boys stood around nervously while Mary went into Jesse's room to make sure he was up to seeing them.

Jesse was awake. Nothing had changed since that afternoon. He lay limp beneath the sheet, staring at the ceiling with eyes slightly clouded, his mouth in a relaxed, straight line. Black, stubby whiskers sprouted from his face.

"The boys went fishing today," Mary said. "Lyle took them to a lake."

"Catch anything?" Jesse asked.

"No," Mary said. "They had a good time, though. They're here now."

"Here?" Jesse turned his head slowly to look at her.

"Dr. Blackwell said they could see you for a few minutes, one at a time."

"Sure," Jesse said. "Send them in. Bring me my sceptor."

Mary smiled. "Marty first."

"Hell of a vacation, isn't it," Jesse said as Marty approached the bed.

"Could have been worse," Marty said. "How you feeling?"

"Tired," Jesse said. "But they say I'm supposed to feel like that."

"You were tired when we left."

"Yeah, I know. You taking care of your mother?"

Marty hadn't even thought about it. "Sure," he said. "She's doing fine."

"Good," Jesse said. "Keep an eye on her."

Marty watched his father's eyes wander off, away from him and up to the ceiling. Marty swallowed, then stared at the bedside commode that sat on the other side of Jesse's bed.

"You're going to have to go over there one of these days," Jesse said, his voice coming from the end of a long tunnel.

Marty felt his palms getting wet. He wiped them on his pants. "Yeah, I know."

"You might as well accept it."

"I accept it." And suddenly he felt resigned, floating in a sea of passivity, breathing air filled with smoke and dust.

"You can come back and tell us all about it," Jesse said. "Go back to college. Take up your music again."

"I'll lose my lip," Marty said.

"You'll get it back."

"Yeah, I guess." It didn't matter anymore.

"You'll be making records some day," Jesse said.

"Sure," Marty said. "Someday. I'll give you all autographed albums."

"Lyle doesn't have you selling real estate yet, does he?"

"Naw. He keeps pretty busy, though."

"He's a hustler," Jesse said, looking back at Marty.

Marty looked at the floor, conscious of his hands hanging like weights on plumb lines. He stuffed them into his pockets. "Looks like they have you wired for sound."

"That's about right," Jesse said. "They all out there dancing to the beat of my heart?"

Marty smiled, relieved. "Yeah. You ought to see them. Playing a full set. You're the bass."

"Good," Jesse said. "Tell them to get Spade Cooley. Without the gun."

"I heard Lawrence Welk was going to try to imitate you," Marty said.

"Won't be any good," Jesse said. "Maybe Liberace could listen to it, though."

"He'd have to bring his own candelabra."

For the first time Marty saw his father smile, a slight, distorted crookedness of his mouth. "Tell Lyle to get him a sequin cowboy hat."

Marty chuckled. "Lyle would know where to get one, all right."

They fell into silence then. Marty studied the EKG monitor above his father's head and his feet shuffled on the floor. Suddenly he looked directly into Jesse's eyes. Jesse was watching him coyly, as if gauging his reaction to this strange, austere place. The penetration in the look startled Marty and he felt vague stirrings of guilt. Whose fault was it that his father lay here in a bed, unable to move, unable to haul hollow metal doors around as he had watched him do when he was a kid and Jesse took him on jobs during the summer.

"Does it bother you," Marty asked, "not being able to move? Just having to lie there?"

"They keep me pretty doped up," Jesse said. "Actually it feels good to be able to rest."

104

"I read all the pamphlets," Marty said. "An artery clogged up for a while and then part of your heart died." He swallowed.

"Only part of it," Jesse said. "The rest of it's doing fine."

"Yeah," Marty said. "You'll be up and around in no time."

"That's what they say," Jesse said.

Marty looked at the floor again. "I'd better let David come in," he said.

"Yeah," Jesse said. "I want to see all of you."

There was an awkward moment of silence. Marty felt he should touch his father, squeeze his shoulder, shake his hand or something. But he was too far away. He would have to step up to the bed, reach his hand out. Instead, he mumbled, "I'll see you again later," turned, and walked out.

David was almost sick to his stomach by the time Marty came out and it was his turn to go into his father's room. He was struck first by his father's weakness, his vulnerability, the whiteness of his face, the relaxed muscles in his arms. Then his eyes scanned the machines he imagined were there to keep his father alive. Infernal machines, he thought, and wondered why he thought that. His father smiled at him weakly.

"So. You didn't catch any fish."

David shook his head. "I don't think there's any in that lake." He walked closer to the bed, stood directly beside it, and looked at his father's face. His father was an old man.

"Well, maybe next time," Jesse said.

"Lyle said there's a better lake somewhere around here."

"No streams, though, huh?"

"No. Lyle said all the streams dry up in the summer."

"Too bad. Stream fishing is the best. Nothing like the feel of a big trout grabbing your line and fighting with the current."

David's stomach muscles relaxed a little. It was his father, after all. He didn't know what he had expected. A smaller man, he guessed, as if the disease would somehow make him shrink. "We had to baby sit. Changed diapers and everything."

"Good. Good experience for you. You guys'll make somebody a good wife before this is over."

"How are you feeling?" David asked.

"Just tired," his father said. "I'll rest up for a while and then be out of here."

"I think you needed it. The rest I mean."

"Not much of a vacation, though."

"There's always next year," David said.

"Sure. Next year we'll do it right. Maybe take a month. Drive clear across the country."

"Sure. We could do that." David looked at the EKG monitor, then over at the bedside commode. His father didn't seem very sick, but he guessed everything was inside where you couldn't see it. "Do you have any pain?" he asked.

"Not any more," Jesse said. "That first night, though. Jesus. I don't ever want to go through anything like that again."

"What did it feel like?"

"It just hurt like hell."

"How long did it last?"

"Until they stuck a needle in my wrist. Then it went away."

"You had it before, though, didn't you."

"Jesus," Jesse said. "You sound like a damn reporter."

David looked at the end of the bed. He could see Aunt Roe sitting in her chair in the little reading room reading the letter he was going to write to her. He would tell her everything—well, almost everything—everything he imagined she would want to know. Last night he had scribbled down a poem he would send her.

cloudy nights and sunless days
keeping time to ancient music

swinging with some bell-like rhythm
tolling out the time
of exhaustion and overwhelming passion
drowning out the silence
manipulating violence
'til she's
gone, gone, gone, gone, gone, gone

He looked back at his father's slack face, the last line of his poem echoing in his mind. Next year, he thought. There's always next year.

"You'll be a good reporter," Jesse said.

"How do you know?"

"I don't know. You have the nose for it, I guess. You like to find things out."

"I don't know," David said. "I don't write much news." Not detached enough, he thought. A reporter has to be objective.

"You ought to do it," Jesse said, a hint of urgency creeping into his voice. "You ought to start now if you like it."

"I don't think I like it much," David said.

"Oh." Jesse didn't move a muscle.

"I like other kinds of writing," David said.

"What?" Jesse asked, tired now, blinking more than usual.

"Poetry," David said.

"You write poetry?"

"Some."

Jesse studied David, as if inspecting him under a microscope. But it was an effort and David saw him relax. "Poetry, huh? I used to read poetry when I was a kid. Never understood it much, but I liked the sound of it rolling and rolling . . ."

"Poetry is almost all sound," David said.

"You ought to get together with your brother. You could write the lyrics and he could write the music. Like Rogers and Hammerstein."

"Landow and Landow."

"Yeah. Landow and Landow," Jesse said. "Not bad." His eyes rolled up to the ceiling as he said it, then shot back to David. "I'd like to see some of your poetry some time."

David looked down at his feet, partially hidden under Jesse's bed. "I . . . I don't know . . ."

"Personal, huh?" Jesse said.

David looked at him for a moment, then back down at his feet. "Yeah," he said softly. His father's eyes had been wet, he thought. He wasn't sure. He didn't want to be sure. He stood there embarrassed, hating himself for even mentioning the poetry. "I'll write you a story, though," he said lamely.

"Okay," Jesse said. "Do that."

David looked back at his father and saw that his eyes were closed. His face was peacefully composed, his jaw relaxed. His springy hair showed more gray than David could remember him having before. He looked tired.

Jesse opened his eyes again lazily. "You better send Gary in." His voice was far away and a little slurred. "I can feel myself drifting off."

"Okay," David said. He moved away from the bed, then turned back and saw his father watching him. David's hand moved from his side almost imperceptibly, a slight, automatic muscular contraction that David's mind caught in the act. The hand returned to its original position.

"Take it easy," David said.

"Not much choice about that," his father returned.

David walked from the room.

Gary had it all figured out what he was going to tell his father when he saw him. He was going to tell him that he wished he wasn't sick, but that it wasn't such a bad vacation anyway. That he still got to use his new fishing stuff and he had fun playing along the bank of the lake with Dawn, even though

Dawn was a girl and littler and kind of a baby. He was going to tell him how he had seen one of those red spiders again right outside Lyle's house and that Lyle had said it really was poisonous and he shouldn't touch it. Lyle said there were snakes around, too. Rattlesnakes. But he would know what to do if he saw one. He would just walk away real quiet. That's what Lyle said to do. Pretty soon Lyle was going to take them to another lake where they would probably catch some fish and then they could eat them for dinner. He would take his cars with him because David fixed up his fishing pole with a bobber and all he had to do was cast it out into the water and wait for a fish to bite. He could play with his cars while he was waiting and make roads and driveways and stuff. Then he would look out and see the bobber gone and know that a fish was on his line and he could pull it in like David showed him. David was being real nice, but Marty was too bossy all the time. Yesterday, when he was outside playing, Marty called him in to eat lunch and he came in and then Marty told him to wash his hands and then he had to sit at the table being real quiet because the baby was sleeping Marty said. And lunch wasn't even ready yet. He could have played outside for a while longer and his hands weren't even dirty and all Marty fixed was peanut butter sandwiches anyway. And then at night, he wanted to stay up and watch a movie on television about a creature that lived in a cave under the water and came out sometimes and scared people. Some men were trying to capture it to take it back to the city and keep it in a cage, but the creature kept getting away from them and he picked up this woman and carried her into his cave under the water and then Marty told him he had to go to bed. Right in the middle of the movie. There was no school or anything. He could stay up and watch movies if he wanted to, couldn't he?

His father would let him. His father would tell Marty to let him do what he wanted sometimes. He didn't see why he had to take a shower every night. He wasn't always dirty and he washed his hands. His father would say he didn't have to take a shower every night. Maybe every other night, or only when he got dirty. He wished he would see a snake sometime.

His mother went with him into his father's room and his father was lying on a bed with just a sheet over him, no blankets or anything, and the room was cold and kind of still, like there was no air in there and it was hard to breathe and it smelled funny, even funnier than the rest of the hospital. There were wires coming out from under the covers that went up to a funny-looking television with wavy lines on it. There was a big green metal thing sitting against the wall and the walls were white and Gary shivered because it was cold. The wires were like in a thing he saw on television once where some scientists hooked wires up to a frog and when they pushed a button the wires made the frog jump, but not like a frog was supposed to jump, not up in the air, but just kind of jerk all of a sudden. He wondered if they made his father do that. His mother had said his father was getting better, and while they were waiting outside his room an old nurse with funny gray hair and a wrinkled nose came over and talked to them. She said his father was getting better, too, and his mother looked at him and said, "See. I told you." But Gary knew she had told the nurse to say that. His father didn't look like he was getting better. He was just lying there.

They walked closer to the bed. He held his mother's hand. He was scared because he felt something funny in the room. Not something he could feel exactly, like you feel hot or cold, but something that made him think of things like the frog. The frog had been dead. They made it jump with the wires even though it was dead.

They got closer to his father but Gary stopped. His father was lying there, real still. His eyes were closed. His face was all white and his hair was gray almost all over. There were whiskers on his face that made him look kind of dirty. He wasn't moving at all. His arms were just lying there outside the sheet. He was wearing a white thing with short sleeves.

He looked up at his mother.

"He's asleep," she whispered.

They stood there a moment longer and Gary was scared. He held his mother's hand tight and tried not to shake.

"We'd better not wake him," she whispered. "He's supposed to rest a lot."

Gary was brave. He stood there waiting, wanting to leave, but waiting for his mother. Finally, they turned and walked from the bed and out of the room.

"It's good for him to sleep," his mother said when they were back in the hall.

But all Gary could think about was the frog.

Marty lay in the overhead section of the camper, his hands behind his head, breathing the cold, crisp night air seeping through the window. For days now, he realized, he had been doing things without thinking. He had been taking orders from Lyle and Ruth. He had fished when he hated fishing, especially when he didn't catch anything. He had been baby sitting that little brat who kept wetting his pants and sticking things into his mouth. He had been trying to keep an eye on Gary and Gary was acting like some kind of monster.

And all the time, his father lay there in that hospital bed trying to come back to life. His father had almost died. Marty realized that now. All the information in the pamphlets suddenly made sense to him. What if he had? What would they have done? He probably wouldn't have had to worry about getting drafted. Or at least he could have contested the notice and won. He would have had a widowed mother and two brothers to support. He would have had to shoulder that responsibility. He would have had to keep working at McMichael's, maybe make it his career, like old Mrs. Poole, who had been sitting in that dark

little booth candling eggs eight hours a day since she was a teen-
ager and now was almost ready to retire. Well, he could probably
work into management. But maybe not. They'd get some guy
with a business degree who would try to run the place like Lockheed or something.

His mother could work, maybe. He didn't know what she
could do besides cook and sew and clean house and raise kids.
She'd done a pretty good job of that but it didn't do much for the
pocketbook. Besides, it wouldn't be fair to Gary to have his
mother at work all day, even though he was a spoiled brat. Hell,
maybe it would be good for him.

Anyway, there would be a lot of changes—for all of them. It
was a strange thing to think about—life without his father.

He put his bare arms under the covers and wondered if he
should close the window. The air was cooler tonight, and a little
damp. The weather was nice here, though. No smog. But it was
such a small town. What do people do here? Almost everyone he
had seen had been old, like the town. Lyle said they have square
dances down on the plaza. Square dances. Jesus. This town
would probably love Spade Cooley.

He could get a group together. Back home he could call
some people from the band. They had jammed pretty good at the
party. With a little practice, they'd be playing gigs every night.
And he'd give lessons during the day. Two-fifty a half hour. If he
had, say, five a day, five days, twenty-five times two-fifty . . .
sixty-two-fifty a week. Not a hell of a lot. But with the gigs at
night . . .

Hell. It was a crazy thing to think about. If he ever wanted
to get married, have kids, all that, he'd need something steady.
Connie would like it, though. She would say, "Go ahead. You
have the talent." Better than Grobin. Well, that's something, but
not enough. Not when people are depending on you.

He could get into something maybe. Not the L. A. Philhar-
monic, but maybe a studio band or a movie orchestra. Have to

be a good sight reader for that, though. It would take a lot of practice at first. Hours and hours of it. And it would be so mechanical—so stifling. "You're selling yourself short," Connie would say. "You're worth more than that. You're not a machine."

Shit. What did she know anyway? Maybe stacking egg crates was all he was good for. One on top of another, five high, building up his muscles and breaking his back every time he bent over. It must be worth something to somebody. They paid him for it, didn't they?

He pulled the covers up over his shoulders, turned over, and cranked the window closed. On the lower bed he could hear David and Gary breathing lightly in their sleep. He wondered what time it was. Probably past midnight. But it didn't matter if he got any sleep or not. There was nothing to do in the morning except more of the same. And his father was lying there in that bed, all white and old-looking, lying stock still, all doped up so he didn't really know what was happening, waiting for his heart to heal.

David woke up early the next morning. It was light in the camper, and he stared at the ceiling, listening to Gary breathing heavily, still asleep, curled up into a little ball beside him. David had been dreaming but he couldn't remember the dream. He felt tired, and had a vague lingering feeling of weight, as if in his dream he had been Sisyphus struggling with his rock.

Sunlight poked through a crack in the curtains over the sink. The line traveled down into the sink, up and out again, fell to the floor, traveled across it, and almost touched Gary's face. A line of light carefully tracing its own image, David thought. He ought to write that down. But there was no paper or pencil. He would have to get up and look through his drawer, but that would wake up Gary, and probably Marty, too, and they would think he was crazy.

He had to write a story. He had told his father he would. It was worse than a feature assignment from Novotny. Worse because he would have to think it up all on his own. He couldn't go out and talk to somebody and take notes and then come back and sit at one of the old typewriters in the back of the journalism room and sift through them.

"A line of light traced its own image across the floor." Not a bad beginning. He would try to remember it. Okay, then what? Somebody sees the light. Who? Some sixteen-year-old kid lying in a little camper sitting in a driveway in front of a log cabin with a forest behind it. Some sixteen-year-old kid with his head up his ass who is even afraid to get out of bed and look for a paper and pencil to write down something important just because somebody might think he's a little weird. Well, he was weird, maybe more than a little.

Gary rolled over and stretched out. He lay on his back, his breathing still heavy, his eyes still closed. Down near his waist something stuck up and made a little teepee out of the covers. David stared at it. He couldn't believe it. God, he thought. Even Gary. He wanted to touch it to see if it was real. But he turned on his side, faced the camper wall, and groaned inside himself.

After breakfast Mary drove the camper to the hospital. Ruth had one of those slow cookers and she had showed Mary how to use it. Mary had made spaghetti sauce and left it simmering. That night, Ruth said, all they'd have to do was boil the spaghetti and dinner would be ready. She had made enough sauce for an army because there was a good chance Aaron and Sybil would be there for dinner.

Mary nodded to the funny little cleaning lady who was polishing a drinking fountain as she walked into Jesse's room. Jesse was asleep. She was surprised. Usually by this time he was smiling and joking in his strange, inebriated way. She looked out the window for a moment, then went to the waiting room and sat down with a magazine. She read a story about a young married couple, Jan and David, who were having trouble with their relationship because Jan's parents were over to see them almost every night and they hardly ever had any time to themselves. It was from David's point of view and he knew he would just have to tell them to butt out of their lives. He was trying to think of a nice way to do it when she decided to go back to Jesse's room.

This time Jesse was awake.

"How are you feeling?" Mary asked.

"Strong as an ox," Jesse said. "Can't you tell?"

"Good," Mary said. "I thought we'd dance a few polkas."

"Sure," Jesse said. "Any time." But he just lay there without moving a muscle, expressionless.

Mary looked down. "How are you feeling, really?" she asked.

"About the same, I guess. Blackwell came. Said I was doing okay."

"That's good," Mary said.

"They're going to take me out of here pretty soon. Put me in a regular room."

Mary smiled. "That's wonderful."

"Yeah. Just great."

"It means you're getting better."

"Sure," Jesse said. "Let's dance a polka."

Mary looked at him closely. He seemed tired today. "You shouldn't be so negative."

"Yeah, well, I was feeling pretty good this morning. Then I sat up for a while. Ten whole minutes. Wore me out."

"Did they say you could sit up?"

"Sure," Jesse said. "It was their idea. Part of the therapy."

"They're trying to build you up."

"Yeah. I'll be hanging doors again tomorrow."

"Maybe not tomorrow," Mary said. "But sometime."

Jesse shook his head slowly. "I don't think so. Nope. No

more hanging doors. Blackwell said it looks like that part of my heart that died was pretty big."

"Did you tell him what you do?"

"He never asked."

"You should tell him and see if he thinks you'll be able to go back to work."

"There's plenty of time for that."

"But you just lie here and worry about it. It would be better to know, one way or the other."

"I already know."

"No, you don't. You haven't asked the doctor."

She watched him look at her silently. She could imagine the wheels turning slowly, sluggishly in his brain, bringing up for the hundredth time what he had been thinking ever since the attack. His face took on a reddish glow, as if a red light bulb had come on inside his skull. There was a minute twitch at the corner of one eye. Mary slipped her hand into his.

"You make everything so hard," she said. "Don't worry. Everything will be all right."

Jesse looked away. "It's lousy," he said. "Just lying here. Watching my family fall apart. I—"

"That's not true," Mary said. "We're doing fine."

"I think about what'll happen," Jesse went on. "Angelo can't keep me on if I can't work. What else have I ever done but work? I'll have to sell Fuller Brush or something. Jesus."

"You make it sound worse than it is."

Jesse looked at her again. His eyes were wide now, his mouth tense and thin. "Like hell I do," he said. "How are we going to live if I can't work?"

"I can work," Mary said. "I'm not helpless."

"Yeah, sure," Jesse said. "You could go up to Salinas and pick lettuce. Take the kids along, too."

"I could find something," Mary said. "It's a big city."

"Yeah," Jesse said. "Some goddamn clerk job or something

where you have to yes ma'am a bunch of fat old ladies and let your boss make passes just to keep your job. Jesus. You don't know what it's like. It's tough enough for a man with some kind of skill. You think a woman can support a family?"

"A lot of women do," Mary said. "Besides, you talk like you'll be an invalid the rest of your life. There are lots of jobs you'll be able to do."

"Sure," Jesse said. "I'll be a night watchman. The old fart burglars always shoot before they break in."

"My God, Jesse," Mary said. "You're only forty-three."

Jesse looked back at the ceiling. "I should have planned better, that's all. I should have known something like this would happen. You know how much life insurance I have? Four thousand dollars. Enough to bury me and that's all. Jesus. The house won't even be paid for."

What is he saying? Mary thought. She watched him sulk like a spoiled child who had had his favorite toy taken away, then sudden outrage surged up in her chest. It brought her to her feet. She wanted to say, you don't have any right to talk like that, not after all the love we give you, not after all you've put us through. And not just us. Lyle, too, and Aaron, and all the other people who would be concerned if they knew. And if you want to feel that way you can just go off and sulk all by . . . But a nurse walked into the room, a short blond with a pimply face. She nodded to Mary and smiled at Jesse.

"How are you feeling today, Jesse?" she asked.

"Great," Jesse said. "Just great."

The nurse picked up his wrist and looked at her watch. Then she glanced quizzically at Mary. Mary nodded a slight, tight smile, and sat down. A minute passed, and the nurse said, "Fine. Your pulse is fine. You look a little more awake today."

"Yeah," Jesse mumbled.

She wrapped a blood pressure cuff around Jesse's arm and pumped it up. It hissed softly while she studied the gauge. Then she unwrapped it, rolled it up, and stuck it into a pocket in her white uniform.

"Blood pressure's normal," she said. "You're doing fine. I hear you sat up for a while this morning."

"Yeah," Jesse said.

"Did it make you tired?"

"Yeah."

The nurse glanced at Mary again, then looked back at Jesse. "That's all right," she said. "You can expect things to make you tired. We have to get your heart back in shape and you have to work at it a little. We'll try it again tomorrow."

"Okay," Jesse said.

The nurse nodded to Mary and left the room.

Jesse forced a smile that Mary didn't believe. "Don't worry," he said. "I'll be all right."

"Aaron and Sybil are coming this afternoon."

"That's good," Jesse said, as if he already knew. "It'll be good to see them."

He's gone now, Mary thought. He had been there for a while, but now he was gone. What had she done wrong? It was the old story. She could never have all of him. For some reason . . .

She stared out the window at Thumb Butte in the distance. A great ache swelled within her, as if she was about to give birth to some misery the way she had given birth to the boys. The misery would be her child to nurture and rear. She would do it on her own.

After Aaron and Sybil called that afternoon, Mary and Lyle drove to the end of the little dirt road to meet them. The air was hot and still and they got out of the jeep to wait in the shade of a big pine tree. Mary was wearing a pair of light blue shorts that she had the feeling were tighter than they should be, although Jesse had told her they looked fine when she bought them. The sun filtering through the pine needles made dappled shadows on her legs.

Before they left Lyle's she had noticed a bank of big black clouds building up in the east. It was about time, Lyle had said. They needed some rain, but it would probably be a couple of weeks before the clouds brought any. It happened every year.

Now, Mary noticed the air was more humid, more like the air in the Valley except there was no smog. Every once in a while a slight breeze drifted past her making her think of the ocean. But still the dusty pine scent filled the air and the dry, brown pine needles made a cushion under her feet.

Lyle was quiet, a little gloomy today, she thought. She couldn't help wondering if their staying there was getting to be too much for him and Ruth. But she didn't know what else to do. It was ridiculous to even think about all of them staying in a motel. She supposed she could park the camper in the national forest somewhere, but she would have to leave the boys there without anything when she went to the hospital. What if it rained?

"You sure they know how to get this far?" Lyle asked.

"I read the directions right from the ones you gave us," Mary said.

"They should be here pretty soon," Lyle said.

If they don't stop off at some bar first, Mary thought. Aaron wasn't exactly the most reliable person she knew. Nothing like Angelo. She had called Angelo as soon as she had returned from the hospital that afternoon. She had kept herself under control while she talked to him. He was concerned, naturally, and shouted to her in his New York Italian accent as if there was no phone, just the distance. He asked if there was anything he could do, and she said no, wondering all the time what he would do about Jesse's salary when his vacation time ran out. She didn't ask, but Angelo told her not to worry. "His salary keeps going," he said. "I'll have Rhoda send it up there."

"Thank you," Mary said.

"And there's insurance," Angelo went on. "Jesse should have a card. Have them call if they want to know."

"I will," Mary said. He had everything under control. The epitome of competence.

Aaron and Sybil's beat-up little Volkswagen came around the corner and Mary stood and waved to them. The car scattered dust as it pulled up beside Mary. Sybil was driving. She looked at Mary with cool, droopy eyes, as if appraising a player in a poker game. Mary couldn't see Aaron.

"How are you, honey?" Sybil asked.

"I'm okay," Mary said. She nodded to the jeep. "Just follow us."

Mary had told everyone that morning that Uncle Aaron and Aunt Sybil were coming and Gary had been looking forward to it all day. He liked Uncle Aaron. He was big and gruff, like Papa Bear in the story, and he liked to grab Gary around the waist, swing him up over his head, and twirl him around and around until Gary was dizzy.

That's exactly what he did when Gary met them in the driveway in front of Lyle's. The ground went around and around and Uncle Aaron laughed his hoarse, deep laughter. Then when he was back on the ground, Gary staggered around like he was drunk and made Uncle Aaron laugh some more. He watched him shake hands, then, with David and Marty and meet Lyle and Ruth. Dawn had stayed in the house. She was being snooty.

At dinner, he talked Ruth into letting him sit next to Uncle Aaron and he told him all about what had happened—that they had come up here on a vacation and his dad had gotten real sick so they stayed here and slept in the camper at night and played outside most of the time during the day, down there in the woods where there were big trees and poisonous spiders and rattlesnakes and chipmunks and squirrels and sometimes porcupines and mountain lions and bears. And they went fishing but they didn't catch anything because the lake was all fished out and because they used the lake for drinking water so they had to keep it clean. And he had a new fishing pole and a reel and he knew how to cast it himself and put the worm on and pull in the fish if he ever caught one. And he and Dawn had a fort out in the woods that no one knew about (he whispered this) and he would show it to him after dinner, okay?

His mother said he should stop and let Uncle Aaron eat, but Gary could tell Uncle Aaron was glad to hear all about it. Uncle Aaron put his arm around Gary, leaned over, and whispered in his ear that he would probably have to wait until tomorrow to see the fort because he was going to the hospital tonight to see his dad. Gary nodded. He didn't like Uncle Aaron's sour breath, but it felt good to have his big, heavy hand on his shoulder. He was glad Uncle Aaron was there. Everything wasn't so scary anymore.

Jesse was surprised when old Martha came in just after he had finished gagging down the slop they gave him for dinner.

"Thought it was your day off," he said.

"It was," Martha said, " 'til they called me in." She grabbed his arm and wrapped the blood pressure cuff around it. "Sit up this morning?"

"Yeah."

"How long?"

"About ten minutes."

She smiled. "I told them you could do it. How you feeling? Any pain?"

"Nope."

"Good."

The blood pressure cuff hissed softly and Martha watched the gauge. Then she said, "Talkative today, aren't you."

Jesse didn't respond.

"You're supposed to fill me in on all the gossip. Which nurses are bitchy, what surgeon screwed up an operation, which doctors are screwing which nurses."

"I don't live here," Jesse mumbled.

"What?"

"I said, I don't live here."

"Like hell you don't."

Jesse looked away while she picked up his wrist and looked at her watch. He wasn't in the mood for her gruff kind of caring tonight. All day, ever since Mary left, he'd been thinking what a rat he was. Leaving his family stranded in this stupid little town, dependent on people they barely knew, worried sick that he might die any minute, and then what would they do? And he kept wondering how he had had this damn heart attack in the first place. Working too hard. It wasn't worth it. Sure, he got a good salary. And it was nice having Angelo think he was important to the company. But look what it got him. He was no good to the company now. He would have to go into something less strenuous. Only once did he ask himself why. And then, why him? But he didn't think about that very much. There was no answer. It wasn't the kind of question he could deal with. He'd leave that to Sister Elizabeth. All his life he'd been dealing with things. He could figure out anything if you put the materials in front of him or gave him a blueprint. But what good would that do him now?

Martha let go of his wrist and his hand fell limply to the bed. "Oh, brother," she said.

Jesse looked back at her round, puffy, white face, made rounder by her short, thick, colorless hair. She stood there looking at him with a disgusted look, her hands on her hips.

"It's the feeling sorry for yourself stage, isn't it," she said.

Jesse looked away from her again.

"Look," she said. "Everybody that has a heart attack goes through it. You think you're no good any more. You think your family's going to starve. You think your days as a big stud are over. You think your wife'll have to cut your steak for you, and then you probably won't be able to chew it."

"What do people do after a heart attack?"

"Oh, they usually go right into an old folks home. They sit around and drool all over themselves."

"I did a lot of heavy work."

"Okay. You might not be able to do that. You might be able to. You have to ask the doctor. But I'd say probably you won't. But that doesn't mean you just roll over and die."

"So what do you do?"

"What do you want," Martha said, "an instruction book? You do what you want."

Jesse smiled a little. "You're a big help."

Martha stuffed the blood pressure cuff into her pocket. Her uniform fit tight and made her look like a stuffed potato sack. "Oh, that's all right," she said. "Just part of the job." She walked around his bed and out of the room.

That's great, Jesse thought. Next thing you know they'll be sending some shrink in here to convince me I'm a normal, healthy person. He looked out the window. The sun had gone down somewhere off to the right of his window and the sky was a filmy gray color. Silhouetted against the gray sky was that little mountain, Thumb Butte, Mary had said it was called. He watched it fade as the sky became darker until he couldn't see it anymore at all. His eyes were calm, but his mind raced. He wondered what kind of medical insurance he really had. How much would it cover? He wished he could increase his life insurance right now, just in case. If he had to pay most of the hospital bill, he didn't see how they would ever make it. Even if he kept working for Angelo it would take years to pay it off, and Angelo needed him out in the field, not sitting behind some desk. What could he do behind a desk? He would have to sell the camper to get that payment off his back. Probably take a loss, though, now

123

that it was used. He might be able to take out a second mortgage on the house. Jesus. He should have gotten mortgage insurance. Mary would have those payments to make, too, along with the hospital. They'd never let her rest. Damn. How could he have been so stupid. But he guessed you never think about dying when you're strong and healthy. He had come that close, and it wasn't over yet. He could take care of other things. If his sex life was over, he could probably handle that. If his kids started to think of him as a sick old man, it would be hard to take, but he could handle it. He could keep from doing strenuous things and take care of himself and probably live to be eighty. But if he couldn't make enough money, if he couldn't work . . .

Mary appeared in his room like an apparition. It startled him.

"How are you feeling?" she asked.

He took a deep breath. "What do you think? That I found some miraculous cure? Jesus. I don't change much in six hours."

Mary looked at the floor.

"Goddamn it, don't pout," Jesse said.

Mary looked up again. "Aaron and Sybil are here."

"Good. Send them in."

"One at a time," Mary said. "You know that."

"Yeah, okay. Aaron first . . . Wait. How is the bastard?"

Mary looked at him quizzically. "He's fine. He's worried about you."

"Okay," Jesse said. He watched her walk away from him, her plump bottom swaying slightly. He pictured her approaching him naked, as she had so often, a little shyly, still, even after all these years. She ought to try to lose some of that weight.

Aaron walked quickly up to the bed, shuffling his big body like a bear.

"Hey, Jess," he said. "How you feeling?"

"Good as I should, I guess," Jesse said.

"Well, you look great." Aaron stood near the bed, his hands hanging limply at his sides.

"Bullshit," Jesse said. "I look like a ghost. Sit down."

Aaron sat down. He looked apprehensively at the big green oxygen bottle behind him, then back at Jesse. His tiny eyes were set deep in his big, round face. Jesse wanted to laugh at him, like he would laugh at a bear lumbering around a cage at a zoo. But he controlled himself.

"Jesus, Jess," Aaron said. "I'm really sorry this happened."

"Why?" Jesse said. "It's not your fault."

"Well, I know. But . . ." He looked down at his hands. "You know. It's no good being sick."

Jesse was tired of watching him. He looked up to the ceiling.

"How you doing?" Aaron asked. "Are you getting better?"

"They say I am," Jesse said. "They're going to put me in a regular room pretty soon."

"How long does it take? I mean to get back on your feet again?"

Jesse met Aaron's eyes soberly. "How long did it take Dad to get a restaurant going again after the fight?"

Aaron looked quickly away. "Come on, Jess. You don't really think . . . Well, hell . . ."

They were silent then. Jesse watched Aaron fidget nervously. He knew Aaron had understood him. In the life of their family—of Jesse and Aaron, their mother and father—events had always been dated as before and after the fight. Before, everything was normal and good; after, everything was different and bad. Jesse could remember the incident perfectly. He was eleven at the time. He was helping his father in the restaurant in Moorpark, the first and only successful one, when Clyde Bellman from the hardware store next door banged on the back door and began yelling obscenities at his father. In between the four-letter words, Jesse heard Clyde claim his father was fooling around with his wife, something that seemed absurd to Jesse. Clyde's wife was fat and dumpy with huge, sagging breasts and dull mouse-colored hair that Jesse could never remember seeing any way but in curlers.

Clyde challenged Jesse's father and Jesse's father accepted. His father went out the back door, solemn and intent. Jesse watched from a window. Clyde swung at his father, clipping his jaw. His father landed a hard punch in Clyde's stomach with his left and almost simultaneously came up with his right in a solid uppercut to Clyde's jaw. Clyde staggered back toward the edge of the yard where there was a stack of old lumber. He grabbed a two-by-four about five feet long and ran at Jesse's father, swinging. If the board had hit his father's head, it probably would have killed him, but it hit his father's shoulder, throwing him to the ground on his back. Clyde stepped back and made a running leap, landing with both feet on his father's chest. Jesse could see the breath leave his father's body and his face contort in pain. Jesse grabbed a mop and ran outside. Tears filled his eyes, nearly blinding him. He swung wildly with the mop, yelling things he couldn't remember, even after Clyde had run back to his own house.

Jesse watched his father pull himself slowly from the ground and stagger over to Clyde's door. He stood there leaning on the door, doubled over, raging, calling Clyde things Jesse had never heard before from anyone. Jesse ran, then, all the way down the block to their house, and got his mother. When they came back, his father was still at Clyde's door, yelling, his face red as a flag, his hair tangled and wet with sweat. His mother led him away and took him to the hospital. He had three broken ribs. One of them had punctured his heart.

It may not have been the fight that caused all the other failures, even though it became obvious, after his father got out of the hospital and had to sell the restaurant to pay hospital bills, that he could no longer work the long hours necessary to make a business successful. The depression came, and then the war. But to the family, it was the fight that had made their life so hard.

Out in the hall, a soft, calm voice called for some doctor over the loudspeaker system. The voice was always like that. Somebody was probably dying, but the voice stayed calm so the other patients, who still believed they could live, wouldn't be upset.

"It's okay," Jesse said softly. "Don't worry about me. I'll be all right."

"Yeah," Aaron said. "I know you will, Jess. You'll get well and be back on your feet in no time. It's just that, you know. I'm sorry—"

"Quit being sorry, will you?"

"Okay." Aaron took a long, deep breath. "Hey, that's a nice looking camper you got."

"Yeah. It's worked good so far."

"I bet you could go anyplace in that."

"Just about, I guess. Haven't had a chance to try it out yet."

"Oh . . . yeah, well, you'll get the chance. I'd like to see the Grand Canyon one of these days."

"They don't have any casinos there."

Aaron grinned. "Yeah, I know. They have bars, though."

"Not a good place to drink," Jesse said. "You might fall over the edge."

Aaron chuckled, his belly rolling like a mountain during an earthquake. "Hey," he said. "I snuck in a flask." He pulled a small, flat bottle from under his shirt.

"I knew I should have told them to search you before they let you in."

Aaron held up the bottle. "Want a snort?"

Jesse shook his head. "With all the crap they give me, I'm drunk most of the time anyway."

Aaron unscrewed the cap. "You mind?"

"Go ahead."

Aaron tipped the bottle and took a quick swallow. He ran his tongue over his lips as he screwed the cap back on and tucked the bottle away. "That's better," he said.

"How long you staying?" Jesse asked.

"Only 'til Sunday. I have to be at work Sunday night."

"You working graveyard again?"

"Yeah. You know. They change shifts every three months."

"How are things going over there?"

"Well, they keep getting worse. Last week, I walked into the rec room and there was blacks on one side of the room and whites on the other, both looking at each other like they were going to kill. And there I was in the middle of them. Jesus. My asshole was going like this." He made an "O" with his thumb and forefinger, then made the "O" open and close several times.

"What happened?" Jesse asked.

"I guess they figured they'd wait. They just filed out of the room. One of these days, though, it's going to hit. I'm just hoping I'll be retired by then."

"You think it'll wait that long?"

Aaron looked down. "No. I try not to think about it."

"You got through the war," Jesse said. "You ought to be able to handle this."

"Hell. The war was nothing," Aaron said. "The war was almost human compared to this. They're animals in there. You ought to feel the tension."

"Maybe you ought to get out."

"Yeah," Aaron said. "If I was smart I probably would. If I was smart I'd probably leave and just say to hell with the retirement. It's not worth it. I'm not that smart, though. I guess I'll stick it out. Eight more years. It's really not that much, you know."

"Well, it's your war," Jesse said.

"What else could I do?" Aaron said. "There's no call for forward gunners anymore."

"You could probably learn something," Jesse said. "Some trade. TV repair or something."

"Naw. It's too late for that. Can't teach an old dog new tricks."

"You're selling yourself short."

"Well, maybe I like what I'm doing."

"You didn't sound like it just now. You haven't sounded like it for five or six years."

"Well, sure. I complain a lot. But it's not that bad."

"Sounds pretty bad."

"Yeah. I guess maybe it is."

"If you want to stay there, that's fine," Jesse said. "I just don't think you should feel like you're trapped in there like a convict—like you're doing some special sentence where you get off on weekends and vacations."

"Yeah," Aaron said. "Sometimes it gets to you like that. You have to watch that."

Martha stuck her head around the door jam. "You're going to have to let this old fart get some rest," she said.

Jesse smiled. "I don't get no respect around here."

"Yeah. I better get going," Aaron said. He stood up.

"I want to see Sybil," Jesse said. "At least for a minute."

"Okay," Aaron said. "Look. I'll come by tomorrow."

Jesse nodded, then looked into Aaron's beady little eyes. "Tell me the truth, Aaron," he said. "How does Mary seem to you?"

Aaron stuffed his big hands into his pockets and looked out the window. Jesse waited. Finally Aaron said, "Pretty good, I think. Yeah. I think she's holding up fine. You don't need to worry about her."

Jesse smiled. "Thanks, Aaron."

"See you, Jess." Aaron left.

Jesse could hear them talking low out in the hall, then Sybil came in. Her bleached blond hair was piled up on her head and

129

teased, as if she still lived in the fifties. She wore black pants that fit her like another skin and a loose white blouse, unbuttoned down the front, revealing a fairly ample cleavage. She smiled at Jesse and her teeth caught the florescent lights like on a toothpaste commercial.

"Hi, Jesse," she said softly. She sat down and took his hand in both of hers. She stroked the back of it lightly, up toward his wrist. "Are you feeling okay?"

"Not bad," Jesse said. "Kind of tired." He was aroused, for the first time since the attack. At least he felt aroused, but nothing happened.

"You're going to be all right," Sybil said. "I just know you are."

"Sure," Jesse said. "It just takes time, that's all."

"That's right," Sybil said. "You should take as much time as you need. Just let things slide for a while. Let the world go on without you for a while."

Jesse looked into her eyes. They were blue. Not bright, but deep, like long, soothing tunnels. She kept her lips parted a little, and they were full, the kind that would feel so good . . .

"Are they taking good care of you here?" she asked.

"Oh, yeah," Jesse said. "Everyone's been fine. It's a fine hospital."

And her hands were long and slender and her fingers moved like little snakes.

"Is there anything we can get for you?" she asked. "Some books or magazines? How about a *Playboy*?"

Jesse smiled. "I can't do any reading yet. Maybe later, though."

She patted his hand and set it down like a kitten she had been petting. "I'm going to let you rest," she said. "Just remember we're thinking about you. We're with you, you know?" She half stood, leaned over, and kissed him lightly on the forehead. Her bra had some kind of filmy lace around it. Then she stood up straight and smiled at him. "We'll come back tomorrow."

"Thanks," Jesse said.

She walked to the door, swinging her slender hips. As soon as she left, Mary came in.

"We're going now," she said. "They want to come back again tomorrow."

"Fine," Jesse said.

She leaned over and kissed him lightly on the mouth, a gesture he could only half respond to. It was late. He was sleepy. She stood up and looked down at him. She was like a cloud hovering over him. Her mouth was relaxed, but straight. Her eyes drooped and tiny wrinkles went out from around the dark places beneath them. She touched his forearm.

"See you," she whispered.

Jesse nodded. "See you."

She went out of the room. Jesse listened and could hear them walk softly toward the elevator. He thought about Sybil. How did Aaron ever get somebody like that? I bet she knows every trick in the book. He felt a brief surge of energy run through his crotch. He put his hand under the sheet. It was limp as a rag. And his hand was cold. He felt tired—and cold. He noticed it now for the first time. He was really cold. They must have turned up the air conditioning. He pulled the sheet over his shoulders. Why was he cold? Maybe he should get a blanket. No. It wasn't that bad. It would go away in a minute.

He couldn't see out the window any more. All he could see was the reflection of his room—the end of his bed with his feet making little white mountains; the blank white wall; the glaring flourescent lights that eliminated shadows. He was glad he couldn't see his own face. He hadn't seen it since before he came here. A nurses aide had given him a shave that morning and they gave him sponge baths. Must be part of the therapy to keep you from seeing how bad you really are.

Damn, he was cold. Were they trying to freeze everybody out of here? He felt icy fingers going down his spine. That old black magic, he thought, and the song started running over and

over in his head. . . . got me in his spell, that old black magic . . .
Maybe his blood wasn't circulating. Maybe his heart . . . What if
they weren't watching that screen out there. He felt his stomach
squeeze together and he began to sweat in spite of the cold. He
reached out from under the sheet and found the button to sum-
mon a nurse. He pushed it, then waited.

Where the hell is she? He stared at the ceiling, wondering if
he should pray or yell or something. What was happening?

Martha came in. "You want something?" she asked.

Jesse turned to look at her. He wanted to hold on to her, to
grab her huge waist so her weight would keep him from floating
away. "I'm cold," he said, and his teeth chattered.

Martha went quickly to the bed, reached under the sheet,
and picked up his wrist. She watched her watch for thirty seconds, then looked at him and smiled.

"You're okay," she said.

She took out the blood pressure cuff and wrapped it around
his arm. The gauge hissed and she watched it.

"Blood pressure's low," she said. "That's why you're cold.
It's the medication. Nothing to worry about." She looked closely
at his face. "You okay now?"

"I'm still cold," Jesse said softly.

"I'll get you some blankets," Martha said, "but it won't help
much. I'll have the resident look in."

"Okay," Jesse said.

He watched her walk away, leaving him to lie there
shivering.

It took Mary and Aaron and Sybil all day Friday just to see
Jesse twice. He was asleep most of the time. He had had a bad
night, the nurses said. It worried Mary. It seemed like a relapse,
but the nurses assured her he was all right. It was the medication. Even so, Mary felt strange. She wanted to talk to Dr.
Blackwell.

They waited all morning for him to come on his rounds. But at two o'clock, when he hadn't come yet, they left for some lunch. They wandered around town and finally ate at a little hamburger stand. When they got back to the hospital they learned that Dr. Blackwell had come and gone. Aaron and Sybil tried to cheer Mary up, but her face was tense, as if she was about to cry. She was wearing the same face when they dropped her off at Lyle's that evening.

Ruth had taken the boys to Lynx Lake to fish. The eight trout they had caught wouldn't break any records, but they were big enough to eat, and Gary was excited because three of them were his. He told Mary all about it while she set the table and Ruth fried them. Ruth seemed to be trying hard to be cheerful. Mary thought she could see the strain—the strain of trying to mother too many children, of having her family's routine disrupted for almost a week now.

Sybil had decided that Mary was spending too much time at the hospital so the three of them had planned a picnic for the next afternoon. Aaron and Sybil would take care of everything. Mary had agreed reluctantly. She was still worried about Jesse, but she knew she had to get the boys away from Lyle and Ruth for a while and that she needed to spend some time with them herself.

Saturday morning, she took the boys with her to the hospital and each one was able to see Jesse for a few minutes. Jesse was better, not so tired. Dr. Blackwell came by and talked to Mary for a long time. He explained about the low blood pressure caused by the medication—that the medication was supposed to do that so his heart wouldn't have to work so hard while it healed. Everything was still progressing normally. There was nothing to be concerned about. Talking to Dr. Blackwell relieved Mary a little, but she still carried with her a vague apprehension she could neither understand nor ignore. It seemed to settle in her face. The wrinkles around her eyes and in her forehead became more pronounced, and when asked a question, she responded with an air of distraction, as if she had been interrupted while solving some complicated problem.

They went on the picnic. Lyle had given Mary directions to Granite Basin Lake. It was more a pond than a lake, surrounded by scrubby pines and oaks and huge granite boulders. They built a fire, cooked hot dogs on sticks that Marty and Aaron whittled from green twigs, and drank lemonade and beer. After lunch Aaron and the boys took off up a trail that was supposed to lead to the top of Granite Mountain. Mary and Sybil sat across from each other at the table. Mary munched potato chips while Sybil smoked menthol cigarettes in a slender wooden holder. The air was warm and still, almost balmy.

"Beautiful place," Sybil said.

Mary looked at her. Jesse is not here, she thought. Somewhere within her there was a dull crash. An emptiness seemed to fill her chest. Jesse is not here. They'd been eating and drinking in this beautiful place, looking at the trees and the rocks and the sky and Jesse was not here. Tears flooded her eyes and she tried mentally to push them back. She studied Sybil's face, which watched her calmly with squinted blue eyes, a thin, steady stream of smoke coming from the full mouth. Mary took a Kleenex from her purse and wiped her eyes.

"It's okay," Sybil said softly.

Mary tried to smile. "Sometimes it just comes over me. All at once like that."

"I know," Sybil said. "It happens to me, too. I think about it a lot. Especially lately. What would happen if Aaron didn't come home from work. If I got a call from the warden and he said . . . Well, you know."

"I guess I never thought about it much before," Mary said.

"I have to live with it," Sybil said. She held up the can of beer she had been sipping. "I guess that's why I need this. I need to forget sometimes."

134

"Maybe I need to forget," Mary said. But something within her shouted, No. Don't forget. Don't ever forget.

"Sure," Sybil said. "Have a beer. It would be good for you."

Mary looked at the six-pack sitting on the table. There were three left. She had nothing against drinking. She had done her share of it. But she couldn't drink now. It would be wrong somehow. And yet, it may be right, too. Good to forget, at least for a while. To try to be normal. To try to act like everything was okay. But she couldn't do it. She looked back at Sybil.

"No. No thanks," Mary said. "No games."

Sybil smiled. "I think I understand that, too. Some things you just have to accept. Things just happen and there's nothing you can do about them."

Things just happen, Mary's mind repeated. Things just happen. She looked up at the deep blue sky. A bank of black clouds was forming on the horizon. What would Marilyn say? Suddenly, she looked back at Sybil.

"Nothing just happens," she said.

Sybil was puzzled. "Well, if there's a reason for Jesse being sick, I sure as hell don't know what it is, do you?"

"He worked too hard," Mary said, but there was no conviction in her voice.

"I see," Sybil said. "He did it on purpose. He had it all planned."

Mary looked at the table. That wasn't what she meant. She didn't know what she meant. She just had to deal with it, whatever it was.

"I'm sorry," Sybil said. "I didn't mean to knock you. We all have our ways of coping, I guess."

"I don't know how much longer we can stay with Lyle and Ruth." She said it without thinking.

"Why?" Sybil asked.

"It's not that they don't want us exactly. They'd do anything for us. But it's not good. There's too many of us."

135

"Why don't you send the boys home with us?" Sybil asked.

Mary was startled. "Oh. I didn't mean to—"

"I know," Sybil said. "It was just a suggestion. We'd love to have them. Really."

"I don't know . . ."

"Mary," Sybil said. "Listen to me a minute, okay? I know it's tough having your man sick in the hospital, and you're wondering if he'll ever really be well again. But he's not here now. You have to realize that. You've got to make some decisions on your own. If it's not good where you're staying, you have to decide what to do."

"I just have to think about it."

"Well, you think about it for a while. But we really do have to leave tomorrow morning. We'd like to have them. It would be kind of fun. Like a borrowed family, since we never had one of our own."

"I have to talk to the boys about it," Mary said.

"Talk to them today, okay?" Sybil said.

"Okay. When they come back."

They lapsed into silence, that awkward silence that follows a vague decision that awaits some concrete action to fulfill it. Mary sipped her lemonade, then got up and walked down to the little lake. There was an old man sitting on the bank on the other side, a fishing pole propped up in a forked stick. He watched his bobber, out almost to the middle of the lake. The lake was deep blue, reflecting the sky.

The boys came down the trail with Gary riding on Aaron's shoulders and Aaron galloping like a horse.

"Whoa!" Gary shouted as they reached the table.

Aaron stopped, panting, and whinnied. He whirled around, and set Gary down on the table.

"Good trail coming down," Aaron gasped. He unhooked a beer from the six-pack, popped off the tab, and took a long drink. Marty poured the rest of them some lemonade.

"Did you get to the top?" Sybil asked.

Aaron shook his head. "Has to be a full day's hike." He walked around the table and sat on the bench next to Sybil. Sweat trickled down his forehead.

"That's more exercise than you've had in months," Sybil said.

"Yeah, but I can keep up with the best of them," Aaron said. Marty smiled.

Sybil turned to Aaron. "What do you think of the boys coming to stay with us for a while?"

Aaron looked at her, then turned to look quickly at Mary. Marty and David and Gary looked at her, too. "I think that's great," Aaron said. "But what does Mary say?"

Mary watched the boys carefully for a moment, then said, "What do you think?"

"I want to go," Gary said.

"Why can't we stay here?" David asked.

"It's too much for Lyle and Ruth," Mary said. "I don't think we should impose on them any more than we have to."

"We have the camper," David said.

"I know," Mary said. "But I have to drive it to the hospital."

"I'd rather stay," David said. He wasn't sure why. He wanted to think it was because he was concerned about his father, but he wasn't sure. More likely it was because he didn't want to miss anything—anything he might be able to write about later.

"I think I should just go home," Marty said. "Somebody ought to watch the place. Besides, I'll have to start work again in a week and if I go back sooner, I get my vacation pay plus what I make working."

"Well, that's fine," Sybil said. "We'll take Gary; David can stay; and Marty can go home to watch the house. It sounds very logical. We should have thought of it." She smiled at Mary.

"I don't know," Mary said. Everybody looked at her again.

She felt the eyes on her. "If that's what you all want." She said it slowly, hesitantly. Jesse is not here, she thought. She looked at Marty. Their eyes met and something within her seemed to release itself from her. "Okay," she said. "That's what we'll do."

"Yeaaaah!" Gary shouted. He ran around the table, jumped up, wrapped his arms around Aaron's neck, and hung there with his feet in the air.

VI

Jesse woke from a deep sleep and stared at the ceiling. The ceiling was light, not dark, so he knew it was daytime, but he couldn't tell what time it was. He had been dreaming a long, vivid dream where he was hanging doors at a school somewhere in the middle of nowhere, where there was nothing but sand dunes as far as he could see. It was a strange school. It was old and run-down, made of stucco, and painted a dirty beige color. The paint was cracked and peeling off in places. He couldn't understand what they wanted with brand new hollow metal doors and frames, but he knew it was the right place because he had been arguing with the damn state inspector about the size of the doors for most of a morning. The inspector kept insisting the doors had to have an eighth of an inch clearance at the bottom because of the air conditioning system, but Jesse knew there was no air conditioning in the buildings. He finally told the inspector, "The hell with you, I'm going to hang them the way I know they're supposed to be hung," and the inspector had vanished. Well, not exactly vanished, but Jesse was hanging the doors then, and the inspector didn't care if he hung them upside down.

He was working on the door that opened into what looked like the foyer of a big auditorium, thinking it must have been a church at one time because there was an unpainted place on one wall in the shape of a cross, when he woke up. Still looking at the ceiling, Jesse thought he could see that cross, but then realized it was only the reflection of sunlight coming through the window and bouncing off the crank handle at the end of his bed.

He sensed he was not alone and glanced to his left. Mary was there. It was Monday, he remembered now. Aaron and Sybil had left and taken Gary with them. Marty was supposed to be on his way back home by bus.

Mary looked up from a magazine. "Hi," she said.

"What time is it?" Jesse asked.

"Almost five."

"Jesus. I'm going to sleep my life away."

"It's good for you."

"Yeah, I know." There was a well, Jesse remembered now, made out of mortared rocks, right in the middle of the playground. It was filled to the top, but the water was stagnant. He didn't think any of the kids should drink it.

"Marty left this morning," Mary said.

"What time's he supposed to get there?"

"Late tonight. Ten something."

No flowers either, Jesse thought. No grass. Nothing green at all. Just a kind of fine, dirty beige sand that the kids were playing in. "Good," Jesse said. "I guess he can get the car tomorrow or the next day."

"He doesn't have to. It can wait."

"Like to get rid of that piece of junk they gave us for a loaner."

"He'd have to drive it with no brakes."

"Power brakes," Jesse said. "Probably leaks fluid. He can fill it up."

"Well, there's no hurry."

140

"No. I guess not." And there was no sun, Jesse thought. Just a strange yellow glow that didn't come from anywhere. Funny that the dream was so vivid. But it was fading now. He tried to hold on to it, but it was like holding on to water.

"I was talking to some of the nurses," Mary said. "They said you sat up again this morning."

"Yeah," Jesse said. "Fifteen minutes this time. I'm supposed to do it again tonight."

"That's good," Mary said.

"Yeah. And tomorrow they're going to move me."

"I know," Mary said. "The nurses say you're recovering faster than most patients with the size infarction you have."

"They do, huh?"

"It's because you're in such good shape."

Jesse smiled, almost laughed. "That's good. The job that almost kills me keeps me in good enough shape to survive. Yeah. That's really good."

"Well, you know, you might have had it anyway, no matter what job you had. Dr. Blackwell said it's not just the physical work that does it. It's stress, too."

"Yeah. He told me that. The only trouble is they don't know what stress is."

"Pressure," Mary said. "Like trying to hang four hundred doors in a week."

"Yeah, maybe. It didn't seem go bother Mac any though."

"Mac's a lot younger."

"Yeah. It's only us old farts that have heart attacks."

"You're not that old," Mary said.

"Oh, yeah? Then why do I feel so old?"

Mary looked at the magazine. "I don't know," she said softly, then she looked up again. "But you're going to recover. You should be thankful for that. Some people don't."

Jesse looked away. He would have said, What good is it to recover if all you are then is some old fart who can't get it up and can't hold down a decent job, but he knew he was doing what Martha had accused him of—feeling sorry for himself. He had to get back on his feet, that was all. Besides, Blackwell hadn't said anything definite about working. Maybe he could go back to work for Angelo after all. Maybe he could work in engineering or something. He could do a little drafting. He'd done some over in Belfast when they got stuck and there wasn't anyone else to do it. He'd learned it by the seat of his pants—the way he learned everything. If he could keep working for Angelo they could probably pay the bills. Maybe they wouldn't have to sell the camper. He looked back at Mary.

"Marty'll probably find his draft notice waiting for him when he gets home," he said.

"It hadn't come as of yesterday. I called Eleanor."

"Maybe he can get it postponed or something."

"I'm sure they'll consider the circumstances."

"Yeah. They ought to." Jesse paused a moment. "Ah, hell. If he gets it he ought to just go. Get it over with. The longer he waits, the more time he'll waste."

"It's really his decision," Mary said.

Run, Jesse thought. He might run. "Yeah, it is," Jesse said. What would he do if he were in Marty's shoes? He didn't know. Things were different when he was Marty's age. He couldn't tell how Marty felt. Marty probably couldn't either. That's probably how *he'd* feel. Undecided. Any little thing could sway him, but then, any other little thing could sway him back. It really was Marty's decision. But, damnit, he was his son.

"You hear from Aaron?"

Mary shook her head.

"Well, call them tomorrow, will you?"

"If you didn't want him to go you should have said something."

"Said something. You had it all figured out. What was I supposed to say?"

Mary looked down.

He shouldn't have snapped. It was probably all right to send Gary with Aaron. What else was there to do? They couldn't keep imposing on Lyle. He was just sick of it, that was all. Sick of lying here staring at the ceiling, thinking about everything and nothing, having crazy dreams. They wouldn't let him read. The television didn't work in here because of all the electronic junk. What was he supposed to do? Jesus. Never before in his life had he had to just lie in one place and do nothing. At least when they moved him he could watch television. Go to the bathroom in a real bathroom. Read the paper. He could hardly wait.

He didn't have to wait long. The next morning they unhooked him from the monitor, let him put on his own pajamas, put him in a wheelchair, and wheeled him down the hall, around some corners, and into a room where there was a television, a bathroom that opened off the room, a small table next to the bed, and another bed with another patient. By the time he climbed into his bed he felt like he had hung fifty doors that morning. As soon as they left him, he fell into a deep sleep.

When he woke up, the first thing he realized was that he had been dreaming that same dream again. He was trying to hang doors, but he kept getting distracted by the kids playing in the schoolyard. He wasn't even sure you could call it a yard; there wasn't any fence. The boundaries were marked off by shallow ditches that the kids didn't seem to want to cross. The air was hot and damp and he was sweating. He tried to work, but the kids came and stood around him, staring at him as if they had never seen anything like him before. It wasn't a very big school. There were only two buildings and neither of them had any windows.

He screwed a screw into a hinge with his Yankee screwdriver, then turned and looked at the kids. They backed away, but kept staring. He stepped toward them and they backed farther away. He smiled at them.

"It's okay," he said. "I won't hurt you."

At that they looked frightened and jumped back. Several ran away. It must be my height, he thought, and got down on his knees. The little group came closer.

"See," he said softly. "There's nothing to be afraid of."

Several came closer still, and he held out his hand. "Here," he said. "Touch me."

A little girl with long, flowing black hair, wearing a bright red dress came a little closer, reached out her hand as far as she could, and touched him quickly. Then she ran back to the rest. She whispered something to a little boy and then the boy came closer, put his hand on Jesse's, and felt it all over. The boy's hand was cold and damp and smooth. Jesse looked into his eyes and saw the fear there. He smiled and watched the fear melt into trust.

Those eyes lingered in his mind as he looked around and saw that he was cut off from the world by a white curtain surrounding his bed. But he felt fine. Hadn't felt this good since the attack. Maybe he could watch some television. He could see just the top of it over the top of the curtain. He'd have to open the curtain.

Without even thinking he pulled the sheet back, swung his legs to the floor, and stood up. The room spun around in circles and he sat down again. His heart. He put his hand on his chest and felt it beating. It's okay, he thought. He sat for a few minutes, waiting for his heartbeat to slow down, then stood up slowly. He grabbed the edge of the curtain and walked with it toward the end of his bed.

He was at the end and starting to round the corner when he saw a small, black figure breeze past the door, return, and storm into the room.

"Get back into that bed this instant, Jesse Landow. What do you think you're doing?"

Jesse looked down at the feet protruding from the bottoms of his maroon pajamas. "I wanted to watch some television," he mumbled. He shuffled back to the side of his bed and sat down. Sister Elizabeth stood in front of him, her eyes glaring out from under her bonnet.

"Well, get into bed," she said.

Jesse swung his legs up and pulled the sheet over him. He smiled up at Sister Elizabeth sheepishly. Her face softened.

"You know better than that, Jesse," she said.

"I just wanted to watch television," Jesse said.

"You have a button," Sister Elizabeth said. "Use it."

"I guess I forgot," Jesse said.

"We've moved you into this room because you're recovering nicely, not because you're well."

"But I thought I could get up once in a while."

"To go to the bathroom, and at our directions. Those are the only times you are to be out of bed. Don't worry. In a few days you'll be able to take short walks down the hall. Then longer walks. Then you can go home."

"I get so sick of just lying here."

"I know," the sister said. She smiled pleasantly. "Lying still is probably harder work than you have ever done before. Here you must prove the strength of your mind, as well as your body."

"Yeah. And my mind has been sitting here like a bump on a log."

Sister Elizabeth laughed. "So you want to stimulate it with a little television."

"Right," Jesse said.

She pointed to the little table beside his bed. "There's a paper with listings, and," she picked up an oblong black box with dials on it, "this is the remote control device to operate the television." She laid the box beside Jesse's head. "Happy viewing."

She turned on her heels, pulled back Jesse's curtain so he could see the television, and walked to the bed next to Jesse's. "Good afternoon, Tom," she said. "How are you feeling?"

"Fine, sister. Really good, thanks."

Jesse looked over at his roommate. He was a young man with thinning brown hair and a thin mustache. His face was thin, too, drawn and pale. A pair of wire-rimmed glasses sat on the end of his nose. He pushed them up when he talked. A book lay open, upside down on his bed.

Sister Elizabeth patted his arm. "Won't be long now," she said.

"I know," Tom said.

"Have you met your new partner?"

Tom shook his head.

"Tom Orason, Jesse Landow. I'll leave you two to get acquainted."

Jesse looked over at Tom. Their eyes met for an instant, then they both looked down. "Want to watch some television?" Jesse asked.

"I . . . uh . . . I was reading," Tom said. "But if you want to, go ahead."

"Thanks." Jesse turned a dial on the box and the television burst into life. The television was large, sitting up near the ceiling so Jesse could lay down and watch it. There was a picture of a globe spinning slowly and a strong male voice said, "And now we return to part one of As the World Turns." There was piano music and a prim, middle-aged woman sitting at a piano looking distraught. She got up and walked around a living room that had the personality of a motel room. The doorbell rang and the woman started. She went to the door, opened it a crack, and the person outside pushed it open more. The woman at the door was foreign-looking, with full lips and dark skin, and she talked with the slight trace of some accent. "What are you doing?" the first woman said. "Wait," the foreign woman said. "I want to talk to you." "Get out," the first woman said. "But it's about Steve and Barry." "Get out." "No, wait. I'll tell you everything . . ."

Jesse switched the channel. There was David Janssen as "The Fugitive" talking to a woman in a lonely farmhouse. Jesse remembered. He'd already seen that one. He changed channels again and there was Gale Storm looking over the rail of her ship. Jesse hated Gale Storm. He changed channels again and he was back to "As the World Turns." He picked up the television listings. Only three channels. What a choice. He turned off the television and looked over at Tom, who was propped up with some pillows holding his book a few inches from his nose.

"What're you reading?" Jesse asked.

Tom put the book down. "Dickens. *Our Mutual Friend.*"

"How is it?"

"Kind of depressing."

"Yeah. Dickens is like that. Ghosts and all that."

Tom smiled. "Yeah. All that."

"You have a heart attack, too?" Jesse asked.

"No," Tom said. "Cancer. Intestinal. Caught it in time, though, I guess. They said they got it all."

"I thought you were too young for a heart attack," Jesse said.

"Wasn't there anything on TV?" Tom asked.

"No," Jesse said. "Maybe tonight."

"The real Fugitive's on tonight," Tom said. "Those things during the day are all repeats. Hey, you want to read? I have some books here."

"What do you have?" Jesse asked.

Tom reached over to the little table beside his bed and picked up three books. "Let's see," he said. "*A Portrait of the Artist as a Young Man* by James Joyce, *The Plague* by Camus, and *Henry the Fourth, Part One,* Shakespeare."

"I don't know about Shakespeare," Jesse said. "Let me have that first one."

"*Portrait of the Artist.*" Tom threw his sheet back and put his feet on the floor. "It's a good book." He handed it to Jesse.

"Thanks," Jesse said. He watched Tom get back into bed and bury his nose in his mutual friend again. He looked at the book Tom had given him, turned to the last page, and read the last two paragraphs.

April 26. Mother is putting my new secondhand clothes in order. She prays now, she says, that I may learn in my own life and away from home and friends what the heart is and what it feels. Amen. So be it. Welcome, O life! I go to encounter for the millionth time the reality of experience and to forge in the smithy of my soul the uncreated conscience of my race.

April 27. Old father, old artificer, stand me now and ever in good stead.

Not bad, Jesse thought. Classy. "Welcome, O life!" Pretty good. He turned to the beginning, settled back on his pillow, and read.

Once upon a time and a very good time it was there was a moocow coming down along the road and this moocow that was down along the road met a nicens little boy named baby tuckoo . . .

What the hell, Jesse thought. "Nicens?" Jesus. He looked over at Tom again. "You don't have any Ellery Queen or something, do you?"

Tom laughed. "No. That's all I have. Sorry."

"That's all right," Jesse said. He laid the book on his table.

"You'd probably like this one." Tom held up the book he was reading.

"Yeah," Jesse said. "Well, I'll wait 'til you're through with it and give it a try. Looks pretty long, though."

"It's easy to read," Tom said. "Really keeps you going."

"Yeah," Jesse said. "Well, I'll give it a try later."

Tom buried himself in his book again. Jesse thought about turning the television back on, but he knew better. There was never anything worth watching on during the day. Then, for the first time, he wondered where Mary was. She should have been there when he woke up.

"Hey, Tom," he said. "You got the time?"

Tom looked at his watch. "Almost four," he said, smiling amiably. "Getting hungry?"

"Yeah. A little. Guess I'll have to wait, though."

Tom went back to his book. She's probably off helping Ruth shop or something. Or maybe she and David went somewhere. Did some sightseeing. There's no reason they shouldn't have some kind of vacation. That had to be it. Something like that anyway, although he felt uneasy in the back of his mind, like something was missing and he didn't know what, or like he had forgotten to do something that was important.

He reached over and picked up the remote control. He was so restless. Maybe they'd let him walk for a while now. He could always pretend he had to go the bathroom. He started to turn the television on when Lyle came into the room grinning.

"They finally let me in this damn place," he said.

Jesse grinned back and watched him walk to his bed. "Jesus, it's good to see you, Lyle. How you been?"

"I'm supposed to ask you that."

"Hell. I'm doing fine. Heart pumping, blood circulating, all that."

Lyle handed Jesse some envelopes. "You got some mail."

Jesse looked at them. "Thanks." There was one from Security Metals Inc., one from Mac, and a post card from Gary. He read the post card first. "Dear Dad, Having a goodetime with Uncl Arone but he sleeps alot. Mis you. Wish you were here. Youre son, Gary." He smiled and felt himself start to choke up. He laid the other envelopes on the table and looked at Lyle, who had pulled a chair beside the bed.

"How's everybody doing?" Jesse asked.

"Great," Lyle said. "I got Mary in my office filing and answering the phone. David's having the time of his life, I think.

149

Goes off hiking all the time. I was watching him the other day from the deck. He just walks around looking at everything. I bet he knows that forest better than I do already."

"That's why Mary wasn't here."

"Hey. You don't mind, do you? She was looking so down-in-the-mouth. I figured she needed some kind of distraction."

"Hell, I don't mind." He didn't think he minded. If she was doing Lyle some good, what the hell. After all, he was just lying up here in this damn bed trying to get better. He didn't need her for that.

"Well, it's good for me, too," Lyle said. "I can see how much time it's saving me. When I open my own office, I might want to hire a secretary."

"You going to open your own office?"

"Sometime. When I get my broker's license."

"You're not paying her, are you?"

"We haven't talked about it, but why not? She's working for me, isn't she?"

"You've done enough for us already."

"Hell. We haven't done much. You didn't have to send the other kids away, you know."

"I couldn't have you taking care of my whole family."

"Why the hell not? What are friends for? You'd do it for me."

"You don't have a family like mine."

"A family's a family," Lyle said. "What's the difference?"

"I got a damn hip musician, a poet, and . . . well, a spoiled kid, I guess."

"Well, I'll tell you one thing. David's no problem. He doesn't even talk much."

"No. He's quiet, all right."

"So don't worry about it, okay?"

Jesse smiled. "Okay. I guess they're in good hands."

150

"You never know," Lyle said. "Mary might like working for me. She might want you to move up here."

"Yeah, well, that depends on what she makes. Ought to be worth a thousand a week at least."

"Sure," Lyle said. "An extra house a week and I'd have it."

Jesse looked at the blank television screen. He had thought he'd feel a lot better in a regular room, but something depressed him and he didn't know what it was. Even with Lyle sitting there, talking like they used to at night in the barracks, back and forth, until one of the other guys would yell at them to shut up. Then they'd whisper until they heard Jones, in the bunk over Jesse, groan and swear under his breath.

"Hey," Lyle said. "Can I get anything for you? A newspaper? Something to read?"

"Yeah," Jesse said. "A newspaper would be great. Haven't read one in a week."

"Hang on," Lyle said. "I'll be right back."

It was Melissa, Jesse thought. She'd laugh and pull on his ear and click her tongue and say, "How are you ever going to learn, Jesse?" He could see her lying on the bed with her brown skin shiny with love-sweat, smiling with her full lips and her brown face. Looking him over with her big dark eyes—dark, innocent, deceptive eyes. "How are you ever going to learn?"

He had learned plenty. And forgot most of it. When he started it with Mary again, it was all back like it had been, like he hadn't learned anything. What good was it? It had left him tired and irritable, with the desire to escape. So he had gone overseas and wrote lovesick letters back to Mary, wanting her so bad that when he went to bed with that Irish girl he couldn't even make anything happen. He had been all ready, had watched her undress and lay down on the bed with a hardon a mile long. But when he got in beside her, he thought of Mary, and of what he had told Mary, and it disappeared.

151

He had had to tell her. Because she knew anyway. Sensed it somehow. Women's intuition. So he told her and nothing was ever the same. Even after he came back and they seemed to be happy together, there was still that thing in the background that made everything kind of distant, like he was living someone else's life. He had tried to be what he had been but it hadn't worked. And he had thought about finding someone else, or looking up Melissa again. But all he did was think about it, because he knew, really, that what was, was. It would never be any different. Mary hadn't forgiven him. Mary wouldn't forgive him. Maybe Mary couldn't forgive him. Even though she said she did, he knew she didn't.

Melissa was really something. Not much better than a whore, really, but a great roll in the hay. "How are you ever going to learn?"

Lyle came back with a newspaper under his arm. He laid it on the table. "It's the local paper," he said. "I would have gotten you a Phoenix paper but they were all sold out."

"That's okay. Thanks."

Lyle sat down again. Jesse wished he would leave. He didn't have anything to say to him and his presence seemed to be keeping him from something important.

"So David hikes around a lot," Jesse said.

"Yeah," Lyle said.

Jesse shook his head. "He's a strange kid. I don't know where he came from."

"He's all right," Lyle said. "Maybe a little smarter than he should be."

"In some ways, I guess. Is he writing anything?"

Lyle shook his head. "Not that I know of."

He wouldn't write that story, Jesse thought. He hadn't really expected him to. It would be too much to expect him to write something special just for his old man. He could write forever for the school paper, but if Jesse was overseas someplace David probably wouldn't write a single letter. What was that kid after, anyway?

"How's Ruth doing? And the kids?" Jesse asked.

"Oh, they're fine." Lyle said.

Jesse nodded. "Good."

"Oh, hey, I almost forgot to tell you. I did some checking around. Your Doctor Blackwell is one of the best in the business. I asked my doctor about him and he said Blackwell knows everything there is to know about heart disease."

"That's good to know," Jesse said.

"Yeah. It made me feel better, too. In a small town like this, you never know what you're going to get."

There was an awkward silence. Jesse looked again at the blank television screen. Funny he had never thought about it like that before—that Mary hadn't forgiven him. She still held a grudge. After all these years. He couldn't believe it. But he couldn't blame her either. It was a rotten thing to do. He shouldn't have told her, that was the main thing. He should have just left it alone. After that night Melissa blew up at him, and said he'd never get a divorce, that he was just using her to get back at his wife. A stupid thing to say. Then she ordered him out of her apartment and threatened to go to the police and claim rape. Stupid. He had worried about that for a long time. It was one of the reasons he went overseas. He should have known she would never do it. What started that, anyway? He couldn't remember. It wasn't important. After that night it was all over. She had been right about one thing, though. He never would have gotten a divorce.

If he had just waited. If he had just given Mary a chance to get over that miscarriage thing. But Jesus. He was young then. A young man has certain drives. What was he supposed to do, become a monk? Even now, just thinking about Melissa gave him a hardon. Well, not now, sonofabitch. But it used to. He was getting tired. His eyes were getting heavy.

Lyle stood up. "Well," he said. "I better get going. Look. Is there anything else you need? Now that they let me in here, I should be able to come by at least once a day."

Jesse thought. "Yeah. Something to read. You know, a book or something. You'll know what to get. Don't buy anything, though. Just something you have around the house."

"Sure," Lyle said. "I'll find something."

"Say hello to Ruth and the kids."

"Will do."

"And . . . Lyle. Thanks, okay?"

"Forget it, Jess. See you tomorrow."

Lyle walked out of the room and Jesse wondered what was wrong. All the good times they used to have, the endless yakking back and forth, back in the days when they were both young and needed each other as sounding boards. He guessed there was nothing left to talk about, which meant they didn't need each other anymore. And so Lyle came out of some sense of obligation or loyalty or something, not because he really wanted to come. Of all the goddamn places to have a heart attack . . .

He reached over and picked up the two envelopes Lyle had brought. He opened the one on Security Metals Inc. stationery first. It was a short letter from Angelo saying he was sorry Jesse was sick, that his pay would keep coming, that he was sending it to Lyle's address, and that he shouldn't worry about his job, he would always have a job as long as he wanted to work there. At least he left that much of it open, Jesse thought. After all, he might not want to work there sometime. Angelo could see to that, too. Angelo had dictated the letter and Rhoda had typed it, probably along with ten or fifteen other letters he dictated that day. Well, what the hell. What did he expect?

He tore open the envelope from Mac. It was a get-well card with a picture of an old man wearing a black suit standing there wringing his hands. It said, "Get well soon." On the inside were the words, "Funerals are so expensive."

Jesse smiled. What a sense of humor. There was a note. "Hey, old man, get back here as soon as you can. This place is falling apart without you."

"Looks like you have another visitor," he heard Tom say. "You're a popular guy."

He looked up and watched Mary walk around Tom's bed. "I can only stay a minute," she said. "I have to get back and help Ruth get dinner."

"How's work?" Jesse asked.

"Oh, it's fun. I didn't do much, though. Filed some papers. Looked up some things for Lyle. Answered the phone a couple times. I'd be more help if I knew what I was doing."

"You don't know how to answer a phone?"

"Oh, sure. But I could have answered questions, you know. If I knew anything about real estate. Or even how to look up things in Lyle's book."

"Yeah, well, stick with it. You'll learn."

Mary's eyebrows furrowed slightly. "You don't like me working there? I thought it was the least I could do after—"

"Hell, I don't care," Jesse said. "Work your ass off."

Mary sat down. Jesse watched her. She looked older to him today. We're all getting old, he thought. There were more wrinkles on her forehead and around her eyes, and her eyes were sad, like some old hound dog.

"Oh, Jesse," she said. "I just don't know—"

"Forget it," Jesse said. "It's okay. Really. You can work as much as you want. It's okay."

She stood up again. "I thought I'd come back tonight. And bring David. If you don't think it'll tire you too much."

"No," Jesse said. "That's fine."

"Okay." She forced a smile. "See you tonight."

As soon as she left, Jesse turned on the television and watched the news. They brought his dinner—real food that he could chew and everything—and he finished watching the news while he ate. He talked a little with Tom, who, he found out, had a bachelor's degree in literature from the University of Arizona and was an insurance salesman. Tom told him all about a course he had taken on best sellers where they read the books and tried to decide if they were literature or trash. Most of them were trash. It made Jesse wonder what Tom would think of Ellery Queen, or Louis L'Amour, but he didn't ask. Then Mary and David came in.

"Well, there's the two fugitives," he said. He didn't know what he meant, except that he had been hoping Tom wanted to watch "The Fugitive" that night. He motioned to Tom. "Tom, this is my wife and son, Mary and David. This is Tom Orason."

Tom nodded and Mary and David said hello. They stood awkwardly at Jesse's bed.

"Tom's got a degree in literature," Jesse said, as if making a general announcement. Then, "David here is a poet."

He watched David shrink almost visibly.

"Never did any writing myself," Tom said. "I just like to read a lot." He got up and started pulling the curtain around his bed. "I'll leave you folks alone. My wife should be coming pretty soon anyway."

Jesse looked at David. "Well," he said. "Done any more fishing?"

David shook his head. "Lyle said something about this weekend, though. There's another lake somewhere."

"Good," Jesse said. "Let me know what happens."

"Ruth said she would like to take him," Mary said. "But she's been gone a lot. They're having some kind of secret meetings. The city council."

"Secret meetings, huh?" Jesse smiled. "Sounds like Mission Impossible."

156

"She won't say what they're about. She won't even tell Lyle."

"She'd make a good spy."

Mary smiled. The tightness left her face for an instant, then returned. "Yes," she said. "I think she would."

There was a lull, and Jesse looked at both of them, his wife and his son, standing there like pallbearers waiting for the funeral to end.

"Why don't you sit down?" he said.

Mary sat in the chair beside the bed. "I think there's another chair someplace," he said to David.

"That's okay," David said.

Jesse lowered his voice a little. "An interesting guy, my roommate. He knows a lot about books." He looked at David. "You ought to talk to him. He loaned me this one." He picked up the book on his table. "But I just couldn't get into it somehow." He handed it to David. "Ever read that?"

David shook his head. "I've heard of James Joyce, but I've never read anything. He wrote a book called *Ulysses* that was banned in this country for a long time."

"Maybe he'll let you borrow it. I don't think I'll ever read it. It's way over my head. You intellectuals ought to understand it, though."

David laid it back down on the table. "That's okay," he said.

"What the hell are you doing anyway?" Jesse said suddenly vehemently. He surprised himself.

"What do you mean?" David asked.

"I mean with your life. What are you going to do? You and your brother. Jesus. You both drift along like you got silver spoons in your mouths."

He watched David's face contort into several expressions of pain at the same time. "I don't know," he said. "I haven't decided yet."

"For God's sake," Mary said. "He's only in high school."

157

"Yeah," Jesse said. "That's what I always said. What the hell, there's plenty of time. And you know what? I never did decide. I still haven't decided."

"It's not the same," David said.

"Like hell. The only difference is that I had to work or I would've starved. Well I'll tell you one thing. I'm not going to support you all your life. You can count on that. Or your brother either."

"I never expected you to," David said.

"Yeah. So you'll do like Marty and work at some goddamn backbreaking job until you decide, just like I did, and then you never decide. Or maybe you'll go to college and then work some shitass job." He pointed his thumb toward the curtain and lowered his voice. "You know what he does? He's a goddamn insurance salesman. A degree in literature and he's a goddamn insurance salesman. He probably has a wife and seven kids to support and he spends most of his time buried in some book. Jesus."

"Can I at least get out of high school before you kick me out?" David asked.

"Jesse, what's wrong with you?" Mary said.

Jesse looked away. "I don't know," he mumbled. "Must be something I ate."

They were silent then. Jesse could hear a female voice floating through the curtain like music. It laughed softly, a low, throaty birdsong, and then was silent. Melissa used to laugh like that. He'd stand in front of her naked, ready to follow her into bed, and she would laugh at him, and he would laugh with her, and she would take him in her arms, her long, dark, slender arms that always seemed to wave like palm fronds. "How are you ever going to learn, Jesse?" He could see her looking at him, her full lips curved up in a seductive smile, her big, dark eyes with the long, dark lashes staring at him, looking deep into him, seeing things he would never see himself, that no one else would ever see.

"I got a card from Gary," he said.

"Lyle showed it to me," Mary said.

"Have you heard from Marty?"

"No."

Jesse took a deep breath.

"He's all right," Mary said. "He probably went to work today."

He probably went to Canada today, Jesse thought. They didn't give a damn what he said or what he thought. He could tell them to sit in a chair and they would stand. He could tell them to stand and they would sit in a chair. They didn't think he knew anything just because he didn't like to read books about nicens little baby Tuckoos. Well, he'd like to see them hang four hundred ten doors in ten days with only one other man. He may not be much good at anything else, but goddamn it, he could work.

"Are you tired?" Mary asked. "It's been a big day today."

"I don't know," Jesse said. "Yeah, maybe I am."

"We can go," she said. "We'll come back tomorrow."

"No. That's okay."

"Maybe you'd sleep if we weren't here."

"No. Probably not." He looked up at David. He was fidgeting with a button on his shirt. Jesus, he was skinny. Had he always been that skinny? He ought to get some wire glasses like Tom had; he'd look like a real scholar. David looked up from his button and Jesse caught his eyes for a moment. He wasn't sure what he saw there. It wasn't love.

Mary stood up. "I think we'd better go. We'll come back tomorrow, okay?"

"Suit yourself," Jesse said.

He watched her look at him, her eyes squinted, her mouth straight and tense. Then, with what seemed like a monumental effort, she smiled. "We'll come back tomorrow."

She walked around the curtain. David followed her. He

heard them walk out of the room. Yeah, he thought. I'm just some sick old man who doesn't know what he's talking about. I haven't been through anything in my life before. I haven't watched myself and everybody else sidestep decisions like they were doing some dance or something. I haven't learned anything from living for forty-three years.

He could still hear low voices from behind the curtain—soft, soothing voices, like that little stream he fished in that time he was on location with the studio, that didn't run, really, just flowed easily over tall grass and smooth, moss-covered rocks and collected in little pools where he would almost always get a nice-sized trout.

He could see the trout swimming around in those pools as he dozed off into a light sleep. He woke up when he heard Tom's curtain being pulled back. He saw Tom smiling at him.

"Did I wake you up?" Tom said. "I'm sorry."

"That's okay," Jesse said.

"If you want to sleep some more I'll pull your curtain."

"No," Jesse said. "If I sleep anymore now I won't sleep tonight."

"Well, The Fugitive's on. You want to watch it?"

Jesse smiled. "Yeah. Let's watch The Fugitive."

Jesse stayed awake until almost the last commercial, then drifted off. Later, he woke up in darkness. Off to his left he saw light coming through the door and could hear the incessant rumble of hospital activity. It was that dream again, he thought. Jesus. It was like a soap opera. But it was already fading. He had been playing with the kids, giving them airplane spins or something. And there was this one little girl in a red dress. Pretty. With long black hair. But that was all he could remember about her. And two girls were walking around the edge of the well, their arms outstretched to keep their balance. Suddenly they both fell in. He saw it out of the corner of his eye. And he could see it clearly now, as he remembered it. He ran over to the well, but the girls had disappeared—sunk like rocks. He had to save them. They were going to drown. He would dive in and save them. He started taking off his shirt and that's when he woke up. He felt hot. He threw the sheet away and lay there staring at the ceiling. David Janssen had almost caught up to the one-armed man, had even seen him, but the man got on a bus and the bus left before he could reach it, and that police detective was on his tail so he couldn't follow the bus. He had to hide. What a life that guy had. Chasing and being chased.

He drifted off into sleep again.

The next morning he woke up feeling sharp and clean, like a brand new drill bit. For breakfast they brought him Cream of Wheat, toast, and orange juice. He tried to con the nurses' aide into bringing him some coffee, but she found out it wasn't part of his diet. After breakfast he got up and went into the bathroom. He had to go, but he stood there in front of the toilet for a long time. It felt good to be standing on his own two feet.

Afterward, he talked to Tom for a while, mostly about the war. Then Tom's wife came in. Tom introduced her. She was tall and blond and slender and beautiful; her hair rippling down to her shoulders in long curls. When she talked she ended every other sentence with a funny little embarrassed laugh that showed her crooked teeth. Her father should have gotten her braces.

Tom's wife only had a few minutes—she was on a coffee break or something—so Jesse decided to leave them alone. He got out of bed again, put on his robe, maroon to match his pajamas, and shuffled slowly out of the room. There was no one in the hall. He turned to his right and walked toward an open door at the end of the hall that showed bright light. He thought it was some kind of waiting room and he could imagine open windows filling the room with fresh air and sunlight. It would feel good to stand in the sun, he thought. He kept looking behind him, expecting some nurse to come by, plop him into a wheelchair, and take him back to his room. Then he would get another lecture from Sister Elizabeth. But the hospital seemed deserted. The lighted doorway beckoned him, but halfway there he started to feel tired and decided the sunlight wasn't worth risking some kind of setback for. He shuffled back to his room.

Tom's wife had left. He climbed into bed and lay there quietly, letting himself relax. He was just drifting off when Tom said, "Hey, I figured it out."

Jesse looked at him. "What?"

"This book. I figured it out. The theme, I mean."

"Oh," Jesse said.

"It's about death," Tom said. His excitement was genuine. "There's death all through the book. They fish a body out of the river. People are always dying or almost dying. That's what Dickens meant. Death is our mutual friend."

"Some philosophy," Jesse said.

"Well, I said it was depressing. Boy, what a paper I could write."

Jesse was about to say the paper would be as depressing as the book when Dr. Blackwell appeared beside him as if he had materialized out of thin air. Jesse tried to keep from breathing hard.

"How are you feeling today?" Dr. Blackwell asked.

"Fine," Jesse said.

The doctor listened all over his chest with his stethoscope. "What have you been doing?" he asked.

"Just went to the bathroom," Jesse said.

Dr. Blackwell grunted and picked up Jesse's wrist. After thirty seconds he put it down and said, "I think we'll get another electrocardiogram this afternoon. Try to lie quiet until then. You seem fine, though. Everything is proceeding according to plan."

"Good," Jesse said. "When do you think I can get out of here?"

Dr. Blackwell stroked his bushy gray mustache. "Another two weeks, I should think," he said. "Maybe less. We'll know more after the electrocardiogram."

"And then I can go back to work?"

Dr. Blackwell smiled. "No. Not then. In fact, you'll have to spend some time here in town resting before you'll be ready for the trip home. Then you should give yourself a few more weeks there. Don't rush things. It's important for your heart to completely heal before you put too much strain on it."

Two months. Jesse felt his stomach sink down to his butt. "And then will I be able to go back to work?"

Dr. Blackwell looked at him for a long time, took a deep breath, and said, "What kind of work do you do?"

"I work for a company that makes hollow metal doors and frames."

"I see. What do you do for them?"

"I'm a field supervisor."

"And what does that entail?"

"Well, I have a crew. We go out on jobs and install the doors and frames."

"Is there much heavy work? Lifting? Carrying?"

Jesse looked away. "Yeah. Some."

"Let me put it this way," Dr. Blackwell said, and Jesse felt the full weight of those innocuous words. "Your heart will heal. That is to say, the infarcted area will turn to scar tissue and the function of your heart will return nearly to normal. I say nearly because the scar tissue is not elastic like the rest of your heart muscle tissue. It doesn't expand and contract. In some ways it works against the normal operation of the rest of the muscle. Do you see what I'm saying?"

Jesse nodded. "I think so."

"What this means is that your heart, as a muscle, isn't as strong as it once was—that it never can be. The damage done by the infarction cannot be reversed."

"Yeah," Jesse said. "I see that. So will I be able to work or not?"

"Of course you'll be able to work. You should never consider yourself an invalid. But you should avoid heavy, physical work. You should also avoid work that causes stress. If those two conditions can be met while remaining with your previous job, there is no reason why you should have to look for another. It appears, though, that they probably can't. My suggestion would be to find another type of work involving less physical labor and less stress."

"You mean like selling pencils or something."

Dr. Blackwell shook his head. "I realize this isn't an easy idea to consider. You may, of course, go back to your old job, continue in the same manner you were before your attack. No one is going to lock you up to keep you from physical work or stress. If you do go back to your old work, however, you can expect another heart attack sometime—which will more than likely be fatal."

"So I can't work," Jesse said.

Dr. Blackwell pushed up his heavy glasses and ran his hand through his gray hair. "That's not what I said, Jesse. I'm telling you to avoid excessive physical labor and stress. However little you may like to admit it, there were conditions in your previous life style which led directly to your heart attack. To avoid another, it is imperative that you eliminate those conditions."

"So what kind of work can I do?"

"I don't know you well enough to make specific suggestions. If you would like to speak to an occupational therapist, we have one here at the hospital. But I would suggest you wait until you return home, until you're more settled and in familiar surroundings. Then you'll need to talk to someone who is familiar with opportunities in your own area."

"You make it sound pretty dismal," Jesse said.

Dr. Blackwell smiled. "It's not as dismal as it sounds. Your life can be every bit as meaningful as it ever was. You need to take stock of your abilities and desires. You need to see them in a new light. Some changes are inevitable. It won't hurt you to at least face that fact now."

"No, I guess not," Jesse said.

"Think about it," Dr. Blackwell said. "And try to stay quiet until this afternoon." He turned and left.

Take stock of your abilities, Jesse thought. Shit. That won't take long. About two seconds is all. Why would Angelo put him into engineering anyway? There were guys with college degrees in there, guys who knew more about how those doors are made than he did, guys who knew how to figure the math and all that. Designers, who knew about stress and everything.

"He sounds like a reasonable man," Tom said.

Jesse looked over at him. He had forgotten he was there. "Yeah, he does, doesn't he."

"I was lucky, I guess," Tom said. "My work wasn't very physical anyway. When I get out of here I'll just go back to my same old job."

Yeah, Jesse thought. Gloat, you bastard. But Tom was looking at him, smiling with big innocent eyes. "Yeah," Jesse said. "You're lucky."

"You'll find something to do," Tom said. "You could always sell insurance."

"I guess I could," Jesse said. "Do you have to go to school or something for that?"

"I went to some training classes," Tom said. "But mostly I just started selling. I worked for another agent for a while, then went out on my own."

"How much do you make?"

"It depends on what I sell. It builds up. We can't quite make it on just my pay yet, but pretty soon."

Shit, Jesse thought. So they starve for five years while he builds up the business. Or he lives off his wife and son. Great. Ahead of him, he could see a huge, yawning emptiness.

Tom stuck his nose back into his book and Jesse stared at the blank television screen. What a goddamned life it was. All his life he'd done nothing but work. He'd supported his family, given them a pretty good house, two cars, enough food to feed three growing boys, toys, clothes. They'd never had to be ashamed of who they were or what they had. He'd given them all a chance to go to college, had started the fund when Marty was born. And he cared about them, goddamn it. He cared about them, all of them. The dreams he had for them. He could remember when Marty was born. He had pictured him playing football, going to college, working hard, becoming something important, like a doctor. Stupid dreams, he thought now. But still, he could do it if he wanted to. He could still get back into college. But he was a big boy now. Hell, he was a man. You'd think he'd see what a goddamn screwed up mess his life was. And he'll go over to the war and fight and never be the same again. He'll learn things over there it would be better he never knew. He could see it happening. He could see Marty going over there like he was now and getting locked into it. He'd become a man in three months time, never able to change again, like some piece of pottery that gets put into the oven too soon and once it comes out you can never change its shape again. He'd be a bum for the rest of his life. He'd sit in his room playing his trumpet all day, living some kind of weird dream where he was a star and could go around snapping his fingers all the time in time to some beat in his head that never left and was always the same. Yeah, sit around his room. Like David does now with his nose in some book like this asshole next to him, never coming out into the real world, learning everything he'll ever know from books so that he ends up like some innocent baby who doesn't know there's a life to be lived, that there are important things to do, to do, not just to read about. David didn't even want to be a reporter. At least that would be important. He could work his way up. He'd have to get out there and see what was real. You can't write newspaper articles from what happens in a book. But David would never do it. Hell, he didn't even realize his old man was sick. He just couldn't see it. He walks in here with his eyes looking the other way, like he never sees what's going on in front of his nose. Jesus Christ. What kind of a life is that? But what the hell, Gary was the same way. Always walking around with that moony look on his face, following any goddamn kid in the neighborhood into any kind of trouble just because he doesn't know any better, because he can't see anything, doesn't listen to what his old man tells him, and doesn't hear what the teacher says. He could see him sitting there in class staring out the window when he was supposed to be learning something. Even when Mary went over to see that kid's mother, it didn't make any difference. Gary would just kind of settle into himself and let the world go by. Mary couldn't make any sense out of that woman. Hell, she didn't care what her boy did. He could burn down the house for all she cared. And then Mary sends him off with Aaron, of all the goddamn people to send a little kid with. Jesus Christ. He'll either come back a drunk or a pimp, and then he'll grow up too fast and before they knew it he'd be a bum like his brothers. And Mary would just look at him and cry, or look sad and screw up her face so she wasn't pretty anymore. But she didn't forgive him anyway. She always held that against him, and he would have to live with it because there was no way out now. If he could go back and change it he would, but it was over with and he had been a bastard and now he was paying for it and Mary was paying for it, and all the rest of them were paying for it.

Suddenly he could see that lighted room at the end of the hallway. There was sun in that room. He craved sunlight the way Mary had craved onions when she was pregnant. He needed to get into the sun, to feel it warm on his body, feel it seep into his bones.

He threw the sheet back, pulled his legs slowly to the floor, and stood up. He would just say he was going to the bathroom and got lost. Sunlight. Jesus. He needed it. He needed to feel it on him. He could think straight in there. There was light in there—natural light, not this goddamn flourescent light that makes everything look like a department store.

He was walking down the hall, realizing how tired he was. He should have taken a nap after Blackwell left. Stay quiet, he'd said. Hell. It didn't matter anyway. Nothing mattered. Only the sunlight. He passed other rooms where other patients lay quietly on their beds. There were nurses in some, but they didn't see him walk by and there weren't any in the hall. Good, Jesse thought. They can't stop him. He'd sit in the sunlight as long as he wanted and the rest of these people who said they cared about him could just go to hell. He had a family to take care of. He had sons who needed direction, who needed a strong father they could rely on, who could tell them what was right. He couldn't just let them grow into bums.

His legs felt like rubber. His feet hurt, as if he was walking over glass in his bare feet. Hell, his feet were bare. And he had forgotten to put his robe on. But it didn't matter. He was getting there. The doorway was getting bigger and brighter. He could see streams of sunlight flowing through a window, bouncing off a brown rug. There was a chair. He could sit in the chair in the sun. He was tired. Maybe he should go back.

No. He'd make it all right. A nurse walked past him and smiled. He almost laughed. She didn't know. He was breathing hard now. Could feel his lungs expand and contract, like his heart, expand and contract, but not the infarcted area. It would never be the same again and he couldn't work anymore. He was almost there. He could feel it, the sunlight flowing over him. He could see it. The door was small. Wooden. Three-O in a wooden jam with four-and-a-half-inch non-template butts. Number twelve screws. But it was open and he walked through the doorway and stood just inside the room.

The sunlight was dazzling. The whole room was filled with windows that overlooked the parking lot, the town, the mountains, that little mountain called Thumb Butte. He felt the sunlight bounce off his body as if his body was made of steel and could be cut and welded into a big door that he would hang on hinges in some frame.

He was breathing hard. His heart was beating fast. Beating. Too fast. Something was happening to it. He couldn't catch his breath. He felt weak. He couldn't stand. He felt himself sinking, as if in water, in slow motion, and the room spun around and the sunlight bathed him in its warmth. He was on the floor. Choking. He couldn't breathe. There were voices coming from far away and something black hovered over him, some big bird, like an eagle or something, flapping its big wings, coming closer, and he couldn't escape.

The bird screeched. "Code . . ."

And then he was standing beside that well with his shirt off wondering why he didn't dive in and save those girls. But he couldn't. For some reason he just couldn't. But he could find someone who could. He ran to one of the buildings, the one he had been working on, but it wasn't the same. The door was a big heavy wooden door. He twisted the knob and pulled, but the door wouldn't budge. The hinges were rusted. He grabbed the knob and pulled hard, put all his strength into it, and slowly the door creaked open.

He went in. The air inside was heavy and stale. He was tired. He wanted to sleep. His feet felt heavy, like lead bricks had been tied to them. He went through a short entranceway and found himself standing in a room large enough to be a banquet hall. A group of adults sat in one corner talking. As he walked toward them, he heard the drone of their voices echoing back and forth along the bare walls. They talked seriously and made ceremonious gestures to one another. One woman was writing in a notebook.

As he got closer, an old woman with a shriveled face and gray hair looked at him.

"Two girls just fell into the well," he said.

"Yes, we know," the old woman said. She looked back at the others and their voices droned on.

"Aren't you going to get them out?" he asked.

"No," she said, without looking back at him. "We just wait for them to float to the top."

He nodded and walked back out of the building.

Outside, the children ran around him again. He played with them. He lay on the ground and they climbed all over him. Then he picked them up over his head and spun them around and around, pretending to be a great giant.

While he was catching his breath the little girl in the red dress approached him shyly. "Why are you so big?" she asked.

He smiled down at her. "I'm grown up," he said. "Some day you'll be as big as me."

At that they all laughed and ran around him as if he was a May pole.

A bell rang. The children stopped, froze almost, then ran to one of the buildings, the one that he had thought used to be a church. They filed through the doors. He was left alone.

Everything was silent. Everything was still. And there was an odor. At first it was faint, but it became more dense until finally it covered the yard like thick fog. He recognized it. It was the nauseating smell of decaying flesh. He tried to see where it was coming from and noticed something lying in one of the shallow ditches. He couldn't see it clearly, but knew it was dead and decaying. He didn't go any closer. He didn't want to see it.

He walked to the well and stood there waiting. The air

around him was hot and wet and the odor of decay wafted past his nose in windless gusts. He could see now there were dead, decaying things littering the yard all over. Some of them were fresher than others. Some looked mutilated, a piece here and a piece there. None of them were forms he could recognize. The air darkened and thickened. The sky itself seemed to press down on him.

Then the bodies of the girls floated to the surface and hung there, suspended like dead jellyfish. Their bright dresses splayed out on the surface of the water and their hair rippled limply with its motion. He waited.

After a long time, a procession dribbled out of the big doorway. Four men, one at each end, carried two oblong boxes, old, with dirty beige enamel paint flaking off in big curls, each one nailed to two long wooden dowels the size of broomsticks. The old woman led them, marching slowly, with measured steps, to the well. There they took the girls out of the water and placed them in the boxes. There was a hole at one end of each box, and the girls' heads protruded from them. The men closed the lids and locked them with padlocks. Only the girls' heads were exposed.

Then they marched, the old woman still leading, her arms outstretched as if she was blind. He walked beside the second box, following the procession toward the border of the yard. He looked at the girl's head, dangling grotesquely from the hole in the box. She was pretty. Her long, black hair trailed along on the ground, her eyes were closed.

Suddenly, the eyelids fluttered, then opened wide. The girl looked up at him, deep into his eyes, and screamed. It was a terrible, hideous scream, inhuman, yet terribly human. It leaped out of her mouth and grabbed at his guts like a leech, sucking his breath.

"Wait a minute," he gasped to the man next to him. "This girl's alive."

The man ignored him. They kept marching as if nothing had happened.

"What are you doing?" he said. "She's alive. Can't you see? Can't you hear? She's alive!"

They ignored him. The procession kept marching; the girl kept screaming. He rushed ahead, up to the old woman.

"What's the matter with you people? That girl's alive. Stop!"

But they marched on. The girl screamed. And he sobbed hysterically, choking in the fine dust. They were almost to the border of the yard. He looked around him with the horror of recognition.

"Sto---p!" he cried, and the word became a scream of abject terror that swirled through the thick air like a whirlwind, surrounding them all, then swirling upward into the dirty beige sky.

But they kept marching. Nothing would stop them. They marched across the border of the yard, and kept marching toward the sand dunes in the distance, the girl still screaming. He stopped and watched them until they became tiny black specks against the sand and the girl's screaming died to a whimper.

Grief tore at him, tearing him to pieces, and he knew he would be left to lie there on the ground, mutilated, dead, to decay along with all the other dead, decaying things, when three words came to him. They came into his mind, but he couldn't say them. He opened his mouth, but they wouldn't come out. He mouthed them without sound. He cried. He strained to say the words. Then he stopped. He felt himself fall softly to the ground like a bunch of feathers and he knew he was dying. He could feel death wash over him like a deep sleep, and he relaxed into it, slowly, peacefully.

"Let them go," he whispered softly. "Let them go."

Suction cups sticking to his chest. A needle in his wrist. Oxygen pouring into his nose. Diffused light. Muddled voices.

". . . almost lost him . . ." ". . . he doing down there, anyway?" "I don't . . ." ". . . watch him constantly . . ." ". . . touch
and go now. Watch that monitor . . ." ". . . any more signs of
arrhythmia increase . . ."

Marty had waited with his mother in front of the bus station for about half an hour before the Greyhound came. They
could have sat inside but the little room was dark and dismal.
Outside they watched the patrons, mostly old cowboys probably
drinking up their retirement, go in and out of the Cattleman's
Bar next door. Down the street a short distance was an old railroad depot, painted the usual light beige with the usual cracks
and peels and windows so dirty you couldn't see through them.
It was apparently used for freight now, because they saw a few
men dressed in overalls and railroad caps come and go. There
were a few boxcars sitting on sidings near the depot, but they
never saw an engine or a real train.

When the bus came, Marty kissed his mother goodbye,
picked up his small paper bag (they hadn't brought any suit-
cases; everything was packed in the camper), and climbed
aboard. The bus was nearly empty. He found a seat near the middle by himself and sat down next to the window. The bus rumbled down the street. He looked back but couldn't see his
mother; he was on the wrong side of the bus.

For a while he thought of her standing there, of her getting
back into the truck and driving on to the hospital, of her sitting
there in that waiting room. He tried to think what she might be
thinking, but found it impossible. What would he think? He
couldn't tell. He had never loved anyone like his mother loved
his father. He could imagine a little the fear she must be feeling,
the fear of losing such a basic part of her, worse than cutting off
an arm or a leg. She really was holding up well.

He settled back then and watched the scenery go by. The
bus was taking a different route than they had taken coming

173

into Prescott. It went to Phoenix, where he would have to transfer to another bus. They passed through a kind of prairie country, then rolled through some rolling hills where small houses sat all by themselves and made him wonder about people who wanted to live that isolated. He wondered if they had telephones or had newspapers delivered. Hermits, he decided. And he knew he could never stand it. Even though he didn't like to admit it, he knew he longed for the bustle, the heavy traffic, the horns and tires screeching, the sirens, and even the smog of the city. It was his home. He belonged there. His mother and father—well, they had come to the Valley when it wasn't any bigger than Prescott. They had an aerial photo of the house sitting next to three or four other houses surrounded by vacant desert. They had watched the area grow, his father always kicking himself because he hadn't bought land when he could have gotten it for five hundred dollars an acre. But five hundred dollars was a lot of money in those days, he'd always say. Now an acre went for fifty thousand, sometimes more, if you could find an acre.

The bus stopped at a little restaurant-gas station where the highway met the freeway, and two more passengers got on. Then it headed down the freeway toward Phoenix. They wound through mountains, across a high desert plateau, and down some steep hills. Sitting alone, Marty became aware of something he had been feeling almost since they left home on the vacation but had never thought about consciously. He was horny as hell.

He thought about Connie, wondered what time he would get home, if he should call her right away or wait until tomorrow. He should probably go to work tomorrow. He could make some good money. But what the hell. He was on vacation. But it would probably be too late to call Connie tonight, and tomorrow she had to work. He'd see how he felt. He could probably take one day to be lazy at home. He could water the lawn, maybe rake some leaves. He'd have to see Mrs. Trimble and get the mail. He could play his trumpet a little. He could put on the music-minus-one record and play with that.

The bus depot in Phoenix was big and hot and crowded. Marty found where he was supposed to catch his next bus, then wandered around while he waited the half hour until it arrived. He bought a sandwich from a machine and when he finished that, he bought a Coke from another. He went to a little gift shop and stood in front of the magazine rack wondering if he should buy something to read on the way across the desert. But he decided people would probably sleep and would want the lights off, so he thumbed through a couple, read part of an article in *Cosmopolitan* about making love after a mastectomy, then realized it was time to go.

At the bus, he gave the driver his ticket and boarded. He could see from the front that nearly every seat was filled, but both right front seats were vacant, so he threw his bag into the luggage rack overhead and sat down. There wasn't much leg room because of a metal barrier between the seats and the door.

Another passenger got on—a young man about Marty's age, wearing Levis, cowboy boots, and a cowboy hat and carrying a dirty orange backpack. He stood in the front a minute, just as Marty had, then tossed his backpack up into the luggage rack, just as Marty had, and sat down next to Marty. He grinned apologetically and in the dim light Marty saw the glint of a large silver tooth in the front of his mouth.

"Ain't no other place," the cowboy said.

"That's okay," Marty mumbled and looked out the window.

Two more passengers boarded and walked to the back. They disappeared back there, so Marty knew there must have been some seats. Then the driver took his seat and backed the bus out of the depot.

It wasn't until they had been on the freeway for about half an hour that the cowboy said something.

"You goin' all the way to L. A.?"

Marty nodded. "Sun Valley."

"Where's that?"

"In the Valley," Marty said.

175

"What valley?"

Marty looked over at him. "The San Fernando Valley."

"Don't know where that is," the cowboy said. "I'm gettin' another bus in L. A. and goin' north."

"Oh," Marty said. He liked sitting in the front, he decided. You could see out the big front window. You could watch how the driver drove. If he got some sleep now, he could call Connie when he got home.

"I live out in Buckeye," the cowboy said.

"Where's that?" Marty asked.

"West o' Phoenix. My ol' man works on a ranch. I work it, too, sometimes. I was goin' to college, though. Takin' agriculture. Wasn't doin' too good, though. Dropped out mostly."

"Oh," Marty said.

"Then I got my draft notice."

Marty's eyes shot over to the cowboy's. The cowboy had a sparse three-day growth on his chin. "When do you report?" Marty asked.

The cowboy grinned. "Yesterday."

"What are you doing here?"

"Like I said. I'm catchin' a bus in L. A. and headin' north."

"You're a dodger?"

"I don't play no baseball. I'm just goin' up to B. C. Figure I can get on at a ranch up there somewheres."

"Jesus." Marty lowered his voice to a whisper. "What if you get caught?"

"You goin' to turn me in?"

"Well, no, but . . . Jesus."

"You think anybody's gonna turn me in?"

"I don't know. Why not?"

" 'Cause it's a bastard war, that's why. Everybody thinks it's a bastard war. We got no business over there and everybody knows it."

"What about the police?" Marty asked.

176

"What do they know? They didn't put out no dragnet for me. They probably ain't even figured out I'm not there yet, the Army's so screwed up."

"They'll figure it out sooner or later."

"By then I'll be in B. C. and they can take their bastard war and shove it."

"Well, it's not a bastard war, really," Marty said, a little patronizingly. "It's a war against communism."

"Well," the cowboy said. "I don't know nothin' about communism, but I talked to guys that was over there. You go around blowin' up gooks and you never know if they're the enemy gooks or the gooks that're on your side or just some poor bastards that happen to have slanty eyes. It's a bastard war."

"How many guys have you talked to?" Marty asked.

"Well, let me see now . . ." The cowboy thought a minute. "Two."

"And you think they know everything there is to know about the war? Just because they were in it doesn't mean they know what it's for."

"I don't give a damn what it's for," the cowboy said. "I ain't gonna fight it."

"You're chicken shit," Marty said.

"Damn right. I like my asshole the way it is."

They turned away from each other then. Marty thought he'd like to clip this asshole's jaw. "Ask not what your country can do for you . . ." In ten years he'd come back and go on welfare.

"What does your father say?" Marty asked.

"My ol' man pulled out mostly his whole savings so I could get up to B. C. I didn't like leavin' him, but it was a mutual agreement."

Marty was flabbergasted. "Your father wants you to run?"

"Hell, he told me to."

"Doesn't he have any patriotism? Jesus, you'd think somebody—"

"Patriotism. What the hell is that? It don't mean shit. You can take that flag and burn it for all I care."

"You think you can just live here free gratis and not do anything to pay for it?"

"I told you. I ain't livin' here."

"Yeah, but you'll be back."

"Maybe."

"And then what'll you do?"

"Well, I'm gonna save my money up there. Save a whole shitload of it. Then, when I come back, I'm gonna buy me a little spread. Just big enough so I can work it myself. Maybe thirty, forty head and enough land for 'em to graze on. Have me a little house all my own. Maybe a wife, a couple kids."

"Bullshit," Marty said.

"You think you can do better by goin' over there and gettin' your head shot off?"

"I think that'd be the right thing to do."

"Right, shit. There ain't nothin' right about shootin' people."

"If they'd just go over there and bomb the place there wouldn't be any shooting."

"Goddamn. Why don't we just blow up the whole world. Kill off everybody. That'd stop the shootin', too. Bloodthirsty sonofabitch, ain't you."

Marty slumped down in his seat and propped his knees on the steel railing. He looked out at the twilight, at the dim lights coming and going. So he runs, he thought. Like a scared dog. It'd be different if he stayed and fought it here, refused to go and took his knocks for it. Burned his flag in the street instead of in some secret room like a goddamn Nazi or something. He decided he'd better stop thinking about it. He should get some sleep. He folded his arms across his chest, leaned back against the headrest, and closed his eyes.

"By the way," the cowboy said. "Why ain't you over there, you're so hot on it?"

"Haven't got my notice yet," Marty said.

"Shit," the cowboy said. "You don't have to wait for no notice, you know. You can enlist. Why don't you get in the Air Force. You could go over there and bomb 'em all. Jesus. Just think of it. You could kill thousands. And it wouldn't matter if they was enemy gooks or not. You couldn't see 'em anyways. You might even kill some good, red-blooded Americans that way."

"Shit," Marty said under his breath. He closed his eyes again.

The bus stopped in Blythe and Marty got off to get a Coke. When he came back to his seat the cowboy and his dirty orange backpack were gone. He wondered if the cowboy was scared that he might turn him in, that he might call the Blythe police department and say, "Hey, there's a draft dodger on this bus and if you get here right away you can nab him." But he knew better. That asshole was probably just some drifter not going anyplace, just feeding Marty a line of bull. Jesus, he'd be glad to get home.

And he got home, finally. After leaving the bus depot in the middle of downtown L. A. at ten o'clock at night, he stood on a corner outside a noisy bar with his hand over his wallet waiting for the city bus that took him to Sixth and Hope where he caught another bus that took him into the Valley and dropped him off at Lankershim and Magnolia. Then he had to wait almost a half hour for a bus to take him the rest of the way down Lankershim to Saticoy, and he walked the five blocks to the house.

It was almost eleven-thirty when he dialed Connie's number. He was surprised when she answered the phone. He had expected her father to answer and tell him he woke up the whole house.

"Marty," she said in a whisper. "Why are you calling so late?"

"I'm home."

"You're home? You're here?"

"Yeah."

"What happened. You didn't get—"

"No. It's a long story." He told her what happened.

"Oh, Marty," Connie said. "I'm sorry."

"Well, anyway, I'm home."

"But it's so late."

"Yeah, I know."

"Tomorrow, okay?"

"Yeah, okay."

"Buy some eggs and stuff. I'll fix your breakfast."

"In the morning?"

"I'll call in sick."

Marty drove to the all-night Thriftymart as soon as he hung up the phone. He bought a dozen eggs, a pound of bacon, and some frozen hash browns. When he got back home he opened some windows, got into bed, and set the alarm for five thirty. He wanted to get up in time to take a shower and change his sheets.

In the morning, fresh from the shower, he met Connie at the door. They kissed long and hard, then, wordlessly, he led her back to his bedroom. The bed was better than the seat of his car. They could move, try different things, look at each other, throw the covers back and feel the cool morning air move softly over their perspiring bodies while they lay there panting like swimmers after a race before they embraced again.

They had a late breakfast. Marty sat in his robe at the kitchen table watching Connie move around the stove. She could be a geisha, he thought. He had given her David's robe to wear. Sunlight streamed through the window over the sink and caught her shiny black hair, making it flash as it swayed with her movements. The thick odor of frying bacon filled the kitchen.

When she put the plates on the table and sat down, Marty looked at her for a long moment. But she avoided his eyes and started eating as if she hadn't eaten in a week.

"So what are you going to do?" she asked between bites.

"What do you mean?" Marty said.

"Are you going back to work or what?"

Marty picked up his fork, broke open his egg yolk, and swished the thick yellow liquid around over the rest of the egg. "I guess. I don't know."

"You're still waiting." There was a strange tenseness in her voice.

Marty picked up a slice of bacon and snapped it in half with his teeth. "What else is there to do?"

"Quit."

He looked at her. Her plate was almost clean. "Just like that?"

"Why not?"

"Why?"

"What are you working for?"

Marty started eating in earnest, even though he wasn't very hungry. "I don't know. To pay off my car, I guess."

"Oh," Connie said. She picked up her mug and sat back in the chair, sipping her coffee.

Marty swabbed up the last of his egg with a piece of toast. He could see smoke swirling in the sunlight. He should open the kitchen window to let some of it out. What was he going to do? Today they could do something. Go to the beach, maybe. "We could go to the beach today," he said.

"I don't have my suit," Connie said. "And I can't go home to get it."

"Well, we'll just stay here then. We can listen to some music. Watch some television."

"What's the matter, you bored?"

Marty looked at her. Her face was solemn; her eyes squinted slightly; her mouth, full and moist, drooped at the corners. "No," he said. "I'm not bored."

She smiled a little. "I'm sorry. We have all day. I don't want to spoil it." She scooted her chair back, stood up, and started carrying the dishes to the sink.

Marty went to her. "Leave them," he said as he turned her

181

around to face him. He untied the string around her waist, opened the robe, and slipped it from her shoulders. She clung to him, laid her head on his chest, and the sunlight streamed over her milky body. They walked slowly back to Marty's bedroom.

At five o'clock she left, dressed as she had come. But she would only be gone long enough to pick up a change of clothes and tell her parents she would spend the night with her girl friend, Jill.

All night, Marty thought, as he stood under the steaming shower. He would have her all night. They would lie together in his bed. Sleep together. He would let her presence soak into his body like suntan lotion or something. All night. He couldn't believe it.

They went out for dinner, to a little Mexican restaurant where the light was dim, the waitress soft-spoken, and the air filled with damp odors of frying tortillas and beans. Marty looked across the table at her. He tingled all over. He longed to run his hands over her smooth body, as if he hadn't been with her all day, he thought. But she looked different in her other clothes—new and fresh. Her eyes sparkled and she smiled more often. They stopped at Baskin Robbins on the way home and had a hot fudge sundae.

Back in Marty's bedroom, they undressed together like an old married couple. They hesitated a moment, just a trifle awkwardly, before they got into bed. But once they were there everything happened naturally—like the song. Marty had played in the orchestra when he was a sophomore in high school and they did "Annie Oakley." He had a hopeless crush on the lead singer but he never even spoke to her. He was just a pimply-faced sophomore and she was a senior, suave, sophisticated, and talented enough to do nightclubs. He always wondered what happened to her, even though he couldn't remember her name anymore. He felt himself moving back and forth—felt Connie beneath him—and thought, what the hell am I thinking about? He should have turned the light out. Connie's eyes were closed, her face expressionless. He stopped moving.

"It's been a long day," Connie whispered.

"You okay?" Marty asked.

Connie nodded. "A little sore."

And then the phone rang. Marty heard it as if it came from the back of his mind somewhere, as if it was in a dream and he had just awakened. He pulled up on his knees, then rolled over on his back. "I'm sorry," he said.

"Aren't you going to answer it?"

Marty didn't reply. He didn't want to get up. But he would have to turn the light out anyway. He thought the phone would stop, but it kept ringing and ringing. Then, suddenly, he thought of his father. What if something had happened.

"Don't go away," he whispered.

He crawled out of bed and loped across the room, down the hall, and into the living room. When he picked up the phone there was a man's voice that he didn't recognize. His mind was clouded and he tried to focus it by eliminating possibilities. It wasn't Lyle and it wasn't that doctor and it wasn't Uncle Aaron, and it obviously wasn't David.

"Is this Marty?"

"Yes, it is."

"It's late, Marty."

"What time is it?"

"Almost midnight."

There was a pause. What was he supposed to say? This was insane, or some prank.

"How did you get my number?"

"Come on, Marty."

"Who is this?"

"You don't know?"

"I'm hanging up, and you—"

"Wait a minute, Marty."

Another pause. He was standing there in the living room naked in the dark. He looked around. Everything was the same as it always was, but it wasn't the same. It was full of vacant places, like holes, not in things, but in the thing that was everything he could see. It was as if he was looking at a photograph that had had something spilled on it while it was being developed that erased part of the picture.

"My wife ran into Mrs. Klinedale at the store tonight."

Something sank in Marty's stomach. He sat down on the floor. It was Connie's father. "Jesus, Mr. Crawford. Why didn't you . . . I didn't know it was you."

"I'm not naive enough to think that my daughter is a virgin. I haven't been that naive for a long time now—since before she knew you. I hope you have sense enough to take precautions, but you're big kids now, and that's . . ." There was talking in the background that he couldn't understand, then everything was silent for several seconds. He waited. He was sweating. "Is Connie over there?"

He could say no and it could never be proved, at least not by anything Connie's father could do. Connie could think up some excuse. She could call Jill and Jill could say that Connie was coming over later and she had forgotten to tell her mother about it. Jill would probably go along with it. Then, just to play it safe, she could really go over to Jill's. Or he could tell the truth. What the hell difference would it make? No difference at all, probably, to Connie's father. He had already lost all his faith in her. Who would it make a difference to then?

"You still there, Marty? Come on. I'm not playing games, you know."

What was that supposed to mean? Who the hell was playing games? "Yeah, she's here," Marty said.

"Well, send her home, will you?"

"I'll bring her home, if you want."

"I don't want to see you, Marty. I don't want you around this house anymore."

"What if she doesn't want to come home?"

"Are you going to marry that girl, or what?"

"Look, Mr. Crawford. I understand how you feel—"

"Like hell you do. I give you ten or twenty years. And even then I doubt it."

There was another pause. He shouldn't have told him she was there. What an ass. He was starting to feel cold, and he felt like a fool sitting there on the floor in the living room naked. He looked down at his hairy crotch and his white, hairy legs and his big feet.

"Send her home, will you Marty?"

"I'll tell her." The click sounded in his ear and he felt exhausted.

Something brushed against his back. He looked behind him. Connie stood over him wearing David's robe. Looking up at her, he felt like one of the seven dwarfs. He turned around and ran his hand up her leg.

"I'd better go," she said softly.

"You don't have to, you know," Marty said. "You can do what you want."

"I have to live there," Connie said. She turned away from him and walked back toward the bedroom. Marty followed her.

Back in the bedroom, he sat down on the bed and watched her dress. He felt as if all the life had suddenly gushed out of him and he was floating in some ethereal dampness like a jelly-fish or something. Connie pulled her T-shirt over her head. It had a picture of a donkey on the front made out of words. The long, floppy ears said, "Ear, ear, ear, ear," and the tail said, "tail, tail, tail, tail, tail." She went into the bathroom. Marty went to the closet and put on his robe.

When she came back he was still standing in front of the

closet and he could tell she was crying. He looked at her as if from a distance, as if he was watching a movie, waiting to see how the plot would unfold. There were these two characters . . .

She wiped her eyes and looked at him silently for a long moment. Then she shook her head and said, "I don't understand you."

"I don't know what I was thinking," Marty said. "Shit. I could have told him anything. What could he do?"

Connie shook her head again. "I don't mean that. That doesn't matter."

Marty watched her pick up her sneakers and walk over to the bed. She started to put them on. "What do you mean?" he asked.

"I guess I want too much," Connie said, tears coming into her eyes again. "I expect too much from you."

There was a vague aching in Marty's chest. "What do you expect?"

"I don't know," Connie said. "Something . . . kind of strong, I guess. Or some feeling." She finished tying her shoes and looked up at him. "I keep asking myself what's wrong with me and what's wrong with you. But that's not it. It's not either one of us. It's both of us. It's us together."

Marty swallowed. He could still taste tacos on his breath. He felt weak and lightheaded and wanted to sit down, but the only place to sit was on the bed where Connie was. "I don't get it," he mumbled.

"Don't you feel it, Marty?"

"Feel what?"

"There's something missing. With us. Between us. Together. Maybe that's it. We're not together. I don't know. I don't understand it very well. I just feel it."

There was something passing over him, some shadow that stretched toward the horizon. It made him shiver. It made him want to curl up in a corner somewhere. It reminded him of a re-

curring nightmare he had as a child. He would be in the house
alone and a giant was outside trying to find him. He would try to
hide, but wherever he went the giant would look in through the
window and see him.

He had been watching the window over the bed. He felt
Connie looking at him. "You feel it, don't you," she whispered.
Marty nodded.

"I'm sorry," Connie said. "I wasn't going to say anything tonight. I thought maybe tonight . . ." She stood up and went to
him. She put her arms around him, but his own arms hung limp
at his sides. "There's something else," she said softly. Marty
looked into her dark eyes. What was behind them? he wondered.
He would never know. "I think I'm pregnant."

"What?" It was a startled cry.

"I'm two weeks late."

"You're taking pills."

"I know. I don't understand it."

"Have you seen a doctor?"

Connie looked down. "No."

Marty moved away. He had to sit down or he would be sick.
He sat on the edge of the bed. His thin, light blue robe didn't
cover his knees. He looked up at her. "Then it's not for sure," he
said.

"No," Connie said. "It's not for sure. But I'm never late. I'm
very regular. Especially since the pills."

"You have to see a doctor."

"I will."

He couldn't believe it. He stared at her, standing there in
her beige corduroy pants tight around her slim figure, her brown
donkey shirt fitting snugly over her small breasts, and he tried to
imagine her pregnant. He remembered his mother when she was
pregnant with Gary and superimposed her big belly onto Connie.
It repulsed him. It made him shudder.

"I'd better go," Connie said.

"I'll drive you home."

"What would I do with my car?"

"I could follow you."

"You think my father's going to beat me?"

Marty looked down at the floor. "No. I guess not."

"You'd only make it worse. It's bad enough as it is."

"Yeah," Marty said. "It's bad enough." He stared at the floor and listened to her pad softly out of the room. He heard the front door close, her car door open and close, and the engine start. He had the feeling he would never see her again, and didn't know how to feel about that. He would talk to her on the phone. She would call him and tell him she really wasn't pregnant and he wouldn't know whether she was telling the truth or not. She might have an abortion. She might try to abort it herself, take a long horseback ride or something. Lift her brother's weights. She might have the baby out of some feeling of responsibility and raise it herself. She would marry somebody who could accept that, some clean-cut accountant or something. He'd be at least five years older than her and kind of ugly and desperate so that it wouldn't matter. She'd have two more kids and they would all live happily as one big family and she would always wonder what happened to the father of her firstborn. The father . . .

He stood up slowly and ambled into the bathroom. He wanted vaguely to take a shower, but he stood at the sink and stared at himself in the mirror. He needed a shave. "You going to marry that girl, or what?" He could always do that. He had more or less planned on it some day. He could marry her and then get drafted and have to leave her here to have their baby alone. She would live with her parents and would have to put up with their low opinion of her, would feel like a whore until he came back and they could get a place of their own. Jesus. It sounded like some soap opera.

He took off his robe and climbed into the shower stall. He turned on the hot water, adjusted it with the cold, and stood there letting the steam rise around him, staring at the blue tile in front of him. Why did she have to say that? If she felt like she did, why did she tell him that? She might not even be pregnant. Only two weeks late. Maybe she was just late. Or maybe there was some other problem.

But he'd read somewhere that the pills weren't infallible. Every time you had sex, you took some risk. He had realized that before they started. He wasn't some naive high school kid who didn't know what he was doing.

Okay. Then he had to take some of the responsibility. If she was pregnant the kid was half his. He ought to foot half the bill.

But why did she tell him? When she wasn't even sure about it? He turned off the water and climbed out of the shower. He had forgotten to use soap. He pulled a clean towel from the shelf and dried himself. He'd say it was a con, some scheme of hers to try to get out of him whatever it was she wanted, but that wasn't like Connie. What would she want from him? Besides, she was too straightforward for that. In fact, that was probably it. Good old straightforward Connie. She probably just thought he should know. Keeping everything in the open. All the cards on the table.

He dropped the towel on the floor, went back into his bedroom, and stood in front of his closet staring at the sliding, pressed wood door. What was he going to do? Goddamn. What *was* he going to do?

He was going to get drafted, that's what. He'd have to go fight that bastard war. And it wouldn't matter whether he believed it was right or not. He'd be there. In the middle of it. Probably just trying like hell to save his ass—and maybe the asses of some other poor suckers. And even Connie . . .

There would be nothing waiting for him at home. That would really suck. Everybody else would have girls waiting for them, some even wives and kids. He'd have nothing but a damn trumpet. And he'd say, Yeah, he could hardly wait to get back home and play in the Valley Youth Band again. The youth band. He'd be twenty-three by then.

If he'd been smart he would have done like Sid Brecht, first clarinet in the band. He got a scholarship to Annapolis and played in the band there. When he got out he'd be an officer playing in the big Navy band. But he was good. He could do that little slide in "Rhapsody in Blue" like he had a slide on his clarinet. Perfectly controlled.

He slid open the closet door and looked at his clothes. He felt like doing something. Except for dinner, he'd been in the house all day. He needed to get out for a while. He needed a beer, that's what he needed.

He put on some clothes, went out to his car, climbed in, backed out of the driveway, and roared down the street. He knew where he was going. He didn't usually go to bars. He was too young. He drank some at parties, but he had never been drunk. Now, in the back of his mind, was the thought that he would like to get plastered, so drunk he couldn't see, couldn't feel, couldn't care, couldn't think.

He drove down Lankershim to downtown North Hollywood—what had once been a nice, conventional shopping area, like his mother said it was when she went to North Hollywood High, but was fast becoming a long row of seedy bars, adult bookstores, and topless joints. He had always been intrigued by one bar in particular. The Hole in the Wall. The front was a brick wall that looked like somebody had taken a sledge hammer and knocked a big hole in it. There were posters on both sides of the door. "Exotic dancers," they said, and there were pictures.

He parked on the street, got out of his car, and looked around him. The sidewalks were deserted. Neon lights blinked here and there down both sides of the street, but many store fronts, the ones that were still stores, were dark. The street looked like a carnival starting to close. The air was warm and a little damp. A city bus, reeking of diesel exhaust, rumbled down the street as he walked up to the heavy wooden door and pushed it open.

Music blared at him, rock music with a heavy sensuous beat, and on a screen behind the long, low bar, a naked woman lay on a bed masturbating. He sat down at the bar. The room was dark. His eyes had to adjust to the light. The music stopped momentarily, and he heard the steady whir of the projector behind him. There was no sound to the movie. The woman writhed around on the bed, her hand between her legs, making a poor attempt at facial expressions Marty assumed were supposed to be rapturous or something.

He was practically the only person there. Behind him, at a table, a group of four or five men talked and laughed. Two pitchers of beer, one empty and one full, sat in the middle of the table. A man sat alone at the other end of the bar to Marty's right and another sat three seats away to his left. Both men watched the movie with solemn, fixed expressions. The man on his left intrigued Marty. He was middle-aged, with shaggy, graying hair. He wore khaki work pants and a dark sport coat that must have come from a Salvation Army store. Marty looked away nervously when he caught his eyes wandering down to the man's crotch.

He glanced at the bottles stacked behind the bar, and a sign, "Shot and a Beer. $1.25," before he looked back at the movie. Then suddenly, a pretty blonde, wearing a tight, low-cut blouse, stood in front of him.

She smiled. "What'll it be?"

"Uh . . . beer. No. A shot and a beer," Marty said.

She turned to pour the shot and the beer. Her hair was teased and bleached and when she turned back, he saw that she was old enough to be his mother.

"Two dollars," she said, setting the glasses in front of him.

Marty fumbled in his back pocket and pulled out his wallet.

191

He laid the bills on the bar and glanced back at the sign. "Happy Hour," it read below the price. He checked his wallet again. He only had ten dollars. He'd have to go to the bank tomorrow.

The bar smelled damp and musty, as if they had collected ocean air the week before and kept it sealed up until it got stale. He picked up the shot glass and sipped the whiskey. It burned his throat and made his breath hot. He swallowed some beer and looked up at the movie. There was a close-up of the woman's face now. Her eyes were wide, her mouth open, and she was breathing hard. Then her face tensed to a rigid mask and she opened her mouth wider, as if to scream. Her eyes closed. Her head rolled back and forth on the pillow. Then, slowly, she relaxed. A fake smile of satisfaction passed over her lips and the camera backed up until her whole body was in view again. She took her hand away from her crotch and licked her fingers.

A slow, languid movement on his left caught Marty's eye. He glanced at the man sitting there, then looked away quickly and felt his stomach sour. The man's hands were big and rough and calloused—and strong. And he was licking his fingers.

Marty downed the rest of his whiskey with a shiver and took a long gulp of beer. He didn't like the taste of the beer on top of the whiskey, but he was already feeling the effects. The music pounded, thudding through his body like an army marching. Electric guitars screeched and shuddered like a traffic accident. The movie faded to black, then blinked off, leaving a lighted square on the screen. The music stopped in the middle of the song and he heard the projector click, clicking behind him. He breathed a sigh of relief and downed the rest of his beer.

As soon as he set the glass down, the barmaid was in front of him. She had freckles on her chest.

"Another?" she asked.

Marty nodded, pulled out his wallet, and laid the ten on the bar. The barmaid moved like a machine, filling the glasses, setting them in front of him, picking up his ten, returning his change, and taking away his two used glasses. After she checked with the other two customers at the bar, she sat down in a chair in front of the cash register with a paperback book.

The lights had come up a little and now floodlights on the ceiling came on, lighting up a raised platform in front of the screen. The music started again, a vocal this time. Some group singing something full of grunts and shouts. The only words Marty could make out were, "Come on, baby (grunt) come on." A dancer came on stage and danced. She was a pretty girl, not more than nineteen or twenty, with short, light brown hair, a round face with a shy, thin-lipped smile, and skin the color of skim milk. She wore a bright red bikini, revealing a straight, boyish figure that was hardly sexy, yet appealing somehow.

Marty began to relax. He sipped the whiskey and watched the girl dance. She seemed to dance mostly for him, although the men at the bar stared at her fixedly. But she smiled at Marty when she took off her bikini top and dropped it to the floor, revealing too small, firm breasts that were even whiter than the rest of her body.

Marty drank and watched her bounce her breasts around for a while, stroking them occasionally with her hands. He was working on the beer when she began inching her bikini bottom down her thighs. The song was almost over and the vocal group was working itself into a frenzy. On the last few chords, the dancer slid her bikini pants down over her cheeks, turned around, and bent over. It was only a flash, but the light was bright and Marty was only a few feet away from her. He could see a bright red pimple in the middle of her left cheek.

She scooped up her top, and ran down from the stage while Marty finished his beer. There was applause behind him and, like magic, the barmaid appeared in front of him. She was plump. Not fat, but plump. He nodded to her and she turned wordlessly to fix him another shot and a beer.

That dancer was cute, he thought aimlessly. He would al-

193

ways remember her as the girl with the pimple on her butt. The barmaid brought his drinks just as the lights dimmed again. The projector whirred and there was another woman on the screen, lying on a bed wearing black underwear and black stockings. It was a different woman, but he knew she was going to do the same thing as the last one. What a drag. He drank half the whiskey and some beer. The men behind him were laughing at some joke. One of them laughed with short, gutteral grunts and Marty pictured him as big and fat, with pants that hung down from his stomach like a curtain. Then the laughter was drowned out by the music blaring through Marty's head like little knives, making his skin tingle and crawl.

He drank the rest of his whiskey, gulped down the beer, and grabbed the rest of his money. Then he turned around on his stool and stood up. The room swam. He walked slowly to the door, watching the floor, trying to put one foot directly in front of the other. He heard the men laugh as he passed their table. He was breathing hard. The bar was so damn stuffy. He needed some fresh air. He reached the door, pushed it open, and stumbled out onto the sidewalk.

The dark night air and the relative quiet rushed over him like water. He picked out his car sitting at the curb and pointed himself in that direction. He walked carefully, but even so, he was weaving. He leaned on his car and tried to catch his breath. He gulped in huge amounts of air, pressed his forehead against the cool metal of the roof. He couldn't drive. Wouldn't trust himself behind the wheel. He pushed himself away from the car and ambled down the sidewalk.

It was no good, he thought. What a depressing place. He should have taken the time to drive into Hollywood to Shelly's Manne-Hole. At least he could have listened to some decent music while he drank. His head pounded. He stopped in front of a sporting goods store. Discount Fishery. It was the one where they were going to buy Gary's fishing pole. He peered through the window into the partially lighted store. There were poles of every size, arranged from long, heavy deep sea poles down to ultra-light rigs, and bins full of other equipment. It was a good store, if you liked fishing. Well, he had gotten out of that. If he had stayed, they probably would have gone fishing every day and he would have spent all his time changing diapers. So he came home.

He came home all right. He walked farther down the sidewalk. His stomach was feeling a little queasy. A few cars buzzed by like lazy flies. If he saw a cop he would stop and look in a store window. That's all he needed, to get picked up for being drunk. Jesus, he felt lousy. He stared at the sidewalk as he walked.

Well, he had screwed up everything. Made a goddamn ugly mess out of his whole life. His girlfriend was pregnant and he was going to get drafted and he was walking down some lonely city street so drunk he couldn't walk straight, like some character out of a Rod McKuen poem. And why not? Who the hell was he anyway? Maybe he was some character in a Rod McKuen poem. That's why everything he did seemed like a big cliché.

There was always the cliché answer. Run. He could get the hell out of there, go to Canada, follow that damn cowboy and work on a ranch up there somewhere. What the hell. Or maybe they have egg companies in Canada. That was the only experience he had. He had about eight hundred dollars in his savings account. That would at least get him up there. The hell with his car payments. They'd never find him in Canada. He could change his name.

He saw it out of the corner of his eye: a police cruiser, black and white with the little red lights on the roof. He turned toward the glass front on his right and stood stock still, hoping he wasn't weaving while he stood there. He stuck his hands in his pockets and tried to look casual. He waited. He was cold.

He tried not to, but he kept thinking about that man on his

left in the bar. Probably some lonely old fart with nowhere else to go, Marty thought. When the bar closed he probably came out and walked up and down these sidewalks and hoped he didn't get rolled. He probably worked some piddly job somewhere, pumped gas or loaded crates or something. Marty pictured him walking down the sidewalk with his sport coat hunched up around his neck as if he was afraid someone would recognize him.

He forgot about the cop and stared into the darkened window in front of him. It was some time before he realized what was behind it. There were desks. It was an office. And there were partitions between the desks with posters tacked to them. He picked out one poster and tried to bring it into focus. It was blurry. The light was poor. He moved closer to the window and leaned his forehead against the cool glass. His breath steamed it up, but he could see the poster better. It was blue, mostly. There was an airplane, a jet, with a man in some kind of dark uniform with a baseball cap standing in front of it. The man was smiling. "In the Air Force the smallest jobs are big ones." The man was holding a wrench.

Marty straightened up and backed away from the window. He started back to his car. He was sleepy. Just all of a sudden, he couldn't hold his eyes open. He blinked off and on as he walked, knowing he must be weaving all over the sidewalk. But he didn't care. He wanted to get home. That was all that mattered now. To get home and go to sleep.

It was late morning before he woke up. A body and fender man was pounding out dents in his skull from the inside. He was in his own bed but he couldn't remember how he got there. He only vaguely remembered waking up there in the dark and trying to make it to the bathroom. But he had thrown up all over the hall carpet. By the time he made it to the toilet he was just gagging. Thinking about it made his stomach churn.

His car. Where was his car? He couldn't remember. He must

have driven it home. He turned over on his side, pulled his legs around, and sat on the edge of the bed. His head throbbed. He was still wearing his clothes. He stood slowly, went quietly into the living room, and looked out a window. His car was sitting in the street—the middle of the street. He trudged out the door, down the driveway, and climbed into it. He drove into the driveway. It was a wonder it wasn't stolen.

Back in the kitchen, he made a pot of coffee, waited while it perked, then poured himself a cup. He took a sip, grimaced, and set the cup down. Then he ambled into the bathroom.

The hot shower brought some life back into him. He put on fresh clothes, then sat in the kitchen drinking coffee for a long time.

It was midafternoon before he drove back down Lankershim and parked in front of the recruiting office. He went in, picked out the Air Force recruiter, and walked over to his desk. The recruiter looked up.

"Can I help you?"

"I want to enlist," Marty said. "I play the trumpet."

Uncle Aaron's car was noisy, especially to Gary, in the back seat. He had taken some of his cars with him and he played with them for a while, setting up a ramp with a couple magazines he found on the floor and letting the cars roll down and crash into the seat. He made the noises softly to himself. "Eeeeyow. Bcewww!" Dust flew into the air and the car was mangled, but the driver always climbed out and walked away. Uncle Aaron said he should look at the scenery, but Gary had seen enough scenery. He had played in it and it was fun, but it wasn't so special. Pretty soon he went to sleep.

He woke up when they stopped at a cafe in a little town in the middle of the desert. He was glad because he was hungry. He had a hamburger and a chocolate milkshake, the good kind with little chunks of ice cream in it. He was sweating when he woke up, but inside the cafe it was kind of cold. Uncle Aaron had a beer with his hamburger. Uncle Aaron drank a lot of beer.

When they started up again Gary sat sleepily in the back seat, looking out the window, feeling the hot air blow against his face.

It was dark when they got to Uncle Aaron's house. Sybil took him into a little room and he helped her put clean sheets on the bed. This was his room, she said. He didn't know he would have his own room. There was even a desk under the window. He went out and got his cars before he went to bed. Sybil kissed him on the forehead and Uncle Aaron stuck his head in the door and waved. Gary put on his pajamas and climbed into the bed.

He closed his eyes to block out the light coming from a fixture on the wall just over his head. He had left the light on on purpose. There was a closet on the other side of the room. It didn't have a door, like his closet. It had a long, blue curtain with white sailboats on it. He was going to look in there before he got into bed, but he forgot, kind of on purpose. He opened his eyes and looked at the curtain. It was neat to have his own room.

Sybil stuck her head in the doorway and smiled at him. "Good night, Gary." She switched off the light and closed the door.

There was still some light in the room. It came through the window over the desk. The window was open and he felt the air moving softly through the room. He could hear sounds outside—a dog barking somewhere far away, a car going down the street, crickets—and then he heard Uncle Aaron and Sybil talking quietly. He felt sticky all over. His pajama bottoms stuck to his butt. Everything got quiet.

He had forgotten to go to the bathroom. And he had to go real bad. But he didn't know where the bathroom was and there was no light coming in through the crack at the bottom of the door so he knew the house was all dark. Maybe he would go to sleep and it would be okay. He put his hand down there and held it and closed his eyes tight. He waited for sleep to come, but it wouldn't. He kept feeling pressure down there. And he kept hearing the crickets go cheep-cheep, cheep-cheep. He opened his eyes. He could see the ceiling above him. Maybe if he turned over on his stomach . . .

He turned over on his side and found himself staring at the closet. The curtain moved. His chest tightened and he tried not to blink. There it went again. The curtain was only a shadow in the dim light, but it was moving, just barely, in and out, in and out, like somebody was in there breathing. He listened. Only the crickets. He should have looked in there while the light was on. Now the pressure was building down there. What if he wet the bed? But he couldn't get up . . .

The crack under the door lit up again. Then he heard them talking. There was Uncle Aaron's deep, hoarse laughter. Then his voice boomed through the house. "That's what he said. It was one of those long black limousines like they put dead bodies in. And when he opened it up there was a bunch of naked hippies in there all tangled up like spaghetti." Sybil laughed. A kind of high-pitched cackle.

He heard them go past his door, then more soft talking. He waited. He heard Uncle Aaron's car start and at the same time, voices—the television.

He pulled his sheet back and crawled along the bed until he got to the end. He glanced back at the closet, jumped to the floor, ran to the light switch, and switched it on. He stared at the closet. The curtain wasn't moving at all now. He took a deep breath, waited a moment, then opened the door quietly and walked down the hall to the living room.

Sybil sat on the couch in front of the television with her legs crossed like an Indian. There was a big bowl of popcorn between her legs, a cigarette smoldering in an ashtray, and a glass of something brown next to it. She was wearing a pink night-gown that didn't cover very much. Her legs were white and her hair was all messed up. She was laughing at the television and didn't see him at first. Then she looked at him and smiled.

"I thought you were asleep."

Gary looked down at the yellow rug. There was a dark stain right where he was standing. "I got to go to the bathroom."

"Down the hall on your right," Sybil said. "Across from your room."

Gary looked at her again. "Is Uncle Aaron here?"

"He went to work," Sybil said. "He's working graveyard."

He turned around and went down the hall to the bathroom. He was thirsty, too. He turned on the water at the sink, cupped his hands under it, and slurped it into his mouth. Then he went to the bathroom.

When he climbed back into bed he was genuinely tired. He fell asleep with the light on.

The next morning he was eating breakfast with Sybil—corn flakes and toast—when Uncle Aaron came home from work wearing his khaki uniform with the patches on the sleeves. Gary ran to him and he picked him up and twirled him around over his head. "There's the kid," he said. "How's the kid?" He almost set Gary down on top of the kitchen table and Gary was laugh-ing. Then Uncle Aaron sat down in a chair at the table.

"Coffee?" Sybil asked.

"I'm beat," Uncle Aaron said. "Think I'll just hit the sack." He stood up again.

Gary watched him walk slowly down the hall and through a door at the end. He closed the door. Gary sat back down at the table. His corn flakes were soggy.

"Well, what are you going to do today?" Sybil asked.

Gary looked at her. "I don't know," he said.

"Well, one thing you can do is write a note to your dad. He'd probably like to know you're all right."

"Okay," Gary said.

He ate the rest of his cereal and drank his orange juice. Then he looked up at Sybil again. "Is Uncle Aaron coming back?"

"He has to sleep," Sybil said. "He worked all night." She stood up and started clearing the table. Gary went into the living room and sat on the couch. It was sure a little house. The living room and kitchen were like one room. But they had a big television. He would see if he could watch it later.

He sat there for a while, staring out the front window at a big bushy tree in the front yard. Then Sybil came in and gave him a postcard and a pencil. He found a magazine to write on and sat there thinking. He didn't know what to write. The last time he talked to his dad, he seemed all right and he didn't see why he had to stay in the hospital all the time. The doctors were doing things to him. Finally he decided he would do like Sybil said and just tell him he was all right. He said he was having a good time and that he missed him a lot and that Uncle Aaron slept a lot, but that was because he worked in a graveyard at night. He didn't know what he did exactly, something with convicts. There wasn't much room on the little postcard. He signed it, "Youre son, Gary."

He took the card into the kitchen to Sybil.

"If you take it to the post office right away, he might get it tomorrow," she said.

"Okay," Gary said.

She told him how to get there and he went out into the bright sunlight. It was hot. Most of the houses on the street were small and old like Uncle Aaron's. Some of them had lawns but most of the lawns were brown and dusty. He finally got to the post office and stuck the postcard into the slot. Then he walked back to the house.

Sybil was on the telephone in the kitchen so he sat on the couch and looked out the window. He heard Sybil say something about three-thirty and he wondered what they were going to do.

There was nothing around the house that he could play with. He wished Uncle Aaron would wake up. Sybil said goodbye and hung up the phone. He went over to her.

"I mailed it," he said.

Sybil smiled. "Good." She looked down at a note pad she had been writing on, then back at Gary. "I have a hair appointment this afternoon," she said. "And then I'm doing some shopping. Pretty dull stuff for you, I guess." She thought a minute. "Well, this is a small town. You can really do whatever you want. Just don't get out on the highway. And be here for lunch."

"Okay," Gary said.

He went back and sat down on the couch. He couldn't think of anything to do. He could play with his cars. But he was tired of that. He wished Uncle Aaron would wake up and they could go on a picnic or something. He got up and went to the window and looked outside. It was sure hot. He stuck his hands in his pockets. She said he could do something. She said he could do whatever he wanted. He looked at the door, looked back at Sybil, then opened the door quietly and stepped outside. He was on his own. Nobody was going to tell him what to do. He grinned and took a deep breath. He hadn't even combed his hair or brushed his teeth. He was on his own.

He strutted down the sidewalk humming "Polly Wolly Doodle."

He walked in the opposite direction from the post office. The street went about three blocks and ended at a big ditch with a little trickle of dirty water running in the bottom of it and green grass on the sides. Three boys were sliding down the bank on cardboard boxes.

He watched them for a while, then one of them let him use his cardboard box and he slid down the hill. It was fun. He wished he had his own cardboard box, but the other kids took turns letting him use theirs. One was named Conrad and one was named Dennis and one was named Jamie. They played for a long time. Gary was sweating and he was thirsty, but he didn't want to stop. They laughed and told jokes, and Gary told them his father was sick and that he was on his own and they all looked at him like they wished they were him.

When Jamie's mother called to him, they all said, "See you," and took their cardboard boxes and ran off down the ditch to some houses over there. Gary walked back to Uncle Aaron's house. He was really thirsty and kind of hungry, too. He went into the house but there was no one there. Uncle Aaron was probably still sleeping, he thought. He looked up at the clock over the refrigerator. It was three-thirty. He got a drink at the sink, then opened the refrigerator. The only thing he could see to eat in there was an apple. He took it out and bit into it. It was hard and juicy and cold.

There was a flower bed in front of the house that would make a neat place to play with his cars. He had seen it when he came up to the door this time. He went into his bedroom and got his cars and took them outside. The dirt was soft and wet and there was a rock there that was a house and he made a driveway going up to it and a road that went around some rose bushes and over to a mine. He dug a big, deep tunnel for the mine. There was a fire in the mine and the rock was the fire station. The truck squealed out of the station and roared down the road to the fire. People were running in and out of the mine, trying to help miners who were trapped in there. The only way they could get to them, though, was to dig a big hole in the top that went straight down into the tunnel. There was a cave-in and the men in there couldn't breathe very good. He dug the hole down into the tunnel and then the whole tunnel caved in and at the same time Sybil growled into the driveway in the little Volkswagen.

"What are you doing in my flower bed?" She nearly screamed it.

"Playing," Gary said. "You said—"

"Not in my flower bed," she said. "Cover it up. Smooth it out." She stormed into the house. She was carrying a bag.

Gary took all of his cars out of the flower bed and filled up

203

the tunnel and the hole and smoothed it out so it looked almost like before. Then Uncle Aaron came out. He was grinning.

"You picked a bad place to play," he said. "She treats those roses better than me most of the time."

Gary looked up at him. He felt like he was going to cry and he didn't want to in front of Uncle Aaron.

Uncle Aaron knelt down and put a big, hairy arm around Gary's shoulder. "Don't worry about it," he said. "Just don't do it again. Come on inside. We'll make some lemonade."

After dinner they watched television. They watched "Gun-smoke" and then there was an old movie on. He sat on the couch next to Uncle Aaron and they ate popcorn out of a big bowl and Uncle Aaron drank beer. The movie was all about these people who were dead but they were alive but they couldn't think or anything. There was a man who really was alive who made them do things. Sometimes they killed people. They lived in a big graveyard. It was pretty scary, but Uncle Aaron laughed at most of it. He probably knew all about those things already anyway. The people in the movie talked funny and Gary couldn't understand what they said most of the time. About halfway through, he went to sleep.

The next day Uncle Aaron slept again. After breakfast he went down the street to the big ditch. He waited around for a long time, but Conrad and Jamie and Dennis didn't come. He slid down the bank on just his pants a few times, but it wasn't much fun. When he thought it was lunch time he walked back to the house. Sybil fixed him a peanut butter sandwich and some lemonade. Then he went back out and walked the way he had walked to the post office.

He turned at the signal and walked past the post office. He was on a street with stores. He went into a dime store and stood around looking at stuff. He wished he had some money. He would buy some of those Batman cards with the big sheet of bubble gum in it. The old man at the cash register kept watching him, so he went out again.

He went around a corner and walked back toward the house on a different street. He was thinking he had probably seen the whole town already when he came to a park.

It wasn't a very big park. Only a square block. And the grass was brown. But there was a cannon at the corner. There were cannons at each corner. And there were swings and a merry-go-round in the middle. There was a bunch of kids playing on the merry-go-round, some riding, others pushing, then the ones pushing would jump on and try to push the other ones off.

He went over and looked at a cannon, but it was old and rusty and the barrel was full of papers and beer cans. He went over to the swings and sat and watched the kids play. They were playing pretty rough. He didn't think he wanted to get into that. Then a big kid, who looked like he was several years older than the others, pointed at Gary and said, "Hey, look."

The kids on the ground looked at him. The others tried to see him, but the merry-go-round kept spinning. The big kid stopped the merry-go-round and everybody got off. They all came over to Gary.

The big kid stood in front of Gary and spit on the ground through his teeth. It just missed Gary's shoe. The kid was dark, with black hair like Manny's, but the kid's hair was long and slicked back and his clothes were dirty and he smelled like sweaty cigarettes.

"What you doing here?" the big kid asked.

"Nothing," Gary said.

The kid looked back at the others. "He says he's not doing nothing."

The others stared at Gary. They all had beady eyes and they were all dark like the big kid.

"You want to do something?" the big kid asked Gary.

Gary looked at the ground and shook his head.

"Here's something to do." He pushed Gary's chest and Gary fell backwards off the swing. His head clunked on the hard dirt. Everybody laughed. From the ground, Gary could see the big kid

205

standing there. It was like looking up at a giant. He got up and brushed off his pants. His head hurt.

"He got his pants dirty," the big kid said. "Too bad, hah?" He started walking toward Gary and Gary backed away. The kid had a big nose and his nostrils were opening and closing, opening and closing. "You don't belong here, you know that, Gringo?"

Gary kept backing away.

"You better run like a rabbit. Bunny rabbit. Little pink bunny rabbit." The others laughed. They all followed the big kid toward him. "We're going to get you, bunny rabbit. Gringo bunny rabbit."

Gary turned and ran. He could hear them laughing behind him and there were tears in his eyes and his head hurt, but he kept running until he got to the house. He sat down on the grass under the big tree. He was crying. He couldn't help it. He could feel the tears running down his face. He turned around to look out toward the street and felt the back of his head. He didn't want Sybil to see him crying. His head hurt.

He'd go back, though. He'd get Uncle Aaron to go back there with him and Uncle Aaron would beat them all up. He wiped his nose on his sleeve. They'd see. He stood up and went into his bedroom and lay down on the bed.

He woke up when he heard Uncle Aaron's voice booming through the house. He rubbed his eyes and slid from the bed. "Well, why don't you do something with him. Jesus Christ. He's only eight years old." Gary walked out into the kitchen. Uncle Aaron smiled at him. "Must be keeping you up too late if you have to take naps."

Gary stood there looking up at him.

"What'd you do today?"

"Nothing," Gary said.

"Did you make any friends?"

Gary shook his head. He sat down on a kitchen chair. Uncle

Aaron looked at him for a while, then said, "Hey, you okay? You're not getting homesick, are you?"

Gary shook his head.

"You been to the park yet? They have swings over there. And a merry-go-round, I think."

"Yeah," Gary said.

Uncle Aaron sat down at the table, too. "Not much fun, I guess, by yourself, huh?"

"There was other kids there," Gary said.

"Oh. Well, you must have made some friends then."

"They didn't want me to be there."

"Why not?"

Gary shrugged his shoulders.

Suddenly Sybil gasped. "Look at his head." She put her hand where his head hurt and he could feel her feeling the lump. "What happened to your head, Gary?" she asked.

"A kid pushed me down," Gary mumbled.

"Over at the park?"

"There was a whole bunch of them," Gary said.

"You mean a bunch of kids chased you out of the park?" Uncle Aaron said.

Gary looked at the floor.

"Jesus," Uncle Aaron said. He got up and opened the refrigerator. Gary heard him popping the top off a beer can. "Okay. Look, Gary. That's a public park. You got as much right to play there as any other kid. That park is for the whole town. Anybody that wants to can go there. Understand?"

Gary nodded.

"Well, you remember that," Uncle Aaron said.

There was silence then. They might still be there, Gary thought. We could go over there and beat them all up. We could go over there and—

"You'd better go wash up for dinner," Sybil said.

Gary ambled into the bathroom. If Marty was here, Marty

would go over there and beat them up. Or his dad. His dad could beat up anybody. He had big strong muscles. Uncle Aaron just had a big belly. He washed his hands and walked back to the kitchen. Sybil was setting the table. There was a big bowl in the middle.

"Well," Uncle Aaron said. "If you're anything like your old man, this ought to make you feel better. Spaghetti."

Something turned in Gary's stomach. He swallowed and sat down at the table. Sybil poured him a glass of milk, then spooned a big pile of spaghetti on his plate. It was white and limp and all tangled up. Then she spooned on the sauce, smiling.

"Smells good," Uncle Aaron said.

The sauce was red, with little chunks of meat in it. Gary's stomach came up into his throat. He swallowed again, tried to hold it in, but it was no use. He ran into the bathroom, his hand over his mouth. He only spilled a little on the floor around the toilet, and when he was through Uncle Aaron came in and said maybe he'd better go to bed.

He was up early the next morning, sitting at the kitchen table drinking a glass of milk when Sybil came in.

"Feeling better?" she asked.

Gary nodded.

They ate breakfast and waited for Uncle Aaron to come home. When he finally came in, he barely looked at Gary. He sat down at the table and stared at Sybil for a long time. Then he said, "I ought to quit."

"I keep telling you," Sybil said.

"They hauled McKenzie out of H with a goddamn sharpened spoon in his gut."

"Who did it?"

"They don't know. Somebody found him in the corridor."

Sybil shook her head.

"I got to get some sleep," Uncle Aaron said. "It's going to be hell tonight. They might call me in early." He stood up and walked down the hall.

Gary went outside and down to the ditch. Conrad and Dennis and Jamie didn't show up, so he went downtown again. He walked through the dime store and stared back at the old man at the register, then walked down to the park.

There was no one there. He went over to the swings and started swinging. He swung high, so high the chains slackened when he reached the top. It was fun but it wasn't even as good a swing as he had in his own yard at home. But he could watch the trees and the brown grass fly by. Then someone pushed him from behind. He turned his head and saw that big kid standing there with the others behind him. When he came back the big kid hit him hard on the back. He scraped his feet on the ground and tried to stop, but he went forward and came back again and this time the big kid hit him on the head with something hard. On the forward swing this time, he jumped out and rolled on the grass. When he stood up the big kid was standing in front of him.

"You don't learn lessons very good, Gringo."

Gary felt tears come to his eyes again, but they were tears of anger this time. "This is a . . . this park is for everybody."

The big kid stepped closer and pushed him. "Not for Gringos. Not for pink bunny rabbit Gringos." The others laughed.

"You're going to get in trouble," Gary said.

"You're going to get in trouble," the big kid mimicked, and pushed him again. He almost lost his balance. He stepped forward and stepped on the big kid's foot. The big kid shoved him hard and he fell on his back.

"You already in trouble, Gringo," the big kid said.

Gary scrambled to his feet, clenched his fist, and looked at the rest of the kids standing behind the big kid. He backed away. They followed him. Then the big kid kicked his leg hard. Gary turned and ran across the street while they all stood at the edge of the park laughing and calling him names.

Gary's blood was boiling. There was a sore place on his calf. They started playing on the merry-go-round and he walked back across the street and stood at the edge of the park. They didn't pay attention to him now. They were knocking each other off the merry-go-round. If it was just that big kid, he'd go over there and beat him up. He could follow him home and wait until he was alone and then hit him hard in the jaw, like in the movies. He walked a little closer. They still didn't see him. He could punch him hard in the stomach and the kid would try to kick him and he would grab his foot and twist it and break his leg. He looked down and saw a rock at his feet.

He threw the rock before he even realized what he was doing. He was amazed when the rock hit the big kid right on the head, but he only had time to grin briefly before the big kid was there. Fists plowed into his stomach, over and over, and he doubled up and staggered back. He couldn't breathe. He was gasping for breath. And still the fists punched into him. Then somebody yelled in his ear.

The punching stopped and he stood there wheezing, trying to keep his balance. A hand grabbed his shoulder and the voice that had yelled said, "You okay, kid?"

Gary looked up at a kid bigger than the big kid. He was David's age, but he wasn't skinny like David. He had big muscles like his dad had. Gary couldn't talk. He nodded. The boy led him across the street. He was starting to get his breath back.

"You better not play in the park anymore," the boy said. "Those damn greasers think they own it." The boy turned away and walked on down the sidewalk before Gary had a chance to say anything.

Gary walked slowly back to the house. Tears were streaming down his face. His stomach hurt. His leg hurt. His head hurt. Uncle Aaron would be asleep. Somebody in the graveyard got a spoon in his stomach. One of the convicts probably. He stopped for a minute and wiped his eyes, then walked on to the house.

But as soon as he stepped inside he couldn't breathe. Something was happening to his throat. It was closing up. He coughed. He gagged. He tried to inhale, but nothing happened. Sybil looked up from the kitchen table.

"What's the matter?"

Gary gasped. He grabbed his throat. Sybil got up and came to him.

"What's the matter?" She looked frightened.

"Can't breathe," Gary whispered.

"You can't . . . Aaron!" Sybil yelled.

Uncle Aaron came stumbling down the hall in just his underwear. "What the . . .?"

"He says he can't breathe," Sybil said .

Uncle Aaron looked at him. "What's the matter, Gary?"

"Throat closed up," Gary whispered.

"Open your mouth," Uncle Aaron ordered.

Gary opened his mouth and Uncle Aaron peered in.

"That's what I thought," he said. "It' s okay. Happens at the prison all the time. Mild case of symbiotic isolation. I know just how to fix it."

He went into the kitchen and took down several bottles from the cupboards. He poured a little of each into a shot glass and added a little water. He handed the glass to Gary. "Drink this," he said. "It's the only cure."

Gary drank what was in the glass. It was sweet and thick. He could feel it sliding down his throat, opening it up. He breathed in. Then he took a deep breath. He looked up at Uncle Aaron, at his grizzled, round face and his big hairy stomach.

"I hit him with a rock," he said.

"Who?" Uncle Aaron asked .

"That big kid."

"In the park?"

"Yeah."

"What did he do to you?"

"Hit me in the stomach."

Uncle Aaron knelt down. "Look, Gary I don't think you ought to go back over there, okay? Just leave them alone from now on."

Gary felt tears coming to his eyes again. He looked at his feet. "Okay," he muttered. He spun around and ran into his bedroom.

He didn't like it here. He didn't like Uncle Aaron anymore. He hated Sybil. He wanted to go home. He wanted to see his dad, and his mom.

Mary stood in the hall outside Jesse's room with the bright lights glaring into her eyes. Her stomach was balled up in a tight knot; her lungs seemed full of smoke; her throat was dry and scratchy. She pulled a Kleenex from her purse to wipe her nose. She had just turned her back on her husband and walked out of his room. Left him lying there by himself to fight whatever it was he was fighting.

David was beside her, his hands in his pockets, staring at the floor. A nurse walked by. A soft female voice called some doctor over the loudspeaker system. The little old cleaning lady walked around the corner, nodded, and smiled. Mary smiled back, then watched the cleaning lady go on down the hall and open a door. She stood there a moment looking into a dark room, then smiled at Mary again, and motioned her over to the doorway.

Mary and David went down the hall and followed the cleaning lady into the room. It was a small storage room smelling of floor wax and disinfectant. Shelves were stuffed with bottles, rags, paper towels, and toilet paper. Mops stood in corners. A huge buffer covered half the floor space. A big white sink stood straight against one wall cradling a big metal pail.

The cleaning lady looked from David to Mary with tiny

bright eyes and a funny little smile. Her gray uniform matched her hair and her gaunt face, full of thousands of tiny wrinkles, made her look like a cadaver in the dim light. She shoved a piece of paper into Mary's hand.

"Are you saved?" she cawed.

Mary started. "What . . . ?"

"Jesus died to save you. You got to get saved."

"Well, I think we're—"

"It don't matter how good you are or what you done. You got to have Jesus in your heart."

"I think we probably—"

"Read that," the cleaning lady said, pointing a red, bony finger at the paper in Mary's hand. "It tells you how."

"Look," David said. "You don't have any right—"

"It's God's right," the cleaning lady said. "It's God makes right and wrong. Jesus died for your sins. He's got the right."

"Let's go," David said .

"Wait," the cleaning lady said. "I got to tell you this."

Mary stared at her. The old lady's eyes seemed to dart out of her head.

"God's got plans for you, all of you. Don't turn your back on him."

"Thank you," Mary mumbled. She followed David out the door, down the hall, and into the elevator.

They drove back to Lyle's in silence. Mary's hands gripped the steering wheel tensely and David stared out the side window. The act of driving calmed Mary's nerves a little and they walked into the house just as "The Fugitive" came on the television. They all watched it together. During the commercials Mary noticed Lyle looking at her strangely. It must show, she thought. She could never hide anything. She couldn't keep track of "The Fugitive." She kept seeing Jesse lying there staring at David with that tight, thin frown on his lips, his eyes bright and beady. Snake eyes.

When it was over, she and David went out to the camper to

go to bed. Since Marty and Gary left they had both been sleeping out there, Mary in the overhead and David on the bed that converted to a table. David waited outside while Mary changed into her nightgown, the short yellow one with little ruffles at the bottom. She watched herself dress in the mirror that hung on the closet door and noticed that her skin was still milky and smooth. She had lost some weight. Without even trying.

She cracked open the door. David was sitting on the bumper. "Your turn," she said.

She climbed into the overhead and David came in to put on his pajamas. He turned out the light and she heard him get under the covers. It was quiet. David's breathing was soft and shallow. Crickets chirped. A breeze whirred through the pines.

"Hey, Mom? "

"What, David?"

"You okay?"

Mary choked back sudden tears, swallowed, and said, "I'm okay."

There was silence again. Something inside Mary was shaking itself loose.

" 'Night, Mom."

"Good night, David."

She wanted to groan. She wanted to cry. She wanted to scream. But she lay there quietly, feeling herself fall through miles and miles of dark nothingness.

It was the end. She had lost him. She had left him. Or he had left her. Long before tonight if she had only seen it. She was empty. The love was gone. What she had counted on, depended on. And Jesse just lay there hissing like some snake. What did he want? She would have given him anything. She would have died for him. But there was nothing to do . Nothing.

She woke up in the middle of the night hearing voices, muddled and far away. She looked out the window. Cool air sifted through the screen. She'd been dreaming. Now she could see a full moon through the bushy limbs of a pine tree. And she could see down the little dirt road and imagined it winding for miles and miles. "Jesse," she whispered. "Oh, Jesse." She sobbed quietly until she drifted back to sleep.

In the morning there was nothing but a steady ache. She dressed distractedly in the best clothes she had with her, yellow pants and a white blouse. She was glad she'd had the permanent. There was nothing to do but wash it every other day or so. She hadn't washed it yesterday. She would wash it tonight. She brushed on some mascara and smeared on some light pink lipstick. Her eyes were bloodshot and her whole body felt limp and exhausted.

David was gone when she woke up. He had left a note that he was going for a hike. She didn't worry about him. She wasn't worrying about anything. She wasn't thinking.

When she went inside, Ruth was sitting at the kitchen table with a cup of coffee. Lyle Jr. was in his playpen in the living room.

"Good morning," Ruth said. "Coffee?"

"I'll get it," Mary said. She went to the electric coffee pot on the counter and poured some into a mug that was sitting there. Ruth looked like she was going somewhere. She wore a smart green pantsuit, had put on makeup, and sat with her legs crossed and her back straight like a receptionist. Mary sat down at the table.

"Where's David?" Ruth asked.

"He went for a hike," Mary said.

"So early," Ruth said. Then she smiled. "He seems to like it here."

"Yes. I guess he does." The coffee was too hot to drink. Mary watched it steam.

"There's cereal," Ruth said. "Or eggs. I'd be glad to fix you some eggs."

"No thanks," Mary said.

"You haven't been eating much lately."

Mary looked up at her. She was smiling like some pseudo wise man. The mayor. She smiled back and felt the hypocrisy of it sink into her stomach. "I'm losing weight."

"Just don't lose too much."

She picked up the mug. Her hand was shaking. She took a sip and burned her lips. Ruth apparently didn't notice.

"Lyle said to tell you he had an appointment this morning but that if you wanted to come down to the office, there are some papers on his desk that need to be filed."

"I'll take care of it," Mary said. She held the mug with both hands, as if she was warming them.

"You don't have to, you know," Ruth said. "I have a meeting this morning, but when I get back we could pack a lunch and go for a picnic somewhere."

Mary thought about it. "No. I'll do it." There was something about Ruth that grated on her, a kind of smugness she hadn't noticed before. She would leave as soon as she finished her coffee.

Ruth stood up, looked into the living room at Lyle Jr., then poured herself another cup of coffee. Her mug was white with little hearts and "MOM" written in big red letters.

"What's your meeting about?" Mary asked. "More secrets?"

Ruth sat down again with her coffee. "It's no secret anymore," she said. "It'll be in tonight's paper. We had to fire the police chief."

"What for?" Mary asked. Not that she cared. She was making conversation.

"Well, it's a little complicated, but the gist of it is, he just wasn't doing his job. The captain under him knew more about what was going on in the department than he did." Ruth shook her head. "It's too bad, too. For a while, he was the best chief we ever had."

"What happened? " Mary asked.

216

Ruth's expression changed. It lost its official air and became simply concerned. "I don't know, for sure. His wife left him about a year ago. That's when it started. I heard then that he would have periodic times of depression. He was seeing a psychiatrist. He may be on pills or something. He just slipped into a kind of apathy."

"That's sad," Mary said.

"Yes, it is. We gave him every chance we could. But we just couldn't let it go on any longer."

They both sipped their coffee thoughtfully.

"Anyway," Ruth went on, "now we have to start looking for someone else. That's what the meeting is for this morning."

"Is that a big job?"

"Well, to tell you the truth, I think the captain will get it. But we have to advertise and accept applications. We'll probably get a lot. There are always young men just out of some police academy who think just because this is a small town we'll take anybody. But Captain Lowe has been here for five years, and he was a policeman in New York for ten years before that. He was some kind of detective there."

Mary drank the last of her coffee and stood up. "Well, I'd better go file Lyle's papers."

"Sure you don't want to have a picnic?" Ruth asked.

"Some other time," Mary said. She went down the hall and into the bathroom. While she brushed her teeth she thought about the police chief and wondered what he looked like, how he felt. He was on his way down. What would he do now? She felt sorry for him.

When she came back into the living room, Ruth was leaning over the playpen picking up Lyle Jr. She held him against her shoulder while Mary walked to the door.

"You know, you're lucky," Ruth said.

Mary looked at her.

"Oh, I don't mean about Jesse and everything. But sometimes I wish I didn't have all these things to do. Sometimes I'd like to just stay home with the kids and be a housewife."

Mary smiled. "I don't think you mean that."

Ruth smiled, too. "No. I probably don't. But I think about it."

Filing the papers took Mary about ten minutes. Then she sat in Lyle's chair and looked at the big map of Prescott hanging on the wall in front of her. The smell of pipe smoke drifted into the office from one of the other salesmen. The ache was still there, a little duller now, and less centralized. The emptiness was spreading like a cancer.

She listened to the soft voice of the salesman with the pipe talking on the phone and felt like she was drifting out of herself, disappearing, like she wasn't real. Nothing was real. It was all phony, like a poorly acted television show. It was all some illusion perpetuated for her benefit.

Why had she fought so long to hold on to something so unreal? Now that it was gone she had the feeling she wouldn't even miss it, that something else, just as unreal, would take its place with barely any noticeable change. She wasn't thinking of Jesse anymore. He wasn't really there. He was some ghost that had crept into her life and crept out again, silently. Everyone did that. Came and went inside her like ghosts. Even Marilyn. Even Jesus, like the cleaning lady had said. They were all just as much a myth as Jesus was.

A hand dropped lightly on her shoulder. She started, and looked up at Lyle standing beside her. Then she looked down to his belly hanging slightly over his western buckle.

"You look like a ghost," he said softly.

She was silent. He took his hand away and walked around her to set his briefcase down.

"Any calls?" he asked.

"No."

He walked back around her and sat in a chair next to the

218

desk. "Slow day," he said. "Everybody looks but nobody's serious."

She looked up at his round face, at his small, dark eyes. He seemed to be studying her.

"You don't have to stick around here if you don't want to, " Lyle said. "I don't expect much to happen today."

"There's nothing else to do," Mary said.

Lyle looked at her quizzically. Then his expression darkened. "No, I guess not."

They were silent then. Mary looked at the electric clock humming softly on the desk. It was ten after eleven. She looked back at Lyle and their eyes met. She held his eyes, gazing into them as if there she would find some meaning to a senseless world. But they were vacant, like everything else, and she felt the emptiness continue to spread.

"I'll bet you didn't eat breakfast this morning," Lyle said.

Mary looked down and shook her head.

"Well, what do you say to an early lunch? I know where they have the best pizza in town."

"Okay," she said. She really was hungry, she realized now. Her stomach felt hollow.

They stood up together and Mary followed him past the pipe smoker and out of the office.

That's probably what it was all along, Mary thought, riding down the road in Lyle's jeep, feeling the wind rush through her permanent. She was just hungry. She'd read in a magazine once that what you eat, or don't eat, often affects you emotionally. She'd get some food in her stomach and then she would feel better.

The restaurant was called Guillermo's Pizza. It was small with faded red-and-white-checkered oilcloth covering the tables. Over her protests , Lyle ordered a pitcher of beer and two glasses, which the waitress brought while they waited for the pizza. Lyle poured her a glass, then himself, then raised his glass for a toast.

"Here's to friendship," he said.

His eyes were smiling. She smiled herself and raised her glass to his. "Friendship," she said softly.

She felt the beer bite at her throat as she swallowed. It slid down her insides, cold and burning at the same time. She took another swallow, then settled as comfortably as she could in the hard wooden chair.

"Wait 'til you see this pizza," Lyle said. "It's even better than anything I ever had in the Valley. Better than Shakey's."

"Do you ever want to go back?" Mary asked.

Lyle looked thoughtful. "Yeah. Sometimes. We had some good times back then. There was always something to do. The pace gets into your blood and it's hard to get it out."

Mary was silent. She took another swallow of beer. All the good times. All the bad times, too, and the times that were just nice and the times of waiting and the times of seeing and feeling. If she had the time and the inclination, she felt she could look back on her life and study it like they used to study paintings in the art appreciation class she took in high school. But she was too young for that. There wasn't enough to her life to study yet. Better to look ahead. But when she tried that, all she could see was herself standing on the edge of a lake looking into muddy water. She couldn't see beneath the surface.

The waitress brought the pizza in a big aluminum pan that looked like it had been run over and then straightened. The crust was thick and there was lots of cheese. Lyle refilled her glass, then took a slice from his side of the pan and settled down to concentrate on his eating. Mary watched him while she ate, feeling a funny little smile creep across her face. When he finished his first piece, he wiped his mouth with a napkin, looked at her, and grinned.

"What'd I tell you? Good, isn't it?"

Mary nodded and swallowed. "Yes, it is."

A giddy, childlike feeling rushed over her. She drank more

beer. She had eaten only one piece and already she felt better. "Do you come here a lot?" she asked.

"Every chance I get," Lyle said, taking another slice. "If I've got somebody that's almost ready to buy, I try to bring them here to clinch the deal. It usually works."

Mary took another bite and chewed thoughtfully. After she swallowed she said, "Do you think I could sell real estate?"

"Sure," Lyle said. "There's nothing hard about it. You have to get your license, but a lot of companies give free classes for that. That's how I got started."

"You put in a lot of hours, though, don't you?"

Lyle shook his head. "Naw. That's what's so good about it. You're your own boss. You work however many hours you think you have to to make as much money as you want."

She drank some more beer and took another slice of pizza. She'd been thinking about it since before Jesse had the heart attack, about getting a job, doing something on her own, apart from Jesse and the boys. She swallowed and pizza stuck in her throat. She almost gagged. She picked up her glass and took a long drink of beer. When she put it down Lyle filled it again. Her eyes were watery.

"You okay?" Lyle asked.

Mary nodded and put the pizza down on her napkin. Her appetite was gone. The one slice of pizza she had eaten lay in her stomach like wet cement.

"You haven't looked too good lately," Lyle said. "Kind of pale."

"It's just nerves," Mary said weakly.

"Yeah," Lyle said. He took another bite, then looked at Mary as if he had had a sudden revelation. "You could make a lot of money in real estate out there in the Valley. Jesus, houses must be going for a low of fifty thousand by now. And businesses . . ." He shook his head. "A guy has to be crazy to be a working fool all his life. You don't get anywhere that way

221

anymore." He took a swallow of beer, then studied his glass meditatively. "If I'd got into it back then, I'd be a rich man now."

Mary smiled at him. "You're not exactly poor."

"No," Lyle said. "But not rich either." He sighed, set his glass down, and picked up another slice of pizza. "Well, *c'est la vie*, as they say. At least we've got Guillermo's Pizza, right?"

"Right," Mary said. But she couldn't eat any more. She sipped her beer and watched Lyle finish off half the pizza. The waitress brought them a bag so they could take the rest of it home and she went outside and got in the jeep while Lyle paid the bill. In the east, she could see a big bank of black clouds building up. She watched them grow bigger and blacker, moving quickly toward her. It wasn't food she had needed after all, she thought, because the emptiness was still there. It was all so useless; eating, drinking, talking, breathing. She could die right now and it would be a blessing. But not die—just cease to exist, as if she had never been. If she believed in God, that's what she would pray for. For some Martian to lift its snake-like neck out of a flying saucer and zap her into a puff of smoke.

Lyle came out, climbed into the jeep, and plopped a six-pack of beer in her lap.

"Let's go for a ride," he said. "I'll show you what this baby can do."

Before she could answer they were roaring up the highway away from town. The wind whipped into her face and the pine trees raced by like frightened stick men. Then they pulled off onto a dirt road and roared ahead at almost the same speed. Billows of dust rolled up behind them and she bounced in her seat, gripping the roll bar above her with one hand and trying to hold on to the six-pack with the other. Up ahead, the road wound up into the mountains, but when another smaller road joined the one they were on, Lyle turned sharply to the right, sliding the big tires over the soft dirt and billowing up more dust. The new road narrowed, crowded by tall pines, and Lyle slowed down. Finally he pulled into a small clearing and turned off the engine.

Silence settled over them like fog. She sat still, frozen in it. They were surrounded by tall trees packed together to make a kind of stockade. Above them, black clouds brooded, blocking the sunlight. A cool, damp breeze blew over them and hissed through the trees. In the middle of the clearing was a fire ring made of rocks and the ground around it was covered with brown pine needles.

Lyle sat watching her, as if waiting for her to see it all. Then he reached over and took the six-pack out of her lap. He slipped a can out of the plastic ring, opened it, and handed it to her.

"You got to loosen up a little," he said quietly. "Give your nerves a chance to untangle."

She started to take a drink, then stopped and waited for Lyle to open a can for himself. She held up her can between them.

"Here's to friendship," she said.

Lyle smiled warmly and clicked his can to hers. "To friendship."

They both took long swallows. Then Lyle got out of the jeep, walked around it, and opened Mary's door.

"Come on," he said. "I want to show you something."

She followed him across the clearing and down a narrow trail that wound around thick pines and big boulders. The trail ended at the base of a huge rock that towered high in the air. Lyle pointed.

"See up there?" He was almost whispering.

Mary looked up at the rock. Near the top, it was painted with symbols—spirals, triangles, and stick figures of men.

"Petroglyphs, they call them," Lyle said. "Indians made them thousands of years ago. They must have had a village near here. Maybe right here."

Mary looked around her. There were more rocks and trees and small green bushes. They all had a hushed kind of life, as if

223

engaged in some ritual, paying homage to something long dead and forgotten. She looked at Lyle and he nodded.

"I know," he said. "Strange, the way it makes you feel. I come here sometimes when I need to think. For some reason I can understand things better here."

Mary didn't know what it meant. She didn't understand what she felt. It was as if for the first time in her life, although only for a moment, she stopped thinking. What she saw looked clearer, sharper, and more three-dimensional, as if her eyes had focused for the first time. It was all there in front of her, a complete, tiny, living universe, and she could see it all. It was all so simple; there were no mysteries to it. It was all sharpness and light and hardness and seemed to pierce through her like knives. This is real, she thought. I'm the illusion. I'm nothing more than a puff of smoke.

Lyle took her hand. "Come on," he said. "Too much of this isn't good for you."

Back in the clearing Lyle took a blanket out of the jeep and spread it on the ground. They sat next to each other with their beer and Lyle took a long, thirsty swallow.

"I've never been here with anyone before," he said abruptly.

Mary watched him set his beer down carefully in the pine needles and wrap his arms around his knees. "Why me?" she asked.

"I don't know," Lyle said. "I guess I thought you needed it like I do sometimes."

"Thank you," she said. She could feel the emptiness again, spreading, engulfing her. She was sinking into it like into warm water.

"Well, I'm not any kind of counselor or anything," Lyle said. "But sometimes it's good to have somebody to talk to. At least I'm safe. I mean, it won't go any farther."

"There's nothing to say anymore," Mary said.

224

"Nothing to say," Lyle repeated. He leaned back on his elbows.

Mary drank down the last of her beer. "I should have said some things a long time ago. It's too late now."

"What's that old song," Lyle said. "Never look back?"

"I can't help it," Mary said.

Suddenly Lyle sat up again, turned her face to his, and looked into her eyes. "You're not as helpless as you think," he said. "You've got a mind of your own just like everybody else. The trouble is, you let other people do your thinking for you. You got to cut that out."

He looked funny trying to be firm and understanding at the same time. His soft, round face didn't fit the part, but his moist hands were holding her up, keeping her out of the emptiness so she could breathe. She looked into his eyes and they reflected a kind of troubled sleep, either his or hers or theirs together, and she felt unless they woke up, they would both drown.

And then he drew her face to his and kissed her, slowly, gently. She dropped her beer can and was about to push him away when she felt the emptiness surge over her and felt herself struggling, grasping frantically for something real. She wrapped her arms around him and clung to him as they fell back together on the blanket with a soft jolt.

The thunder had been rumbling for a long time, but the rain waited until they were back in the jeep before it hit. When it did, it was a torrent. They were drenched instantly. Lyle backed the jeep out of the clearing and splashed down the little dirt road as fast as he could while Mary clung to the roll bar with both hands.

Back on the highway they looked at each other and Lyle grinned. "Won't need a shower tonight."

Mary had been preparing herself for guilt. She was surprised now that she didn't feel any. All she felt was the rain streaming

225

against her face and an ecstatic gladness that she could feel it. She wanted to run to the top of some mountain, take off all her clothes, and stand there letting it splash all over her. It was real, this rain, and she could feel it.

When they drove into Lyle's driveway Ruth was at the door waiting for them. They climbed out of the jeep and ran to the porch and stood there dripping like wet puppies.

"Where have you been?" Ruth asked.

"I took Mary out on a showing," Lyle said quickly. "And then we got caught in this." He waved his hand up to the sky.

"I've been trying to get you for hours," Ruth said. "Jesse had another heart attack or something."

"What?" A searing, freezing pain shuddered in Mary's chest.

Ruth looked straight at her. "You'd better get down there."

"We'll go in the Volkswagen," Lyle said.

"No, wait," Mary said. "I have to change my clothes."

"Me, too," Lyle said. "Make it snappy."

Mary ran to the camper, opened the door, and climbed in. She stripped off her clothes and dropped them on the floor in a puddle, then noticed herself in the mirror, standing there naked and white, tiny goose bumps on her thighs. Jesse, she thought. Jesse. Oh, Jesse. She burst into sobs that doubled her over and wrenched her insides. She lay down on David's bed, sobbing, her arms wrapped around her head, holding in the violence she felt there.

It was almost half an hour before she came out of the camper. Lyle had pounded on the door and she had yelled at him twice to go away. When she finally dressed and opened the door, Lyle was still standing there. The rain had stopped and Lyle's shiny boots stood in a puddle. She looked at him for a moment without saying anything, feeling a strange kind of strength and wondering if she would ever get used to it.

"Stay here," she said. "I'm going alone."

That crazy old woman, David thought. On top of everything else she had to bring religion into it. As if they didn't already feel guilty enough.

He lay on his back in the camper in the lower bed, staring at the dark ceiling and listening to his mother breathe with short little gasps. He had gone to sleep trying to figure out what had made his father explode. Now he was awake again, in the middle of the night, still wondering about it—and about everything else.

You got to have Jesus in your heart. Great. But nobody knows who Jesus was for sure, or if there even was a Jesus. But the woman was some fanatic and if you tried to explain anything like that to her she wouldn't even listen. And if you asked her to explain what she meant she could probably never make it clear. So there you'd be. Some kind of communication gap. It was like she talked some private language of her own that no one could ever translate because no one knows both languages—his own and hers.

That's what it was with his father, too. A translation problem. An unsolvable problem, he thought. At least it was beyond him.

He was getting sleepy again. The fugitive had finally caught up to the one-armed man and let him slip through his fingers like a klutz because he was afraid of that cop who always followed him. He could have gotten on the bus and grabbed the one-armed man and taken him to the cop and said, "Here's the guy that shot my wife. Ask him." Well, he might not confess. Maybe there was other evidence, he couldn't remember. That chase had been going on so long you couldn't remember how it started. The fugitive probably wondered sometimes, too. When he relaxed enough to sit down and take a crap he probably thought, Why am I chasing that guy, anyway?

He had to write a story. He hoped he could write one better than that. One that made some kind of sense. One that didn't need to be translated. A line of light traced its own image . . .

It was still dark when he woke up again. He could hear his mother breathing heavily above him. He sat up in the bed, twisted around, and looked out the window. The sky had just a tinge of gray in it. He looked at his watch lying on the counter next to the sink. It glowed in the dark, but he couldn't tell which was the big hand and which was the little hand.

He was wide awake. He would write the story today. That's the only way he'd ever get it done—set a deadline. He got out of bed and dressed as quietly as he could. Then he rummaged through his drawer and pulled out a spiral notebook and a ball point pen. He stood a moment looking at the dark mound in the overhead that was his mother. She was another translation problem he would like to solve. She didn't move.

He took a deep breath, quietly tore a page from the notebook, and wrote a note that said he was going for a hike. He would find some quiet place to sit under a tree, someplace where he could think clearly, and write his story. He stepped out of the camper, closed the door softly behind him, and started up the road.

There was a chill in the air and he wished he had worn more than a T-shirt and cutoffs. But he knew it would get hot later, as soon as the sun came up. The sky gradually became lighter and the pines rose like spires silhouetted starkly against it. Birds were beginning to chirp. Every so often he would hear a faint rustle in some dry bush beside the road. He watched for a trail that led away from the road into the forest, but after he had walked for about half an hour and the road became narrower, he figured he would probably never find one. He stopped for a moment, took a breath, and plunged into the woods on his own.

The trees were close. He threaded his way through them, walking softly over the cushion of pine needles, brushing invisi-

228

ble spider webs, scraping his bare legs on scratchy scrub oak branches. He was already thinking about his story. It would be about a boy, about his age, who gets lost in a forest and meets a lot of strange . . . No. He probably shouldn't write a fantasy. He had to remember who the story was for. It ought to be like his poetry. It ought to mean something. What kind of story would his father like to read? He didn't have the slightest idea. Not James Joyce.

There was a strange noise. David stopped and listened. It sounded like somebody trying to start a lawn mower. There it was again. He looked around. The sky was light now, although the sun still hadn't peered over the mountains. Then what was obviously a small gas engine burst into a steady, rattling purr, revved several times, slowed down, and stopped. David headed toward the sound.

He weaved through the pines, stepped over dry, fallen logs, plowed through a small thicket of scrub oak, and almost ran into a large, thick-muscled, bearded man holding a chain saw.

The man looked startled. He stared at David a moment, then smiled slowly. "Thought you was a goddamn forest ranger."

"I . . . I'm sorry," David said. "I was just out for a hike."

The man looked at David's notebook. "You one o' them artists?"

"No," David said. "A writer."

"Oh." The man looked disappointed. The chain saw hung at the end of his thick wrist like part of his arm. "If you was a artist I got somethin' here might make a good pitcher."

"Sorry," David said. "I can't draw." He started to turn away but the man spoke again, his voice lowered conspiratorily almost to a whisper.

"Well, lookee here anyways."

David followed him to a big pine tree and the man pointed to two white animal skulls lying on the ground.

229

"Found 'em yesterday," the man said. "Know what they are?"

David looked up at him. The man's eyes were small and glassy and seemed to peer out of his beard. "What?" he asked.

"Camels," the man said. "One of 'em might be ol' Big Red hisself."

David looked back down at the skulls. They could be camels for all he knew.

"Bet you didn't know there was camels around here," the man said.

"Camels?" David said.

"Sure," the man said. "Back in the eighteen fifties the army brought in a whole troop of 'em. Used 'em fer pack animals. Not up here, though. Down south, around Yuma and Quartzsite. They didn't work out too good so they let 'em all loose and fer years they was wanderin' all over the state wild as coyotes."

"I didn't know that," David said.

"Camels," the man said, looking at the skulls and shaking his head slowly.

"So, uh, who was Big Red?" David asked.

"He was a big red camel, started off carryin' a body around tied to his back. Somebody's idee of a joke maybe. Sick. Somebody'd see him down around Tucson, then somebody'd see him up around Payson, then somebody'd see him over in Kingman. People was still seein' him a long time after he should of been dead."

They both looked at the skulls, then the man looked back at David.

"Yer pretty young to be a writer, ain't you?"

"I write for my school paper," David said.

"Oh." The man started back toward the wood he had been cutting, then stopped. "I got a thermos of coffee. Want some?"

"Uh..no thanks," David said. "I have to be going."

"Guess this ain't no big scoop," the man said.

230

"It's interesting," David said. "Thanks." He started back into the forest.

"Gonna rain today," the man called after him. "Watch out fer flash floods."

David waved and smiled. "Thanks. I will."

He walked on. He heard the man laugh, then yank on the cord. The chain saw burst into life and ripped through some logs. It was a long time before he left the sound behind him.

Remember your audience. That was what Novotny always said. What are your audience's interests? What do they need to know? He had been walking downhill for what seemed like miles. It was hot. He stopped on the edge of a dry stream bed. Small shoots of grass sprouted up from the sand around a large boulder that sat on the bank. If there was water in the stream, you could sit on that boulder and dangle your feet in it. Farther downstream he could see where the force of the water had cut a deep trench in the sand, exposing the gnarled roots of an old oak tree. Arizona was famous for flash floods, he thought. They could come roaring down stream beds like this one like a tidal wave. California had flash floods, too. Out around Palmdale and Lancaster.

Lancaster. He climbed up on the rock and looked around him. *What the hell were you going to Lancaster for anyway?* The forest was thick, but up the stream to his left there was a trail cutting through some high grass and around some trees. He climbed down from the rock and started up the stream bed. *I was running away.* Grass tickled his calves and thistles got into his socks. The trail wound deeper into the forest, uphill now.

Westerns. That's what his father liked. He'd write a western. But it wouldn't be your usual shoot-'em-up bank robbery and the character wouldn't be your usual tough, silent hombre. It would be about a kid who lives in a forest like this one. Mines. There used to be mines around here. He'd write about a kid whose father is a miner. His father would be stocky, with big, hard muscles from swinging a pick all day. *Running away from what?* And his mother would be pretty, with long, flowing blond . . . no, black hair. That's all. Just the three of them living alone here in this forest in a log cabin that just has one big room with three beds, a couple of chairs, a table, and a fireplace. No. Two beds, one big one and one small one. *Sex, I think.*

The trail ended in a clearing. David crossed it and stood on the edge of a steep dropoff. Below him the forest glistened dark green in the sunlight, rising steeply to the peak of some mountain, meeting the blue sky like the edge of a serrated knife. *You think? You don't know?* He sat down in the pine needles and stared at the forest.

Death would be the theme. His story would be about death, what it is, what it means. He drew his knees up to his chest and wrapped his arms around them. *No, I don't. The destruction melted me like it was acid. I was scared. I left her lying there, a whimpering baby crying out for the consolation of something lost in the endless miasma of time which circles and circles but never arrives. I ran.*

You take all the responsibility yourself?

I have no choice.

You have a choice.

What?

You can choose to be free or to be caught in a web you've made yourself. But it's your choice, and only for you.

What about the other?

The other makes its own choices.

Then I choose freedom.

He didn't know how long he had been sitting there leaning against a tree, staring out at the forest. When he came to himself and went to look at his watch, he realized he had left it in the camper.

Above him the sky had turned black. Clouds mulled around, tumbling over themselves, like a huge brain ruminating on some cosmic problem. A damp wind blew over him and made goose bumps on his legs and arms. He stood up, stretching his cramped muscles, trying to make himself aware of his sensations.

He hadn't written anything yet, but there was still time. He would find another place. He started walking.

The forest was alive, friendly and strange in the filtered duskness. Thunder rolled across the sky, muffled by the clouds like the light. Birds fluttered from one tree to another. A big blue jay appeared as a shadow silhouetted against the clouds, and jeered at him.

He followed the edge of the dropoff to where it became a sloping downhill slide. There was a narrow trail there, but the rocks were loose. He turned sideways and slid most of the way down to where the slope leveled off. When he came to a boulder big enough to sit on, he emptied the sand from his tennis shoes.

The wind was blowing a little harder and he knew the best way to keep warm was to keep walking. He tied his shoelaces and stood up. He couldn't see the trail. He had thought he was on a trail. He studied the ground around him but couldn't tell where he'd been. There were too many pine needles for footprints. He looked up again and froze.

About twenty-five feet in front of him stood a small, gray deer. A doe, he thought. There were no horns. Her eyes were round and dark. Her ears twitched slightly. Stand still, he thought. If you don't move, they don't see you. But he couldn't help believing she did see him, and that she was watching him as closely as he was watching her. What does she want? he wondered. And his next thought was, That's stupid. It's a deer. But still she watched him, trying to stare him down, trying to communicate with him. What do you want? he thought. But the deer wasn't telepathic. She turned slowly and gracefully, and trotted off into the forest.

David ran after her, knowing if the deer began running and leaping, she would leave him far behind, but feeling an exhilarating rush he wasn't used to. He couldn't see her, but he could hear her rustling through the underbrush. He followed the sound, running as fast as he could, dodging around trees and bushes, feeling the wind pushing him on, taking deep breaths of moist air, feeling the cushion of pine needles under his feet. Something was bubbling inside him and if he hadn't been running, he would have laughed.

A big raindrop splashed on his forehead, then another on his shirt. He hardly noticed. He was concentrating on the noise ahead of him. But the wind kicked up stronger and whistled in the trees. He stopped to listen. The wind sound drowned out everything else. He peered ahead into the forest, but the deer was gone. He stood there panting, gasping, while the raindrops fell on him and around him, glistening like diamonds.

He was at the edge of a clearing. A man-made clearing, he realized, when he saw the stumps of trees sticking up from the ground forming a small semicircle around a hole in the mountainside. A mine. He walked across the clearing to the opening, stooped, and peered in. He could see the sides of the hole, solid rock shored up with rough, squared timbers, for about five feet. Beyond that was dense blackness. But the ground inside the mine was sandy and dry. He stepped in out of the rain and sat down.

Water dripped from his hair. But he was out of the wind. He decided to stay there to wait out the storm, hoping it wouldn't last all day. He was hungry and was afraid his mother would worry if he wasn't back soon. He didn't have any idea what time it was. With the clouds so thick and black, he couldn't even guess.

He hadn't written his story yet. He took out his pen. If he could stop shivering he would write some of it here. He opened his notebook to a dry page, set it on his raised knee, and wrote.

David lost himself in the writing. The rain stopped and the clouds moved on. He glanced out the opening of his cave, took note of the blue sky, and kept writing. When he finally came to the end he turned back to the beginning and started reading.

He read it slowly, making a few changes as he went. The story was about a boy named Daniel who has problems with his father and wants to avoid him. On his way home from school Daniel sees the famed camel, Big Red. Seeing Big Red is like meeting Death, and Daniel knows he will die soon. But the following day he learns that there has been a cave-in at the mine where his father works. His father has been killed. Daniel searches through the forest until he finds Big Red again. "Who in blazes are you, anyway?" he asks. Big Red tells him he is merely a figment of Daniel's imagination, although it is true that he killed Daniel's father. Daniel is stunned by this, but finally whispers, "I want my father back."

When he gets home he finds his father there, alive and well. There was a mistake. It was really his father's best friend, more of a brother, really, who died. That night, after they are all in bed, Daniel hears stifled sobs coming from the big bed where his mother and father sleep. "And Daniel knew that his father, whose strength had so intimidated him, was crying like a baby."

David crawled out of the cave and stood up. His back was sore. His clothes were still wet, but the sun was out and already the ground was drying.

He walked away from the mine, across the clearing, and into the forest in the same direction he had come. The forest shimmered and when he brushed against bushes or trees water shook loose and sprayed him. He figured it would take a couple hours to get back to the road. He could tell by the sun it was way past noon. He was really hungry now, but he would easily be home in time for dinner.

He walked for more than an hour. The sun was sitting on top of the mountains now and he was getting worried. He knew the general direction because the sun had always been behind him. He had figured if he walked with the sun behind him now, he would come out at the road. But he should have come to the road. He sat down on a sawed-off tree stump and wiped the sweat from his forehead.

He was lost. What a dope. Lost in the forest like Hansel and Gretel. He wouldn't be home for dinner and he was starved. Everybody would be worried and Lyle would come out looking for him and they'd have to call the forest rangers and maybe send up a helicopter. Damn. He slugged his thigh with his fist. What an ass. He was always causing trouble.

He started out again. He wove around trees and bushes, trying to keep his general direction as straight as he could. Even if he was going the wrong way, if he walked long enough, he had to come to something—a trail, a road, a building, something.

The sun set behind him and the sky darkened. Hunger bit at his stomach and he tried to ignore it. But he was thirsty, too, and he couldn't help longing for the coffee the woodcutter had offered him. If he could find that dry stream bed, there might be water in it now. But he only walked up and down hills, into gullies and out again, and everywhere the ground was covered with pine needles that soaked up the water like a sponge.

The sky turned black and filled with more stars than he could ever remember seeing before. A chill settled over the forest and the air was absolutely calm. He was cold. His clothes were still damp. He stopped walking. Something was wrong. He looked around him, staring into the darkness, straining to see through it as if it was a wall. That's it, he thought. Silence. No birds. No breeze. No rustling bushes. He shivered. This was a new world, the dark side of the bright, shimmering one he had walked through all afternoon.

He went on slowly, quietly. He had no idea what direction he was going now, but a vague fear drove him on, and his thoughts circled around his father, lying in the hospital, waiting.

Ahead, in the blackness, he thought he saw something, a break in the tall, straight shadows that were pine trees. The road? He walked faster, already feeling a tingle of relief poised to surge through him and understanding how much he had dreaded spending the night in this dark forest.

He broke through into the open space, looked around him, then sunk to his knees in disappointment. In front of him was a clearing—a man-made clearing with tree stumps sticking up like fire hydrants clustered around a steep mountain bank that had a large round shadow in it. The mine.

The entrance stared at him like the eye of a cyclops and seemed to open into unimaginable depths of futility. People could have died in there, he thought, like in his story. He sat down on the ground. He couldn't take his eyes off the hole, as if he expected something to slither out of it.

There was no point in going on. He would have to wait for light. In the morning he could follow the sun again. But tonight . . .

Death, he thought. That obscure glass through which we see darkly. The phantom that haunts us all through life. We begin by wandering, searching for our way back, and we wander through a maze, sometimes thinking we have found ourselves, or learned something, and in the end we arrive back where we started, and learn that that place is death. We crawl back into the hole and follow it into its depths and it is nothing but blackness and the light we thought we saw was an illusion. Death is the reality. Out of death we create our world the way we want it to be, but when we return that world is gone forever.

Sure, he thought. It's like Aunt Roe's story. It all depends on whose tree it is. And you can have anything, even Jesus in your heart, if you want it bad enough.

A strange peace settled over him. He lay down on his back in the pine needles and looked up at the night sky, where millions of tiny stars blinked at him through the pine branches. It's all right, he thought. Everything is going to be all right.

In the morning, he woke up curled in a little ball, shivering.

He uncurled and stood up slowly. He felt weak and a little nauseous and his throat was dry and scratchy. His clothes were wet where he had been lying on the ground. He walked around the clearing, trying to bring his body back to life. The sky was gray and there was no sun yet. He was tempted to walk off into the forest, but he waited. Patience, he thought. Wait for the sun.

When the first signs of the sun showed over the mountains he started in that direction. His body limbered and warmed up as he walked. He didn't expect to find any familiar landmarks now, but he realized he was going in a different direction than the previous afternoon. After he had walked for several hours he heard a faint, familiar sound that made him smile. Someone was starting a lawn mower.

He walked in that direction and found the woodcutter slicing through a thick pine log with his chain saw. The woodcutter looked up at him and smiled through his beard. He finished cutting the log, then turned the chain saw off.

"Out again, huh?" he said.

"I got lost," David croaked.

The smile left the woodcutter's face. "Goddamn," he said. "You been out all night?"

David nodded. "Have you got some water?"

"Sure."

The woodcutter led David through the trees to an old beat-up pickup sitting on a small dirt road. He gave David some water from a dented aluminum urn and David drank four glasses. The water soaked into his empty stomach and the nausea returned. He sat down on the running board.

"You okay?" the woodcutter asked.

David nodded.

"Bet you ain't ate nothin' neither."

David shook his head.

The woodcutter rummaged through the cab and pulled out a paper sack. He unwrapped a sandwich and handed it to David.

238

"Thanks," David said.

"Where you from?" the woodcutter asked.

"California," David said.

"Jesus," the woodcutter said. "You walked all the way from California?"

David smiled. "We're staying with some friends."

"Well, if you tell me where they are, I'll take you back there."

VII

Mary spent the evening and all night sitting in the waiting room down the hall from the coronary care unit. She only left twice to get coffee, and four times, for ten minutes each time, she had sat next to Jesse's bed and watched him sleep. He was hooked up to the monitor again. The oxygen catheter was in his nose and the IV bottle was plugged into his left wrist with the big needle. He breathed lightly and slept, his face relaxed and blank.

That big nurse named Martha had come in several times to check on Jesse and had whispered reassurances to her. Once she touched Mary's arm lightly, her enormous frame lending credence to a gentle kind of understanding.

Mary had talked briefly with Dr. Blackwell. "The damage to the heart muscle apparently extended into that area of the heart which controls the heart-beat," he told her. Jesse had suffered a kind of arrhythmia called "fibrillation" which in turn led to cardiac arrest. She couldn't understand all of it, but he led her to believe that Jesse had actually died and been brought back to life by Sister Elizabeth, who had found him lying on the floor in the waiting room at the end of the hall and had pounded on his chest until they could get equipment there to start his heart beating properly again. Now they were watching him closely, controlling the arrhythmia with drugs through the IV.

Right after she talked with Dr. Blackwell, she called Lyle. She wanted to talk to David and have him call Marty, but David wasn't there. He hadn't come back from his hike. Lyle was worried about him and said he was going out looking for him. Mary said she would call back later to see what happened. Sitting back in the waiting room she realized with amazement that she wasn't worried about David. She wondered what he was doing, but inside she was calm and she couldn't explain it. She had felt this way once before—twenty-two years ago—one night after she had talked to Marilyn for a long time. But Marilyn was in Texas now . . .

She talked to David late the next morning and told him everything she knew about Jesse. He, too, accepted it calmly and said he would call Marty and Aaron. He told her a little bit about getting lost in the forest and about the woodcutter who had taken him back to Lyle's. She wasn't concerned. She knew she would hear more of the details later.

She was sitting beside Jesse's bed at about eleven o'clock when his eyes fluttered open and he looked at her sleepily. She smiled and laid her hand on his.

"I love you," she said.

He looked confused. His eyes traveled up to the IV bottle. "Where's Marty?" he asked.

"He's at home," Mary said. She paused a moment, watching his eyes. "We're in the hospital. In Prescott, where Lyle and Ruth live."

"I know," he said. His eyes closed again.

She held his hand lightly until she had to leave. Two hours later, when she came back, he woke up again. He studied the ceiling for a long time, then asked, "What happened?"

"You had trouble with your heart again," Mary said. "But you're getting better now. You have to stay quiet."

"Yeah," Jesse said. "I'm going to sell insurance."

"Fine," Mary said. "That sounds like a good idea."

He turned his eyes to hers and the sadness she saw made her want to curl up and hide. But she held his gaze.

"You never did, did you," he said finally.

"Never did what?" Mary asked.

"Forgive me," Jesse said.

Mary looked at their hands for a moment, curled together, then looked back to Jesse's eyes. "I forgive you now," she said.

His eyes dissolved into cool, liquid pools and the trace of a smile stole across his lips. Then his eyelids closed and he slept again.

That afternoon she drove back to Lyle's for some much-needed rest. She walked into the living room just in time to hear David saying, "Oh, hey, wait a minute. Here she is now." He handed Mary the phone and whispered, "It's Gary."

"Hi, Honey," Mary said. "How is—"

"Did Dad die?"

"What?"

"David won't tell me."

"No. Of course not. He got real sick again. He had something like another heart attack. But he's getting better now."

"You sure?"

"Gary, I wouldn't lie to you."

There was a pause.

"What did David say?" Mary asked, looking over at David, standing in the living room with his hands in his pockets.

There was another pause. Then Gary said, "About the same thing."

"Why do you think we would lie to you?"

"I don't know."

"He did almost die," Mary said. "But he's getting better now. He really is."

"Okay."

"How do you like staying with Uncle Aaron and Aunt Sybil?"

"Can I come back there?"

"Don't you like it there?"

"No."

"Aren't you having fun with Uncle Aaron?"

"No."

"Why not?"

"It's a real drag."

Mary smiled. "Well, you'll have to stick it out for a while longer, okay?"

"I could take the bus," Gary said.

"Just a while longer," Mary said. "A couple weeks or so."

"Can I call you sometimes?"

"Sure. I'll call you sometimes, too, okay?"

"Okay." Another pause, then Gary said, "Here."

"Hi ya, Sis." It was Aaron. "What happened, anyway?"

Mary explained what had happened to Jesse.

"Goddamn," Aaron said. "Maybe we ought to come back up there."

"I think it would be better if you didn't," Mary said.

There was no reply.

"He has to stay calm," Mary said.

"Yeah. I understand," Aaron said.

"Is Gary giving you any trouble?"

"Naw. He's a good kid. Getting kind of homesick, though, I think."

"See if he can stick it out for a couple more weeks, okay?"

"Sure. We'll keep him so busy he won't have time to think about you."

"He can think about us sometimes," Mary said.

"Don't worry about him," Aaron said. "He's okay."

"We'll keep in touch," Mary said.

She hung up the phone and turned to David. "Where is everybody?"

"Working," David said. "How does he look?"

Mary sat down on the couch and rubbed her eys. "Calm, I think. Calmer than before."

"He's going to be all right," David said.

Mary smiled. "Yes. I think so."

Marty wasn't sure how to feel when David called.

"Do you think I should come back up there?" he asked.

"I don't think so," David said. "Everything is over now. He's doing pretty good again."

"Well, okay," Marty said. "If you need me, though, be sure and call. I can get off work easy."

"We will," David said.

Marty was a little relieved that he wouldn't have to go back to Prescott. Tomorrow he was driving out to Riverside to March Air Force Base to audition with the band director there. If he made it, there was an opening for a trumpet player in a field band at SAC headquarters in Omaha. The recruiter was kind of excited about finding the opening. They didn't come up very often, he said. The band plays mostly for reviews, where everybody dresses up and marches past some general and salutes. So Marty knew he'd be playing mostly marches and dull military stuff, but it was a better way to put in his time than digging foxholes and latrines and shooting people. Besides that there was a jazz band called "The Airmen of Note"—the band that started with Glenn Miller back in World War II—that he could try out for if there was an opening later.

It was a good thing he had talked to the recruiter yesterday because today, when he went over to Mrs. Trimble's to get the mail, his draft notice was sitting in the mailbox. He called the recruiter who told him to bring the notice down and he would take care of it. He had been on his way out the door when the phone rang.

Now he climbed into his car and drove to the recruiting office. He handed the notice to the recruiter and the recruiter looked up at him.

"You pretty good on that trumpet?"

"I was second chair in the Valley Youth Band."

The recruiter shook his head. "I'm no musician. That doesn't mean anything to me." He looked down at the draft notice, then back at Marty. "Well, if you don't make it and change your mind about enlisting you'll probably get this thing again later."

"I have one other problem," Marty said. He told the recruiter about his father being in the hospital.

"No problem," the recruiter said. "We'll set you up to report some time in the middle of September."

"You can do that?"

"Sure. The Air Force has a heart, you know."

Friday afternoon, David went with Mary to the hospital. He had typed two copies of his story, with only a few strikeovers, on Ruth's little portable typewriter, and given it the title, "Daniel's Camel." He had it with him when they walked into Jesse's room. No one else had read it. He wanted his father to be the first.

Jesse looked at them and smiled. "Pull up a chair," he said.

Mary sat in the chair next to the IV bottle and David carried one over from the other side of the bed.

"How's everything going?" Jesse asked.

"Fine," Mary said. "How are you feeling?"

Jesse shook his head. "Boy, I'll be glad when people stop asking me that."

"Won't be long," David said.

"No," Jesse said. "Blackwell said I'm doing okay."

"Did he say how long you'd be here?" Mary asked.

"No," Jesse said. "They're going to take it easy this time. Nobody trusts me anymore." He smiled sheepishly, then looked at David. "We all do dumb things sometimes, I guess."

"I wrote a story for you," David said.

Jesse looked surprised. "You did?"

"I brought it with me." He held up the manuscript.

"Damn," Jesse said. "They won't let me read yet."

"No," David said. "But I can read it to you."

"Would you do that?"

"Sure," David said.

Jesse settled in the bed and took a deep breath. "Well, go ahead, then, Mr. Author."

David read the story, slowly and clearly, looking up every so often at his father's face. Jesse watched the ceiling thoughtfully. When David finished, there were tears in Jesse's eyes. He wiped them with his free hand, looked at David, and cleared his throat. When he spoke, it was almost a whisper.

"That sounds kind of personal," he said.

"It is," David said, just as quietly. "It's very personal."

"You going to leave it here?"

"Sure," David said. "I wrote it for you."

"Thanks, son," Jesse said.

Marty wasn't too worried about the audition. He had called his old teacher who told him what to expect. "All the major and minor scales and arpeggios. There'll be some sight reading. Can you still do the Haydn concerto? Okay. Oh, one more thing. Practice those diminished seventh chords." He'd practiced all day Thursday.

On Friday, after driving all over the base, he finally found the band director sitting at a desk in a small block building painted light green inside and out. He was an old geezer, some kind of officer, wearing a khaki uniform, with hair obviously dyed black and slicked back, probably with Bryl Creem.

He played a few scales and arpeggios and the first trumpet part of "The Stars and Stripes Forever." Then he played some classical music by Prokofiev he had never heard before while the director tapped his desk with a pencil. The director asked if he had a solo prepared and he played the whole Haydn concerto from memory. Finally the director smiled sarcastically and said, "Run through the three diminished seventh chords." Marty did it without blinking an eye, covering the whole range of his instrument. When he finished, the director looked at him closely.

"You've had a good private teacher, I see."

"Yes, I have," Marty said.

"Do you play any jazz?"

"That's what I'm mostly interested in," Marty said.

"I suppose you want to get into The Airmen of Note."

"I'd like to try to sometime," Marty said.

The director sighed. "They all do." He studied his pencil for a moment then looked back at Marty. "There's no room to specialize in an outfit like the one you'll be going to. You'll have to play everything from Dixieland to Mozart."

"I think I can do that," Marty said.

The director thought a minute. "Yes," he said finally. "I think you can." He smiled a silly, phony smile. "I'll tell the recruiter you made it. You'll make a fine addition to the excellent tradition of Air Force musicians."

"Thanks," Marty said.

What a lot of crap, he thought, driving back to the Valley. A fine addition. Shit. They found somebody good enough to fill their vacancy and that's all they care about. But at least he made it. That much was over.

He stopped at the recruiting office before he went home and

signed the papers. He was in. There was no backing out anymore.

When he drove into the driveway he was surprised to see Connie sitting on the front porch.

"I wanted to see you," she said.

"You want to come in?"

"Okay."

Marty unlocked the front door and they went into the living room. Connie sat on the couch and Marty sat across from her feeling awkward.

"I'm not pregnant," Connie said.

Marty looked at her. "You sure?"

"I started my period yesterday."

"Did you go to a doctor?"

"No." Marty felt the skepticism on his face and Connie's expression tightened. "What do you want," she fired. "You want to see the blood?"

Marty looked down. "No. I believe you."

They were silent. Marty fidgeted with a button on his shirt, then looked at her again.

"Tomorrow I'm going to quit work."

"Why?"

"I joined the Air Force."

"You did?"

"I'll leave in September some time. I'm going to be in a band."

Connie's eyes widened. "That's good, Marty. I'm happy for you."

"At least I won't lose my lip."

"I think you did the right thing," Connie said.

Marty took a deep breath. "I sure hope so." He smiled. "Are you doing anything tonight?"

Connie shook her head.

"You want to go get some dinner?"

"You sure you want to?"

"Sure, why not?"

Connie smiled, too. "Okay. Nothing expensive, though."

Jesse spent the next two weeks trying to figure out what he was going to do when he got out of the hospital. Selling insurance wasn't a bad idea. He'd sold vacuum cleaners for a while, when he was really hard up, and kind of liked it. Insurance would be even better because it was something everybody needed. He wished Tom was there so he could talk to him about it, but he never saw Tom again.

A lot of his worry had vanished like magic. He guessed it was because Marty had finally decided what he was going to do, and then got into the Air Force Band, which made him proud. David had written a story that was damn good—at least he thought it was. Maybe he really could be a writer. He still didn't like Gary staying with Aaron, but Mary said she checked on him by phone every other day or so and that kept him from getting too homesick. Mary came every day. She wasn't helping Lyle anymore. She said he didn't need her anyway.

Sister Elizabeth came every day, too. He was grateful for what she had done, although she told him any other nurse who happened to be there at the time would have done the same thing. The first time he saw her he expected another stern lecture, but she was all smiles and warm words. When she prayed she didn't ask God to make him well, she just thanked him for sparing his life.

Jesse felt strange about that. The "why" question he had avoided before suddenly became important to him. He felt a sense of destiny. Why didn't he die? Why had Sister Elizabeth been there at just the right time? What was he to make of the rest of his life, considering he'd been given another chance? What was he supposed to do? Support his family was one thing, he could still do that. But that was obvious. He would keep the family together, but he had the feeling he had already done that, or that they had been more together than he thought all the time. There are other ways of being together than doing things.

Anyway, it was old Martha who gave him the lecture. Two sentences. "That was a damn stupid thing to do," she said. Then she smiled. "Bet you won't do it again."

Well, he had always learned things the hard way. But she was right. He was going to do just what they said from now on. Two weeks in a regular room, then a week in town, and he could go home. That's what Blackwell had said.

When they moved him out of CCU and into a regular room, the first thing he did was to call Marty and Gary. He talked to them both for a long time. He was talking to Gary when Mary came in. He waved to her.

"There's no place to fish or anything around here," Gary was saying.

"We'll do some fishing when I get home, how's that?"

"Okay."

"Your mom's here. You want to talk to her?"

"Okay."

Jesse handed Mary the phone. His bed was next to the window. There was another bed in the room, but it was empty. He looked out the window at the blue sky while he listened to Mary explain to Gary that she and David would pick him up in a couple days. They had decided that she and David should take the truck and camper home, then she would take the bus back to Prescott. Blackwell didn't think Jesse should make the drive across the desert. He said they should fly home. When she hung up he watched her sit in a chair next to the bed.

There was something bright about her. She was wearing white shorts and a bright yellow blouse, but it was more than her clothes. It was her eyes and her smile, her little pug nose and the roundness of her face. It was her small hands and short arms, her nice legs with just a slight tan. And there was something else he couldn't see, that he could only feel, that drifted out of her and wrapped itself around him.

He took her hand. "Come here," he said, and drew her to him.

Feeling her lips pressed against his was like reliving a sensual dream. His hands moved up her back beneath her blouse. He held her close and kissed her neck. The familiar scent of her perfume flooded him with memories. He felt the excitement in his crotch and knew that something was happening down there. He turned slightly on his side to keep it from pushing up the sheet.

"I love you," he murmured. "When I get out of here we'll stay in a motel, not with Lyle."

Mary was sitting beside Jesse's bed watching the five o'clock news with him when Lyle stumbled in and set a whole stack of old Ellery Queen mystery magazines on the table.

"That ought to keep you out of trouble for a while," Lyle said.

Jesse grinned. "I knew you'd know what to get."

"I want them back when you're through, though," Lyle said. "I'm saving them for posterity."

"That trash?" Jesse said.

"Yeah," Lyle said. "I use them to start my fireplace in the winter."

Jesse picked up one and thumbed through it. "The Killer Wore Roller Skates, A Pink Silk Stocking, Nurse Brackett's Revenge. That sounds like it might get me in trouble."

"You can handle it."

Mary smiled at their banter. It was good to see them together again. Lyle had been distant with her lately. For her the struggle was over. She had hated herself for a while, then realized she couldn't live that way and had simply stopped. She hoped Lyle had done the same.

252

She and Lyle left Jesse's room together to go back for dinner. They went down the elevator and into the parking lot. Lyle walked with her to the truck, then waited awkwardly while she unlocked the door.

"Mary . . ." he began, but she covered his mouth with her hand.

"There's no need to go into it," she said. "It happened. We learned from it and we're friends."

She took her hand away and Lyle smiled a little sheepishly. "I was going to ask you if you could loan me a couple bucks 'til we get home. Ruth wanted me to pick up some milk and I'm flat broke."

Mary felt her face grow hot. She looked down. "I . . . I thought . . ."

"Hey," Lyle said. "I was only kidding. You're right, you know. You said it so much better than I could have." She looked at him again. "I hope we'll always be friends," he said. "I mean that."

"So do I," Mary said.

"So, could you loan me a couple bucks?" Lyle asked.

Mary laughed. "Sure." She opened her purse.

Two days later Mary and David pulled into Aaron's driveway and Gary ran out to meet them. Mary was out of the passenger side of the truck almost before it stopped. She knelt down and hugged Gary, glad to feel his small, bony body pressed against hers again.

"I got three new cars," Gary said.

"Well, we'll have to see them," Mary said, smiling.

Aaron and Sybil came out, Aaron grinning, and then they all went inside for dinner.

The first thing David noticed as he drove up to the house was that the gates had been straightened. The second thing was that the old clunker was gone and the little blue Renault sat in the carport where it belonged. Marty opened the gates and David drove the truck on up the driveway. He was glad to see Marty, and the house, and the car, and everything else that was familiar.

It was late, so Mary suggested they go to McDonald's or something for dinner, but Marty had the barbecue going in the back yard and was all ready to put the hamburgers on. When the burgers were ready, they all sat outside at the old redwood table and ate and talked.

Afterward, and late into the night, David lay in his own bed, staring into the darkness and thinking. It had certainly been an unusual vacation, as he was sure Aunt Roe would say. And the time, which he had expected to drag, had flown by. He thought he understood a little of what happens inside people—of what happens inside himself, at least, which was really all he could ever know. But relationships were complicated because they always involved others and some kind of a mixture of his desires and theirs. Some day, he thought, he would find the key to those relationships. In the meantime, he couldn't wait to show his story to Aunt Roe.

The next afternoon they took Mary to the bus depot in downtown Los Angeles. David stood with Marty and Gary and watched her climb aboard and waved to her as the bus pulled out of its parking space and rumbled through the terminal. He knew she would be happiest when she was back with his father.

Gary thought it felt good to sleep in his own bed again, and he kind of liked David being there, even though he didn't talk very much or anything. He slept good the first night, but after his mother left again he didn't sleep so good. For one thing, he kept thinking about those kids in the park and how he should have gone back there and beat them all up.

When morning came he got up about the same time David did and they sat in the kitchen and had cereal for breakfast. When his mom and dad came back they would have pancakes and stuff on Sundays like they used to. His dad always made the syrup, all different kinds—strawberry, grape, lemon. Once he even made chocolate.

Marty was telling them about some kind of thing for the truck and camper, but it wasn't on yet.

"There's a guy in Reseda that builds them in his back yard. He calls it the Come Along Camper Loader. It's a winch that goes in the truck and there's rollers on the camper. You winch the camper up some long steel tracks and right into the truck. It's really easy."

"How much does it cost?" David asked.

"Two hundred bucks, installed. I already paid him."

"Two hundred bucks," David said. "Where'd you get the money?"

"I had it in savings. Besides, I'm going to sell my car."

"You are?" David said.

"Yeah," Marty said. "I won't be needing it in the Air Force."

"Can we come and see you sometimes?" Gary asked.

"I don't know," Marty said. "I'm going to be a long ways away from here."

"Oh," Gary said.

"What are you asking for it?" David asked.

"Five or six hundred, I guess," Marty said. "I have to check a blue book."

Gary picked up his bowl and drank the milk that was left. Marty looked at him funny. Then he got kind of excited and looked back at David.

"Hey," he said. "You want to buy it?"

"Where would I get six hundred dollars?" David said.

"You wouldn't have to pay me right away," Marty said. "You could pay me a little at a time or something."

"I thought you still owed on it," David said.

"Not very much. I'll pay it off with my savings. Five hundred dollars and it's yours. All we have to do is transfer the pink slip."

"I'd have to ask Mom and Dad," David said.

"Ask them next time they call. I don't see why they'd say no."

Gary scooted his chair back and stood up. "I'm going over to Manny's," he said.

"Put your bowl in the sink," Marty said.

"I thought Manny was gone for the summer," David said.

Gary put his bowl in the sink. "He might be back," he said.

"Come back at least by noon," Marty said. "This afternoon we're going over to Reseda."

"Okay," Gary said.

He went out the front door, down the driveway, and out the gate. It felt good to be in his own neighborhood again. It was hot. Smoggy, too, but it still felt good.

Across the street, Mrs. Trimble was watering her flowers with a long green hose. "Hi, Gary," she called, and waved.

Gary waved back and kept walking. There wasn't any sidewalk, like they had around Uncle Aaron's house, but it was just as good to walk in the street. He would talk to Manny and tell him all about what happened, except maybe about the kids in the park. Manny probably would have thrown firecrackers at them all. He smiled to himself and stuck his hands in the pockets of his cutoffs. Anyway, he would know what to do if anybody tried anything like that again. He'd wait and get them one at a time. It would have been neat if Manny had been there. They could have taken them on together. They'd stand back-to-back, like he saw in a movie once. Manny could fight good. Then, when it was over, they would go back to Manny's bar in his den and have some whiskey. He wondered if Manny had caught any fish fishing off the pier with that big pole. In the ocean you caught big fish. Sometime his dad would take him deep-sea fishing in a boat way out in the ocean. Maybe he would take Manny, too.

He passed the second stop sign. The houses were nicer here than they were around Uncle Aaron's. Around Lyle's there weren't any other houses. He'd tell Manny about the forest and the fort he and Dawn built. And about how they went fishing and how he caught three big trout and what it felt like to have them pulling on your line and reeling them in with the pole bent until he was afraid it would break. And then eating them for dinner.

He was in front of Manny's house and he went up on the porch and rang the doorbell. The door opened and a real tall, skinny woman with blond hair piled on her head and a long, skinny nose and bright red lipstick stood there looking down at him. For a minute he didn't know what to say. Then he said, "Is Manny here?"

"Who?"

"Manny," Gary said.

"I don't know any Manny," the woman said.

Gary looked around. It was the right house. "Manny lives here," he said.

"Oh," the woman said. "Is he a little Mex?"

"Huh?" Gary said.

"Is he a Mexican kid about your age?"

"Yeah, I guess," Gary said.

"He doesn't live here anymore," the woman said. "We live here now."

"Why?" Gary asked.

"We bought the house," the woman said. "Why do you think?"

"Where's Manny?" Gary asked.

"How the hell would I know," the woman said. She was starting to look mad. "He didn't leave an address."

"Oh," Gary said.

He stood there a minute, looking up at the woman, and then the woman said, "Is that all?"

"Yeah, I guess," Gary said.

"Then get off my porch." She slammed the door.

Gary trudged down the street. Maybe Manny was going to stay with his aunt and uncle forever. He wasn't going to come back and live with that woman, that was for sure. There was water running down the gutter and he stopped and looked for a twig to put in it and watch it float. He followed the twig on down the street. It was a fishing boat and they were way out in the ocean and they hooked onto a big fish that was pulling them all over. A whale. Then the whale would slap his tail around and the ship would turn over and there would be a big whirlpool and the ship would go around and around and then finally sink. And then there was just one person left floating on a coffin.

He left the boat behind and walked on, kicking a rock ahead of him. The rock went across the street and he was almost home. Mrs. Trimble had left her hose lying beside a rosebush and she wasn't there anymore. He went through the gate, up the driveway, and into the house.

He sat on the couch. David was sitting in an easy chair reading a book.

"Isn't Manny back yet?" David asked.

Gary shook his head. He could hear Marty in the bedroom playing his trumpet.

"Well, you can try again in a few days," David said.

"He doesn't live there anymore," Gary said.

"He doesn't?"

"Some woman lives there."

"You mean he moved?" David asked.

"Yeah, I guess," Gary said.

They were quiet. Then David said, "Well, I bet he didn't move very far away. You'll probably see him in school again."

"Yeah," Gary said. "Maybe."

David went back to reading his book and Gary went back to their bedroom. He guessed he would get out his American Bricks and make a house or something. He took the box out of the closet.

Manny wouldn't come back. He would never see him again. He dumped the bricks on the floor. He would make a ranch house and then get out his cowboys and horses and put them around and there would be a big fight because some bad guys were trying to get some gold they had in the house.

He did that for a while and then he went out to the back yard and sat at the redwood table. It was hot. He watched a fly buzz through the air, then a bird perched on a branch of the elm tree in the middle of the back lawn and chirped. After a while Marty called him in for lunch.

Gary sat down and Marty put a plate with a tuna sandwich on it in front of him. There was already a glass of milk there.

"I told him I'd be there around one," Marty said to David.

"It'll be interesting to see how he does it," David said.

"It's a pretty simple outfit," Marty said.

"Yeah," David said. "One of those things somebody just figures out and then makes a bundle with it."

David and Marty were making their own sandwiches. Gary looked at his, then took a drink of milk. It tasted funny. He looked at Marty and then at David. He knew what they were trying to do. They were trying to poison him. They were acting like everything was okay, but his sandwich was poisoned.

He didn't eat the sandwich.

David was driving the little Renault over to Aunt Roe's. It had taken the guy in Reseda only about two and a half hours to install the camper loader. He drilled a hole in the side of the truck for the winch handle. Then he took the camper off with jacks and put rollers in the front and back of the camper and on the truck. He put angled steel along the bottom of the camper for the rollers to roll on. He lowered the camper to the ground and winched it up the tracks onto the truck. When they got the truck and camper back home, they winched it back down to the ground and left it sitting there safe and sound. David was anxious to see what his father thought of the system. He knew he would like it.

Aunt Roe met him at the door and ushered him into the living room like he was a prince or something.

"I spoke with your mother on the telephone. She said you wrote a wonderful story."

"I brought it with me," David said.

"Yes," Aunt Roe said. "I thought you would. But first you must tell me everything."

David wasn't sure where to start. He thought for a while, then began with his drive home from her house and running into the gate. She laughed at that and he went on with the whole story. When he finished she looked at him for a long time.

"You've changed," she said quietly.

"You think so?" he asked.

"You've grown," she said. There was a nostalgic sense of loss in her voice. But her face brightened. "So. You sat in a mine shaft and wrote your story. That's wonderful. Would you like some coffee? I may even have some ice cream in the freezer."

He heard her in the kitchen pouring the coffee and dishing the ice cream. She came back and handed him a cup and dish. The ice cream was chocolate chip. They ate quietly, and when Aunt Roe had finished hers, she set the dish on the table beside her chair.

"Well, I've enjoyed the anticipation long enough. Let's see your story."

David handed it to her, smiling. She settled in her chair and read it slowly. David watched her face. When she smiled he knew she had come to the first mention of the camel. Then her face grew serious and the tiny wrinkles around her eyes became more pronounced. She finished the story, laid it in her lap, and looked at him. Her face glowed, as if she had just become a proud parent.

"It really is wonderful," she said. "You are a writer." She

paused thoughtfully. "And I think I see what is different about you. There is no violence."

David didn't know what to say. He sat there watching her, imprinting her features on his memory.

"You know," she said. "Stories originated as a religious act. It was once thought that they had the power to change circumstances. I think you have tapped that power."

David felt a slow thrill move through him.

Aunt Roe smiled. "And if you ever stop writing I'll shoot you."

Gary sat with Marty and David at the breakfast table. He could eat the cereal and milk because he had poured them himself. And he was hungry. Last night Marty cooked hot dogs and put them on the plates before he put them on the table. He would have put something in the ones he gave Gary. Gary didn't eat them. Later, when David was gone and Marty was watching television, Gary sneaked into the kitchen and ate some lunch meat and cheese.

Now he watched them because if he looked away they would put something in his cereal, too. When Marty asked him if he wanted some toast he said no. He didn't know what he was going to do today. It was a drag with just Marty and David home. There was no one to play with. He guessed he would hang around and watch David read and listen to Marty practice his trumpet.

After breakfast he got his fishing pole out of the camper. He tied a weight to the end of the line and practiced casting it on the back lawn. He made a circle with some leaves and pretended it was a deep pool in the lake. That was where Lyle said the fish always were. They liked the deep water because it was colder. He practiced for a long time. Pretty soon he was getting the weight into the circle almost every time.

When his father came home they would go fishing, just

261

them, not David or Marty. He wished he could take Manny, too. They would catch some big fish and eat them for dinner. His father told him on the phone that he used to smoke them. He said he had a big rock thing up on a mountain and he built a fire in there and let the smoke get on the fish. He wondered what that tasted like.

When it was lunch time everybody forgot, so Gary went into the kitchen and ate some more lunch meat and cheese. He wanted to have peanut butter, but they would have put something in that. Then he took his cars out to the back yard and made a bunch of roads and stuff. He played there until he got tired of it, then sat on the redwood table and tried to think of something else to do. Connie was coming over for dinner tonight and then she and Marty were going to a movie or something. He wished he could go to a movie. But it wasn't any fun unless you went with somebody.

Marty wanted him to change his clothes for dinner and when he came out of his room, Connie was setting the table, just like she lived there or something.

"You look sharp tonight, Gary," she said.

He looked at the floor. He could hear Marty in the kitchen cooking dinner. And he could smell what it was. Spaghetti. His stomach tied up in a knot.

When they sat down to eat, Connie took the plates into the kitchen and Marty dished up the spaghetti. She set Gary's in front of him and they started eating. Gary didn't eat any. He drank some of his milk and just sat there.

"What are you going to see?" David asked Marty.

"The Sound of Music," Marty said.

"I've heard it's good," David said.

"Something nice and light," Connie said. "Old military man here wanted to see The Dirty Dozen."

"I'm not military yet," Marty said.

"Yes, sir. Sorry, sir," Connie said, and saluted him.

262

They were almost finished with their spaghetti and Gary still hadn't eaten any.

"Aren't you hungry, Gary?" Connie asked.

Gary shook his head.

"It's good spaghetti," she said.

"Yeah," Marty said. "Right out of a jar. I didn't have anything to do with it."

Connie looked at Marty. "Maybe we can bring something back afterwards. Some ice cream or something."

"Sure," Marty said. "We can make sundaes."

"I bet you'll be hungry then," she said to Gary.

Gary didn't know how much longer he could stand the smell of the spaghetti. He wanted to go to his room, but he didn't want to act funny in front of Connie. Finally they got up from the table and pretty soon Marty and Connie left. He and David went into the den to watch television. He was really hungry, but he didn't think he could sneak out to the kitchen with David there. If they found out he was eating stuff they would watch him close and not let him. Then he would either have to eat the poison or starve. Besides, it was hard to tell what they would poison. They could have poisoned the lunch meat and the cheese, too, especially if they found out he was eating it.

He glanced at David and slumped down on the couch. It would be better not to eat anything.

David didn't care whether Gary went to bed or not, so he was still up when Marty and Connie came home. They brought ice cream and chocolate syrup and peanuts and whipped cream. They went into the kitchen and made big sundaes but Gary didn't have one. He looked at the others and felt the hollow place in his stomach, but he knew what they were doing. They thought for sure he would eat ice cream. But he just went into his room, put on his pajamas, and got into bed.

David came in right after he got in bed.

"Are you feeling okay?" David asked.

"Yeah," Gary said.

"Why didn't you want some ice cream?"

"I don't feel too good," Gary said.

David sat on his bed. "What do you mean? You have a stomachache?"

"Yeah," Gary said.

"What kind of a stomachache? I mean, do you feel like you're going to throw up or does it just hurt?"

"It just hurts, kind of," Gary said.

"How bad does it hurt?" David asked.

"Not too bad," Gary said.

"Maybe you should take some Milk of Magnesia," David said.

Gary shook his head.

David stood up and looked down at Gary. "Okay," he said, and walked out of the room and turned off the light.

Gary turned on his side and stared at the closet door. He hadn't gone to the bathroom yet, but if he got up, the door knob would start turning. He wasn't sure, but he thought it was turning now. He didn't like not eating. He thought about the sundaes they were having. He wished his mom and dad were there.

Marty, Connie, and David watched Johnny Carson while they ate their sundaes, but Marty had a hard time concentrating on it. All evening he had been wondering what Connie was thinking. They hadn't talked much since he told her he joined the Air Force. He had thought it would be good to have somebody waiting for him back home, somebody he could write to and call once in a while. But it wasn't fair to string Connie along just for that. It was strange, her not talking. He had the feeling she was waiting for something.

When it was time for Connie to go, Marty walked her out to her car. They stood beside it a moment, and he drew her to him and kissed her lightly.

"You'll be leaving pretty soon," she said.

"Pretty soon," he said.

She took a deep breath. "I don't know how I feel about that. I don't even know if I love you or not anymore."

"I don't know either," Marty said. "I don't think I ever did."

"I always suspected that."

"I know."

A car drove by, stopped at the stop sign, then drove on.

"I don't expect you to wait for me or anything," Marty said.

"No," Connie said. "It wouldn't be any good to do that. A lot can happen in four years."

"We'll keep in touch, though," Marty said.

"We can do that," Connie said. "We can be friends."

They kissed again lightly and she got into her car and drove away. Marty watched her taillights go up the street. The beginning and the end, he thought. It's always kind of the same.

Gary didn't eat anything the next day. He wandered around the house and the yard trying to think of something to do, but he was tired of everything. Once, he was in the kitchen and he heard Marty and David talking about him in the living room.

"We have to figure out some way to get him to eat," David said.

"Maybe if we went to McDonald's or something," Marty said.

"Yeah. Maybe he doesn't like your cooking."

"It isn't that bad."

"No. It's pretty good."

"What does he like?"

"I thought he liked spaghetti."

"Me, too."

"Tacos. He likes tacos."

"That's a lot of work."

"I'll do it."

That night David made tacos for dinner, but Gary didn't eat any. He went to bed early. He didn't feel good. His stomach really did hurt. David and Marty were in the den watching television. He felt like sneaking out to the kitchen and getting some lunch meat and cheese, but he knew what would happen if he ate it. If his mom and dad were here it would be okay. They wouldn't try anything if they were here. But his mom and dad were in Prescott and wouldn't be home for a while. When they called he could tell them, but they wouldn't believe him. He could go ahead and eat something and then when his mom and dad did come home, Marty and David would be in a lot of trouble. They would go to jail. They would go to the electric chair and when they died they would go to the bad place.

He was getting a funny feeling thinking about Marty and David. He wished Manny was home. Something was wrong. It wasn't right that Marty and David would do something that would get them in that much trouble. Gary stared at the ceiling. He looked hard, like there was some writing there he couldn't see too good. Why were they doing it? he wondered. Even in a movie, when they killed somebody they always did it for something. To rob them or something. He couldn't figure it out. He didn't have anything they would want. But he knew they were doing it because . . .

He couldn't think of anything. How did he know? How did he start thinking that anyway? The tuna sandwich. He hadn't eaten any. He just thought they were doing it. Is that right? Maybe they weren't doing anything. He was just pretending and he forgot he was pretending. Is that right? What was he thinking? He had to start thinking right.

He swallowed and his mouth was dry. He would go out to the kitchen and get some water. He got out of bed and went into the kitchen. He got a glass of water from the sink. He drank it, but it made his stomach feel funny. He looked around. Marty and David were still watching television. He went over and opened the refrigerator and got out the lunch meat and cheese.

Then he got into the bread drawer and got out a loaf of bread and made himself a sandwich. He looked around again and took a bite. He chewed it slowly and swallowed, then opened the refrigerator again and got some milk out. He ate the whole sandwich, then made another one and ate that and drank all the milk. Nothing happened except his stomach felt better. He went back to his bedroom and went to bed.

He lay in bed and looked at the closet door. The door knob wasn't going to turn anymore. He went to sleep.

When he woke up in the morning David was already up and he could smell something cooking. He got dressed and went into the kitchen. Marty was pouring coffee from the big silver pot and David was standing at the stove pouring pancake batter onto the griddle with a big spoon. The table was already set and he was really hungry. He looked from David to Marty. Neither of them said anything. David turned the pancakes and Marty sat down at the table. There was a little pan on the stove that Gary knew was syrup. He wondered who made it.

David took the pancakes off the griddle and put them on a plate. He put the plate in the middle of the kitchen table, then brought the pan of syrup.

"Go ahead and eat," he said. "I'll make some more."

Marty passed the plate to Gary. "Go ahead," he said. "Have some."

Gary took three and put them on his plate. Then he put butter on them and poured syrup out of the pan. He cut some away with his fork and put it in his mouth. He swallowed and looked up to see David and Marty watching him.

"You must be feeling better," Marty said.

"Yeah," Gary said. He took another bite.

Marty smiled. "Good. I didn't think our cooking was that bad." He put three pancakes on his own plate.

"We were thinking about going to the beach today," David said from the stove. "You want to go?"

Gary looked at him, then at Marty. "Okay," he said.

267

Jesse and Mary sat in green metal chairs in front of room eight at the Breezeway Motel, looking across the highway at the steep pine-covered slope on the other side. There was a breeze blowing and they knew that behind them, clouds were building. But the sky above them was deep blue. The sun shone on them and they felt the warmth seeping in.

Jesse was still weak, but his strength was coming back. They took short walks around the parking lot and this morning they had walked down the highway a little ways. In a couple days he'd be ready for the flight home.

"I'm going to kind of miss this place," Jesse said.

"Me, too," Mary said.

"I don't think we'll ever move up here, though," Jesse said.

"No," Mary said.

"We'd have to sell the house."

"It wouldn't be good for the boys."

"With David graduating . . ."

They both became quiet, then aware of clouds moving in front of the sun. They knew it was going to rain soon. The breeze was damp and the rain smell was in the air. They would go inside then, and Jesse would lay on the bed, and they would confront what they had been avoiding until this day.

When the first drops of rain splattered on the ground they stood together and went into the room. They stood just inside the doorway a moment, and Jesse pulled Mary gently to him and kissed her.

"It's okay," he said softly. "Blackwell said it would be okay."

"I know," Mary said. "I was waiting . . ."

They kissed again, then undressed and, together, climbed into bed.

VIII

When Mary and Jesse flew home, Marty and David and Gary drove to the airport to pick them up in Marty's car, David's car now. Jesse had told them on the phone that he would pay Marty the five hundred dollars and David could owe it to him. Jesse looked tired coming down the steps off the airplane, but they had flown into the Burbank airport so they didn't have far to drive to get home.

After Jesse rested a while, they took him out to see the Come Along Camper Loader. Marty explained how it worked and how easy it was and Jesse grinned and shook his head and said, "I never would have thought of that."

For a while, it felt like Christmas around the house. Jesse spent a lot of time sitting on a lounge chair in the back yard and the rest of them did their best to make him comfortable. He took walks around the yard and found a lot of things for the boys to do.

269

"You're going to have to stop that walking," Marty said to him once. "Every time you go for a walk you find more weeds to pull."

Jesse grinned back at him. "I have to keep you busy or you all hang around me like a bunch of nurses' aides."

But he liked walking through the house to see Mary washing up the breakfast dishes, David sitting in a chair reading, Marty practicing his trumpet, and Gary busy making a card house that covered the floor of the den—something Jesse had taught him since he came home. This is my family, he would think. Here we all are.

Then school started again and David and Gary were gone most of the day. Jesse was feeling stronger and started looking into insurance companies he could work for. Mary learned of a part-time job at the public library near Valley Plaza and, after much debate among them all, took it. Marty was trying to figure out what to take with him to basic training.

On the night before Marty was to leave Jesse stood with the rest of the family around the barbecue watching the smoke rise from thick steaks. They were having a party. Nothing elaborate, but they had invited Connie, and Mary had made a big salad to go with the steak, and baked beans, and there were gin and tonics and Coke.

Jesse raised his glass and said, "Here's to all the right notes."

They clinked their glasses and laughed.

"No faking it," Jesse said.

Marty grinned and shook his head. "No. No faking it."

They were quiet again.

When the steaks were done Jesse put them on a platter and carried them to the big redwood table. They all sat down to eat. Jesse looked around the table at them all. It would be strange without Marty around, he thought. One son grown into a man.

He pictured the three of them in his mind, lined up, standing at a military at-ease, David and Gary smiling slightly, Marty's face kind of fuzzy—fading.

"We have a mouse at school," Gary said.

They all looked at him with puzzled expressions. He cut a piece of steak and put it in his mouth.

"What about it?" Marty asked.

Gary looked at him. "I don't know. It's in a cage. Sometimes we put it in a maze and it learns stuff."

"Oh," Marty said.

Jesse watched Gary. He felt like he was seeing him for the first time. As if something had been hiding inside him and suddenly popped out grinning. He glanced at Mary. She smiled.

Goddamn, Jesse thought. Who is this kid, anyway?